Second Act

by

Rhonda Strehlow

Published by
Melange Books, LLC
White Bear Lake, MN 55110
www.melange-books.com

ISBN: 978-1-61235-918-2

Published in the United States of America.

Cover Art by Caroline Andrus

To my family who give me so many ideas.

Prologue

I hold the glass to his lips because he no longer has the strength to lift it. He grimaces trying to find a comfortable way to sit; there is no comfortable position.

"Are you sure?" I whisper.

"Cassie." His voice is low, tired. In it is a warning. We have been over this ground so many times.

"But I'm not ready." My voice is thin, cracking.

"It is not about you, sweetheart."

The term of endearment makes me swallow hard. His hand guides mine as he swallows the contents of the glass. I wrap my arms around his skeletal ribs. He sighs and settles against me.

"I will always take care of you," he murmurs.

"And, I will always take care of you," I whisper fiercely into his hair, but already he is leaving me. His breathing becomes shallower until it stops altogether. I let out a deep breath I didn't know I was holding.

"Gordie?" I start to shake. What have I done?

Chapter One

What day is it? It is spring? Possibly early spring I think. Or is it late winter? It has been a long time since I knew or cared what month it is let alone what day it is. I didn't know I could feel this tired. It has been a long time coming. How long? I have to think, almost nine years. I looked in the mirror and do not recognize the person I see there: lank gray hair, when did I color it last? My skin is sallow; I look ill. I can't remember the last time I slept through the night. Always listening. And waiting. When was the last time I exercised? Or saw the sun. Even my brain feels fuzzy.

I squint as I step onto the deck. Lassie walks out behind me; poor, neglected dog. She needs a walk and a good brushing. She looks hopeful so I pick up the leash and clip it to her collar. She starts tugging and I let her; all of the obedience school tricks escape me now. It is just the two of us walking down the street. Tentatively old Mr. Kamps waves. I know he wants to talk but I just nod, point to Lassie and walk on. My friend, Juliet, is weeding her flowers but doesn't look up so I dodge that bullet, too. I don't want to talk. No more words of sympathy, thank you. We walk faster. Lassie's excited. I'm numb.

The neighborhood is quiet, well it is Tuesday at—I check my watch, and it isn't on my wrist. I don't know where I put it; where I have been time didn't matter.

It is two hours before we get back to the house. Lassie is spent; she walks in a neat little circle then lies on the carpet in front of the sofa. That used to be her watch station since Gordie spent so much of the last few years in that same spot.

I'm still numb. When we enter I experience incredible quiet—the quiet of emptiness. Except for Lassie, I'm alone. I take in the fact that I'm alone for possibly the first time in all of my adult life.

I feed Lassie, look into the refrigerator and take of note of the casseroles and jellos; people are still, generously, bringing food. My stomach churns at the sight so I grab a can of Monster and quickly shut the door. When did I become addicted to this drink that makes me hyper-vigilant? But I sigh as the first sip gives me a pleasant buzz. This must be how alcoholics feel. I can picture myself at a Monsters Anonymous meeting. "Hi, I'm Cassie Burns and I am a Monster addict." I take two long swigs and put the rest in the refrigerator. I'm pacing myself.

It is time I do some work; clean the living room; strip the bed, the kitchen floor needs scrubbing, the refrigerator needs cleaning. And when was the last time I did the laundry? Do I have any clean underwear left? I sit down. Where should I start? There is so much to do. I walk into the bedroom and shut the door. I can't sleep but I'm beginning to unwind. I hear the phone ring but don't move. I don't care who is calling. They can leave a message.

"Mom, answer!" It is my oldest daughter. She sounds impatient. She's often impatient. A rising young healthcare executive she plans to be CEO of her hospital by the time she is 30. She is calling to give me more well-thought out advice. I'll listen to it later. Courtney's advice always goes down better with a long cold drink. Courtney often acts like she is the mother; some days it is easier to just let her believe that.

I drift off. I awake with a start. I didn't know where I am and it is dark. Lassie's wet nose touches my hand. O.K. I'll feed you, but the bed won't let me go. She whines a little and then the lights go on in the kitchen. I'm not expecting visitors. Lassie doesn't seem concerned so I tousle my hair with my fingers as Lucas, the baby at 22, knocks on the door and gives me one of his enveloping hugs.

"Were you sleeping, Mom? Are you O.K.?" He looks tenderly into my face.

I give my stock answer, "Always."

"M-o-o—o-m," He drags out the single syllable word.

I smile at my soft-hearted son and run my fingers through his crazy hair. "The question is how are you doing?"

"I miss him." His expressive face droops.

I don't say anything. Instead, I rummage in the refrigerator, "Chicken pot pie, tuna casserole, orange jello with oranges, orange jello with pineapple, orange jello with fruit cocktail. Choose your orange jello," I challenge him.

He takes my hands and leads me to the couch. "Later, Mom what's next?"

I shake my head. Suddenly I don't know if I can talk. I check out the peeling wallpaper and squash a particularly large dust ball with my sock-covered toes.

"What do you want?" he persists.

"Rest, quiet, peace on earth, the end to all wars and pestilence. By the way, what do you think pestilence is?" I say trying for a joke.

"Alright, it doesn't look like we're going to have a normal conversation so I guess I will have to challenge you to a game of Scrabble."

"Fine with me but, no looking up words. Smart as you are you know I can whoop you with one eye closed."

"Well I can whoop you with both eyes closed and one hand tied behind my back."

Lucas is my sweet blond-haired, blue-eyed youngest child. So tiny at birth we didn't know if he would survive. As clear as yesterday I remember Dr. Korth taking Gordie and me aside. "This young man is a fighter. He doesn't know that he is the littlest guy in the nursery, so don't tell him. We're going to pull him through." Eighteen days later he hit the five pound mark and we brought him home. And he hasn't stopped eating. By the sheer volume of food he puts away every day he should weigh 300 pounds. Instead, he tops the scale at 165 pounds of muscle on a six foot one inch frame.

I bring myself back to the present. I look at the score and he is`ahead twenty points. He has a doughnut in one hand, is watching Wheel of Fortune, and scanning the newspaper.

The phone rings, I check caller I.D. It is my mother-in-law, Delia. She's called three times today already. I understand she needs someone to talk to but I can't talk to her again today. I let it go to voice mail. I'll deal with her later.

Lucas raises one eyebrow; I point to the board, and say, “It’s your turn.”

I beat him by three points. I have to pull out the big guns, quire, ibex. I’m pretty sure he let me win.

Lucas routinely drifts in and out of the house. He has a steady girlfriend, Cora. Cora is a very beautiful woman with perfect skin, honey-colored hair, a size two maybe. I think she is a bit of a lightweight but they seem to get along.

Lucas has a BA in chemistry, is studying to be an EMT and he’s applied to medical school. He is a dichotomy; a handsome, loveable, driven man who hasn’t quite figured out where he fits.

“Mom, I have something to tell you.” He wiggles exuberantly in his chair, like he did when he was a toddler with something important to impart.

He sounds serious. “O.K.”, I say.

“I was accepted to medical school at Creighton.”

I smile. “Oh, Lucas that’s wonderful!” I hug him hard.

“I’m packing. I want to get settled. I can finish my EMT certification there and be ready for school by fall. Cora is going with me.”

I’m silent. My baby had decided to leave the nest. I take a deep breath. “You will be a wonderful physician, Lucas.” Then I add,” I’ll miss you.”

“And, I will miss you,” he says but his eyes are shining with anticipation of his anything-is-possible future. “I feel bad leaving you now.”

“We can play Words with Friends over the internet. And, I’ll Skype you.” He squeezes me hard like he did when he was a little boy.

“Go, be free,” I say as I shoo him out the door. “I’m sure Cora is waiting for you. You’ve got lots of plans to make and packing to do. Just call me before you leave.”

Lucas leaves a void. He is Lassie’s favorite—always willing to toss the ball or run around the yard. Lassie lies down facing the door eyes expressing hope that Lucas will return momentarily. I give her a treat which she eats gratefully but she doesn’t move away.

I straighten the pictures and knickknacks, fluffing up the pillows on the sofa. It has been so long since I've had time to be domestic: dust, rearrange furniture, put up new curtains. The house feels neglected, and it has been. But I'm determined to change that; just not today; as soon as I've had my fill of sleep. I figure twenty-four undisturbed hours will do it.

There is a knock and Lila shuffles in with all three kids. Sandy shrieks, "Grandma," and attacks my legs. Then she climbs up my body like a jungle gym. We've done this rough housing since she was little, but now, at forty-two pounds, I'm having a hard time holding her.

"You're getting too big to climb on Grandma like that," Lila admonished Sandy.

Sandy snuggles up to me and says, "I'm not too big, am I, Grandma?"

I hold her close. "You will never be too big to snuggle," I offer. She smells like baby shampoo and sunshine as she crushes her sinewy little body to mine.

"Let's play cribbage, Gram, I've been practicing."

"Lila, do you want to play?"

"No, thanks, I'll feed Jesse and get out some games for Ashley." She looks through the refrigerator. "It's nice of people to keep bring you food, Mom. It doesn't look like you have eaten much since the last time I was here."

I shrug. "I think they are just glad that it didn't happen to them."

Lila gives me a hard look.

"Sorry, sweetie, this is just not my best day."

Sandy and I play a rousing game of Cribbage which takes forever because she is still learning the game and how to count. I admire her as we play—her crazy blond hair pulled back in pony tail with a purple scrunchie, her enormous blue eyes and her concentration. "I have the picture you drew for me and the letter you wrote is on the refrigerator," I tell her. She is carefully counting her cards so she doesn't answer.

"Where's Grandpa?" she asks unexpectedly.

"Honey, you remember…" I start but she interrupts, "I remember he is gone. And not coming back," she continues to count her cards. She only has six points; I can see that from here.

"Sandy," Lila calls a warning from the living room. "We talked about this on the way over here. Have you forgotten?"

"No Momma, I was just making conver… convers… What was I doing, Grandma?"

"Making conversation."

"I'm making conversation with Grandma, Momma."

"We're O.K., Lila," I call out.

Sandy beats me by four points and dances around the table chanting, "I beat Grandma, I beat Grandma."

"Sandy." Lila warns again, then gets up from the rocker. "Mom, we've got to get going. Ashley's got dance in 20 minutes and Sandy's got swimming. I just wanted to see that you're doing O.K."

I smile. "Thanks, sweetie, I'm doing just fine."

"You always say that."

"That's because I always am."

I unload most of the refrigerator on them and then they are gone. The silence is deafening; I hear the mantle clock ticking, the refrigerator humming and the water softener kick in. I turn on the radio. Snitch two more swigs of my Monster. Maybe it will keep me from sleeping tonight. Or, maybe it will keep away the nightmares.

Swiftly, I change the bedding and capture the biggest dust bunnies with my mop. I run warm water and take a long bath. I drink hot cocoa. My eyes feel gritty but tonight I feel uncomfortable in my skin. Clumsily I shuffle my way to the bedroom. Lassie follows her nails clicking rhythmically on the hardwood floors. She's finally realized that Lucas isn't coming back tonight.

I wake at two a.m. and note the spider web on the ceiling fan; I have taken to sleeping with the light on. The house is incredibly quiet. I hear Lassie running in her sleep, probably chasing Frisbees. I get out of bed, exhausted. I click on the computer and turn on the stereo. I surf the Web but nothing captures my interest. I find my favorite music, a mix of oldies and country irritating so I turn off the radio.

In a burst of energy I take everything out of the refrigerator, scrub it down but suddenly find myself too tired to put everything back. I sit down for a moment and fall deeply asleep.

I'm awakened by pounding on the door and I start. Who is at the door in the middle of the night? Then I hear the door opening. "Mom?"

"In the kitchen, Courtney."

She walks in and eyes the messy counter, the cold water in the pan and the open refrigerator door.

"What are you doing, Mom?"

I look around, confused. Damn, what am I doing? This place is a mess. Then I note the ketchup and milk on the counter and remember.

"Cleaning the refrigerator."

"You must have gotten a very early start."

I check the clock. "It's 6:30." I am defensive; Courtney is making me out to be some crazy old person.

"Were you sleeping? This stuff is warm. You have got to throw it out. You cannot keep warm mayo."

"It is fine, Court," I enunciate clearly as I haphazardly stuff condiments into the refrigerator.

"Well, then let me help you." I can hear the irritation in her voice.

"I've been doing this for …" I hesitate, I'm so tired I don't know how long I have been doing this, thirty-one years?

"Mom, you're swaying."

"I'm dancing," I lie and try do a little jig.

"There's no music."

"There is in my head," I snap more sharply than I intend.

I take her hands. "Come tell me what you have been up to."

"Mom, I'm on my way to work. I can't chat. I just stopped to see how you're doing. And don't give me your pat answer.

"O.K., I'm hunky-dory."

She gives me a look of admonishment and I begin to cry. Where do the tears come from? I thought I had no tears left.

Her voice softens and I see the little girl she had been—all elbows and knees, eager to please, always wanting to be the best.

She lets me cry. I get her tailored navy work suit wet.

"Mom, you need a break. Why don't you take a vacation? Lila and Anston and the kids are going to Florida, why don't you go along?"

Heavens, Disney World with three little kids? I gulp. "I need to get the house in order. I have neglected the flower beds. Besides," I decide to go for honesty, "that wouldn't really be my idea of a vacation."

She smiles. "Honestly, me neither. How about a spa? There is one my boss raves about in Campbellsport. Let me give it to you as a gift."

"I'm not ready yet."

"It's been nine months, mom."

Nine Months? It can't be nine months. My mind goes blank. Courtney sees the confusion in my eyes and compassionately changes the subject. "Are you looking forward to starting at the community college?"

"Yes, and I'm going to use the spring and summer to organize this place, spruce it up and decide if I want to move into a smaller place. Did you hear Lucas's good news?"

"Yes, golden boy strikes again." She sees my frown. "Teasing, mom. Now I've got to get to work. I'll check in later. Are you going to finish the refrigerator?"

I stick out my tongue. "No, I'm going dancing. Of, course I'm going to finish the refrigerator. I haven't lost all of my marbles." I'm exasperated; she's treating me like an idiot.

She puts up one hand, cop style. "Just checking." I throw a wrinkled grape at her and she brushes it fastidiously from her jacket. Grinning, she picks it up and throws it back at me. "Food fight" she says, and then she is gone.

Dutifully, I put all of the food back into the refrigerator and move to the rocker on the porch. The sun gets warmer and still I rock. Twice I get up to go to the bathroom and to feed and water the dog. Otherwise, I'm content to rock and rock without thinking. I'm cold but it is too much trouble to get a sweater. I rock faster. At some point I feel myself crying. Lassie licks my hand. I hear a cardinal singing. The sun goes down so finally I get up and go into the house. I lie down on the bed and pull the comforter over me. I sleep a restless sleep and wake up tired.

I dreamt about Gordon; before he looked like a gas chamber refugee. This dream is about a fight we had when he was no longer able to complete even the easiest chores. I remember I was exhausted and he wanted another blanket, then a soda and finally a book from the basement. I had just finished shoveling the walk and making dinner. I was still working full time then. I couldn't find the book he wanted and he was impatient. "I'm sure it is on the top shelf of the bookcase." To me he sounded petulant. "It's not always about you," I yelled back. He was quiet. I covered my mouth and started crying. I apologized. He accepted. But I had broken some marital trust. I wake up, sick again at my quick mouth. It had all happened years ago but I feel like I could never make up for the pain I caused that day; and now, of course, I can't.

It is morning again. I open the refrigerator to get my Monster and feel the warmth of the can. I have forgotten to turn it back on and now everything truly is spoiled. I dump the milk down the sink, recycle everything recyclable and put the rest in a trash bag. I wash the dishes. I turn the refrigerator back on but it is too late. It is too late for so many things. What am I going to do with 180 empty days before I become, once again, a functioning member of society?

Lila calls. I call my mother-in-law; there isn't much more to be said. The tie that once bound us is broken and already I'm out of her circle of influence. I don't know that I'm sorry about that. I can no longer envision myself at one of her typical endless holiday rituals. Something inside of me stirs and I smile. Mine and Delia's always tenuous relationship is unraveling.

I accomplish a lot on this nice winter day; all of the pruning gets done, I scrub the windows, and now I'm headed to the grocery store since I have nothing in my clean refrigerator to eat. I run into Sarah, a former neighbor, who hugs me warmly and we talk quietly for a few minutes. Then verbose Mr. Gracon, an acquaintance of Gordon's, insists on telling me about a person I don't even know who has just been diagnosed with cancer. I hate cancer stories. I close my ears and focus on a point over Mr. Gracon's head and don't breathe again until he is quiet. I murmur something mundane and push past him, rudely, I suspect.

I check my cart, I have a dozen cans of low-carb Monster, I buy a quarter pound of ham and two rolls in the deli, four oranges and a container of strawberries and I'm done. My cart looks empty, especially when I compare it to the two carts I would fill up when all of the kids were home. I must have been standing for too long looking lost because one of the stock boys asks if I need help. I shake my head ruefully, of course I need help, just not the kind he can give me.

I unpack my meager stash when I get home. Then I call Dr. O'Reilly whose receptionist puts me down for a four o'clock appointment. I take a shower, but it is just 1:30. I drop by the hair salon on the off chance that

Julie can cut my hair. She's busy so I get Bart who looks about twelve and has a blue streak on the right side of his part. He asks me what I want; I shrug and tell him to surprise me. He cuts my hair short and layered then brushes on some kind of warm caramel color for me to try. I tentatively shake my tousled hair. I give him a twenty dollar tip and leave feeling lighter.

Dr. O'Reilly is about 60 and looks a bit like a Bassett hound, bags under his eyes and lank dark hair. I talk for my allotted 45 minutes. He asks if I'm taking my medications. I say no. He asks why. I just shrug. Then tell him the truth, "I'm done feeling drugged. I have lost so many days already to that other-worldly fog."

He presses me about my plans for the summer. Impulsively I tell him.

"I'm taking a trip—by myself."

"Where are you going?" he asks.

I answer, "To northern Wisconsin." As a child I had been to Eagle River, Wisconsin, and at that moment I impulsively decide to return.

"Are you running away?" he asks.

"I don't know," I answer him as honestly as I can. We hug, he wishes me well and I wish him well, too.

As I head back home I wonder where I got the idea to go on a trip to Wisconsin, of all places. While I remember the weeks in Eagle River as exciting and fun, I couldn't have been more than 12 or 13 at the time, and my vision of excitement and fun has changed a great deal in the last thirty plus years. I sit down at the computer and pull up the Chamber of Commerce for Eagle River. I download a map and a list of places to visit.

I call my eldest son, Mark, to ask if he will board Lassie for a while because I'm thinking about taking a little trip. Mark immediately agrees. He is a live-and-let- live kind of guy; a throwback to his grandfather, a big guy at 220 pounds, six foot three, long dark hair, dark brown eyes and at one time my biggest worry. He drove fast cars, drank and tried drugs, and dated every girl within an hour of the city. But last year his best friend had gotten killed in a car accident and Mark became a changed man. A talented carpenter he enrolled in night school and is studying to complete his CPA. He lives on a dead end road in a three room cabin with a loft he built himself. He raises his own vegetables; belongs to a food co-op and now mentors boys on the same path he followed ten years ago.

"Do you know anyone who can keep the lawn mowed and check on the house every once in a while?"

"Sure I do, Mom; me."

"You'll be remembered in the will," I tease him.

"I always knew you loved me best." I can hear his slow, sassy grin.

"Who wouldn't?" I reply.

"Love you, Mom."

"I love you, too, Sweet Man. I'll talk to you before I go. And Mark, the rest of the crew doesn't know about the trip yet so just let me break the news."

"You got it. When are you thinking about leaving?"

"Tomorrow," I say impulsively.

"I'll pick Lassie up tonight then. In an hour?"

"I'll make you dinner."

I take Mark to a restaurant instead because I have so little food in the house. We have a wonderful discussion on politics, pruning fruit trees and the Lincoln novel we both read. Lassie is excited about leaving with Mark because he is always taking in strays and undoubtedly she will have lots of company.

It's just 9 p.m. when I return home so I curl up on the couch and call Bailey. Bailey is my best friend from middle school; we were two nerds who didn't have a lot of other collegial options.

"Bay," I sigh his name.

"Cass, how are you doing? No bullshit."

"I couldn't bullshit you even if I tried. Read me a poem before we catch up. Please."

Bailey is a poet who owns two restaurants, a farm, and an e-mail business. He is an odd mixture of steely business man and gentleman. We talk at least once week. His wife, Georgia is O.K. with our relationship but he and Gordon only ever established an uneasy peace. Deep opposite sex friendships are an anomaly in my circle. It doesn't matter; my friendship with Bailey transcends most all of my other relationships.

He slowly reads a poem about butterflies and their ability to break out of their cocoon into something stronger. I haven't heard this one before.

"It's wonderful. Is this new?"

"It's yours, Cassie, for your next blossoming phase. I wrote it for you." Only Bailey can get away with using an expression like "blossoming phase."

I have maybe a dozen poems from Bailey. All of them signify some significant change. The first ten related to the changes in our relationship. One was about physical changes as we worked our way through puberty and another was about making love for the first time. The last two were encouragement to get me through to another plane.

"Thanks, Bay, may I have a copy? And, I've made a rather unlikely for me decision, dear one. I'm going on an extended vacation to northern Wisconsin."

He is silent for so long that I say, "Bailey, wake up…"

"I'm going through a hard time now, Cass. Nothing seems to make sense anymore. I want to stay in bed with the covers over my head. How am I going to cope if you're gone?"

"I'll take my phone."

"But what if I need you right away?"

"Then you just have to ask and I'll come back,"

He sighs. Bailey is prone to bouts of dark depression. He's tried medications, shrinks and light therapy yet still there are days when no sunshine gets into his world. Sometimes I'm able to coax him out, but lately my own world has been pretty bleak so I have been neglecting him.

"I'll take you to dinner tomorrow night."

"Bailey, I'm leaving early tomorrow."

"Then let's have a drink tonight. Or, I could be over in 30 minutes."

There is one problem when Bailey and I get together; we revert back to our intense, sensual relationship. He was my first lover and we never stopped caring deeply for one another. I'm feeling pretty vulnerable now so I decline his offer.

When he was a newlywed and I was a wandering student, he asked me to be part of a threesome. Too sexually inexperienced and too much

Catholic guilt stopped that experiment before it started.

We hold hands, hug frequently and talk in our own shorthand. Since we've been married to other people we're a bit more reserved especially since old gossip Mrs. Giles once went on and on about "the odd relationship" to Gordon.

No one would call Bailey handsome but he is captivating; solid and barrel-chested and everyone is drawn to his eyes which are an electric blue. When he looks at you it is like being caressed. Bailey loves all women no matter shape, size or age. Women fascinate him and he never tires of learning what we're feeling and thinking. Being with Bailey makes you feel like the only woman in the world.

For years, I had made it a point to meet him in loud and crazy restaurants. We've eaten our way across the city, tried every new dive and rated them each on a one-to-four fork tine scale. But that's going the long way around to say that I never entertain Bailey alone in my house. We have a long history that connects us so closely that when we're together I always feel like the adventurous, sensuous creature he ascribes to me.

The downside of Bailey is he is impetuous, spends every penny he earns and is totally unreliable.

"O.K., Little Cairo in thirty minutes."

We talk until midnight. Waltz around the bar to some country music on the jukebox at the second or third beer joint we hit and laugh longer and harder than I can remember.

"Are you sure that you need to go?" he asks plaintively.

I nod. Of course I'm not sure. I could be persuaded to stay. I don't know what I want.

He slips his Swiss Army knife into my hand. "Then take this for luck, call me when you need me and come back whole." We hug and he is gone, tearing out of the parking lot like a sixteen year old.

"I love you, Bailey Walker, always have and always will," I murmur to the retreating tail lights.

Chapter Two

I sleep well and awake at 6 a.m. realizing that I'm ready and anxious for something. I try to pack but find I have very little of the past that I want to take along. After throwing three pair of underwear and two bras into the garbage, I realize I need to go shopping. Any kind of shopping has been on hold for a very long time. Besides, I never go anywhere. I amend that; I never went anywhere. Today I'm changing that.

I put on my best jeans and a newer tee shirt from one of the kids and throw a mostly empty suitcase into the car. First stop, the mall. Five hundred and twenty two dollars lighter I'm back on the road. I set the GPS and am off. Because of construction it takes forty-five minutes to get out of the city. Ms. GPS keeps telling me to follow roads that are closed. Then she starts repeating, "Recalculating, recalculating, recalculating…" I unplug her and drive in the general direction I believe to be north.

For lunch I eat a sandwich from the vending machine and drink a Monster. That's my first mistake. I get pulled over for speeding, seven miles over the limit, and I'm not even out of the state. I grit my teeth, write a check for $125 and promise to reduce my speed. I drive a stately 60 mph for the next four hours. I need to find a hotel. I have never done this alone. Oh, I have taken the kids on numerous overnighters for athletic events, forensics or music and we've gone on vacations but I've never tried this on my own.

Did I mention I hate to drive? I'm not intuitive. I don't have the map in my head so many people claim to see. I take the same route to my children's homes because taking a different one scares me. I hate getting lost. I feel so undereducated when it comes to driving that I once sat at a broken stoplight for five minutes and only sped away when a large, angry man in the car behind me got out and waved his fist threateningly.

It starts to rain and of course there are no hotels. Now it is 8:30 p.m. and I'm hungry and tired. An hour later, I find a Motel 6 and decide tired trumps hungry. I fall soundly asleep after my first day's adventure only to be awakened by my children, one after the other, who want to hear about my day. There is not much to tell. How can I explain the lightening of my mood? The first tiny thrill of excitement?

Now I can't sleep. I click through the channels on the television and watch a story about pythons. As I remember Gordon's struggle to breathe, I turn off the television when the python wraps itself around a small deer.

I wake up at 7 a.m. with a sun so bright and promising I am eager to get started.

I stop at a little diner. There are two other people eating, a tiny grandmotherly lady and a gentleman around my age. They both look up when I come in; the gentleman does a double take. I smile and take a table away from both of them. I'm half way through my waffle when the gentleman stops by my table. He hesitates and then asks, "Jane Roberts?"

I swallow a bite of my waffle and shake my head no.

"You look just like I remember her. We went to school together and then we lost touch with each other. Did I say you look just like her?"

I smile ruefully. "I would have remembered you," I say honestly.

"That's the nicest thing I have heard for a long time. May I sit down? Honestly, it's O.K.. I'm not one of those crazy dudes. I just want to talk a minute. Do you have the time?"

"I doubt that those crazy dudes announce themselves." I reply drily "But please sit down."

"I'm Jonah Willes, I'm a gastroenterologist in Granite, the next town over. Last weekend was our class reunion and I've been reminiscing about who we all used to be. Jane and I were good friends and when you walked in I thought I had conjured her up. But, tell me about yourself. I can't keep thinking of you as not Jane Roberts."

I take a drink of coffee to buy some time. Who the heck am I? I feel my throat closing up. I will not cry. So I shrug. "I'm just passing through, I'm on my way to Eagle River, Wisconsin."

"Visiting family?"

"Revisiting childhood memories."

"Alone?"

I hesitate. Too much information for me to share in my vulnerable state so I just shrug again. Let him think what he wants to think.

He catches my hesitancy and apologizes.

"I've got to get going," I say, rise and grab my bill.

"Not from Peatsworth? No relation?"

"No, sorry. But I hope you find her some day."

He is standing at the door as I drive away and I wave. He waves back and gives me a sad little smile. What an odd but a strangely invigorating event. It's not the first time I have been mistaken for someone—once someone's cousin and another time an ex-wife. I guess I'll always look like the woman next door.

I get on the highway and drive until 2 p.m. when I stop at a convenience store, buy gas, chips and Twizzlers. I plan to drive around Chicago and spend the night in Wisconsin. Somehow I find myself in downtown Chicago during rush hour. After inching along for an hour I take the first exit I can find. Ms. GPS admonishes me. I ignore her and then turn her off. I am hopelessly lost and my gut clenches. Did I mention I hate to get lost? And I'm so lost. I see a hotel and turn in gratefully. $250 a night! I haul my suitcase up to my beautiful room and bounce on the bed. I make the mistake of lying down for just a minute and waking up at 10:30 p.m. Now I'm starving. I ask the concierge if there is a place I can walk to for dinner. She draws me a map to a pizza place.

I put on my new purple shirt, tousle my hair, brush my teeth and am off. I feel energized. There are a lot of people on the streets so I feel safe as I go straight for two blocks then turn left. I smile at a young couple who pass holding hands so intent on each other they don't see me. I feel a pang and try to remember, did Gordie and I ever look like that?

My musings are interrupted. "You shouldn't swing your purse when you walk. It makes you very vulnerable to thieves."

I gasp and turn to face the speaker who has dared grab my arm. I pull away with a jerk.

"I didn't mean to scare you. I just want you to be safe. You don't look like you're from around here."

There are two of them. One a bald, buff Latino and the other, the one who held my arm, a handsome, well dressed blond gentleman.

"Thank you," I say backing away clutching my purse to my midsection.

"Where are you going? Let us walk you. It is late and you shouldn't be out all by yourself."

I hesitate. I have gotten so turned around I'm not sure where I'm headed.

"What's your name?" the Latino asks gently taking in my frightened posture.

"Cassie."

"Well, Cassie, I'm Eduardo and this…." He hesitates when the blond shakes his head slightly.

"And this is my old friend … Tom." I know that he is lying and he is not good at it. His eyes shift to some spot over my right shoulder.

"Well Eduardo and, uh, Tom, I believe I'll be just fine but thank you for your fine offer." I sound like a blathering idiot and now I'm standing at the corner not knowing which way to go. I start going right but realize the right side of the street is very dark. I walk half way into the middle of the street and stand frozen.

Tom gently takes my hand and says, "Bully's Pizza Parlor is down a block. We were going there ourselves. We'll just walk you there."

"How did you know I was going to Bully's?"

"Everybody visits Bully's at some time or another."

They arrived at their destination when Eduardo says, "And, viola, we're here! Since it is just the three of us, let's eat together. "Eduardo finds us a table and Tom gets us settled.

The place is very busy, filled with an upscale, older crowd. I try not to wince when I read the prices on the menu.

I look around. It's a funky little place, warm and smelling like heaven; my empty stomach rumbles.

"The sauerkraut pizza is wonderful. And, we'll get breadstick to start. Alcohol or not?"

I shake my head. All I need is one glass of wine and I'll be acting pretty darn silly as hungry as I am. I spot the familiar black can. "Low carb Monster, please." The two men order Stella Artois.

I take the first long drink, sigh, lean back in my chair and study my companions. They look carelessly wealthy with nice fitting jeans; Eduardo in a polo shirt with some kind of symbol on the pocket and Tom in what looks like some kind of bowling shirt. I squint in the semi-darkness to read the embroidered name; Kurt.

"I hope Kurt knows his shirt is out having a good time without him tonight."

"Pretty lame wearing someone else's shirt, you think?" Kurt replies.

I shrug and ask rhetorically, "What's in a name? Be whoever you want to be tonight. In fact, I no longer feel like being Cassie. Tonight I'll be…" I hesitate; it has been a long time since I've been silly. I cast around wildly for some crazy, fun-loving, sexy name but nothing comes to mind.

"Princess Laia," Eduardo starts, "No, too common, Elizabeth, Barbie, Cat Woman, Sunshine, Wilderness, Hemingway, Frostie…" Encouraged by our laughter he gets crazier, "Cookie Monster, Captain Kangaroo, Sid, Oreo, Boy George…" Kurt cuts in, "I have the perfect name…" He does a drum roll on the table with his index fingers. "Darth," he declares with an air of finality.

"As in Vader?" I think of the scary character and then my second thought is I'm grateful that he didn't say Jabba the Hut or Yoda or R2D2.

"No just Darth," he caresses the word. "It conjures up visions of strength and determination. Now, choose a name for us. Ed first. "I study Eduardo. He is all angles, cheekbones, jaw, almost warrior-like except for intelligent brown eyes.

"The Lone Ranger."

Kurt slaps his leg. "Perfect! Now me."

Eduardo and I turn toward Kurt but I feel them both looking at me. A delicious feeling of power runs through me. I'll not waste this opportunity to openly scrutinize the interesting character in front of me. The pizza comes but I'm too distracted to eat. Eduardo is the only person who takes a slice.

Kurt gets up and offers me his hand. "Maybe if we danced you would know me better and naming would be easier." There is no one else dancing. I can't even hear any music over the thrum of voices. Yet I take his hand and step into his first move. I used to love to dance. Gordon was tone deaf, could never hear the rhythm so it has been years since I have danced with anyone other than my kids or Bailey. However, my body moves in perfect synchronization with Kurt. It is disquieting to be held so close. A strange vibration starts. It startles me. I feel as if the first layer of my skin has been removed. It is an eerie but invigorating feeling. Kurt draws back and looks at me long and hard; he feels it. I smile and shrug suddenly feeling exposed. I see a shadow pass behind his eyes that's gone in a flash. He turns a rakish smile on me, but I know what I saw. He is in pain; something has hurt him so deeply the real Tom or Kurt chooses to hide behind surface charm. But I think who am I to call him on it? Then I wonder what he sees in my eyes.

"Let's eat. My brain needs fuel. Your new name will come when I'm no longer distracted by my growling stomach."

I pull my hand out of his and the humming quiets. He puts his hand on my back to guide me to our table and it starts again. When I turn I catch him grinning slyly—he is deliberately teasing me. I move to the far chair, equidistant between the two men. The lighthearted bantering continues.

Eduardo is respectful but not deferential. I cannot interpret their relationship, though it is deeper than typical male friendship.

"Well…" Kurt is impatient.

"Thor and you have streaks of Attila and some Opie but nope, I'm sticking with Thor."

Eduardo cuts his eyes to Kurt. Kurt has a bemused smile on his face, "All of that from one short dance?"

"You should see what I could come up with if I had dessert," I tease.

"I know just the place." He reaches for my hand but I hesitate.

"It must be the wee hours of the morning," I protest. Kurt checks the most elaborate watch I have ever seen. He notes my interest, takes it off and hands it to me. I listen in fascination as he describes the dials and the buttons. When I go to hand it back he tells me to keep it.

"Thank you, but on this trip I plan on moving beyond time." I hand the watch back. Lord, where did that pious sentence come from?

"Well, that's quite a philosophical observation, which suggests that we have all the time in the world to get dessert." He's changed his voice to that of an English professor.

I tuck my hands beneath the arm of each man and say, "O.K. then gentlemen, we're off to find dessert."

"Crème brulee drizzled with caramel sound right?"

"Only if we split it." I have a theory about sharing food and I'm always testing it. Here is my theory: people who are willing to share food are able to move to a different level of intimacy than those who can't. I know that might sound like a crazy way to judge friendships but so far that test has served me well. Gordon and I always shared. Bailey and I often eat off the same plate using the same fork. Hence, my children think that the food on anybody's plate is fair game. Sharing food disturbs some people; I don't care, those people will just stay acquaintances anyway.

I'm tickled when Eduardo orders one crème brulee and three spoons. Soon we sound like kids arguing over the last bite. Kurt gets up and brings back another dish. I'm not hungry but still try to hoard more than my share while Kurt and Eduardo attack my spoon. Finally I pick up the dish and lick it. "This always worked with my brother," I announce smiling smugly. Then Kurt picks up the crème brulee, licks the dish and passes it to Eduardo who gracefully finishes it off. We're hooting with laughter by this time and people at the nearby tables are glancing our way. A teenage girl at the table next to us picks up her dish, tables of patrons are holding up their licked clean dishes. Eduardo and Kurt bow so I curtsy as we walk out the door.

I'm laughing so hard I sit down on the sidewalk. I look up at the sky and see that dawn is breaking. I feel a tremendous peace. I can feel some hard lump in my chest begin to loosen up; I'm immeasurably lighter. I take a deep breath and fill my lungs. I get up.

"Well gentlemen, this has been a night I'll always remember. Thank you for being so kind to a lost soul, one who doesn't know enough not to swing her purse in downtown Chicago. Now it is time for me to begin the rest of my journey." Although we had walked for more than a mile suddenly I know exactly how to get back to the hotel.

"Let me call our driver." Eduardo's cell phone is in his hand.

"Thank you, but it is a glorious night to walk." I'm swinging my purse in an exaggerated arc.

"But here is the car now." A car of a vintage I do not recognize pulls up.

"Mr. …"

"Hello Roscoe," Kurt interrupts, "Could you take us to the Captain's Walk hotel, please?"

"Really…" I protest.

"Really, it is dangerous," Kurt counters imitating my inflection.

We're seated together in the back of the large old car. I marvel at its comfort and size.

"So, Ms. Burns, where will your journey culminate?"

"Well, Thor, my plan is northeastern Wisconsin, but after tonight I've learned that you don't necessarily have to stick to a plan."

We reach the hotel and get out of the car.

Suddenly I feel out of my element. What an odd and exciting night but now it is over. Without looking at either of them I murmur a thank you and turn to go. Eduardo touches my arm and gives me a gentle hug.

Kurt steps up and carefully pulls me to him. The humming starts and I try to pull away but he holds me closer. I gently disengage myself. His hand rests on my cheek; he tilts my face and touches my lips with his. The humming is so strong that my lips burn. I don't want to pull away but prudently I do.

"Thank you for the wonderful evening, Cassie," Kurt says softly, "I'm sure we will meet again."

I search his face and then nod. Perhaps, I think. Slowly I enter the hotel without looking back. I never look back. It is a matter of pride with me. Too often looking back hurts. Tonight is a night for looking forward.

In my room I stuff the few things I took out back into my suitcase. $250 and I didn't even spend the night. The phone rings and I stare at it for a moment. No one knows I'm here; except… I quietly shut the door as it continues to ring.

I ask that my car be brought around the back. The traffic is very light and within five minutes I'm heading north.

Chapter Three

I sing along with the radio as loud as I can. A semi passes; the driver honks his horn and does a little boogie with shoulders. Everybody is feeling good on a day like today. Sunshine and warmth, a promise of spring.

My cell rings. I'm sure that it is one of the kids. I press talk and listen for one moment before quietly turning it off and stuffing it into my purse. Yesterday's encounter belongs to yesterday I decide. Sometime when it is not so fresh and confusing I'll take out the memories and examine them more closely. Today I just slam that door shut; today is a new adventure.

I drive through southern Wisconsin admiring the scenery. I open a can of Monster and remember to set the cruise control. Why was it I hate to drive? I remember; it takes too much concentration. At least it used to feel that way. Today is different. Or maybe I'm different. For the last twenty miles I'm following what must be cow paths. I travel through one little town after another. I roll up the windows when the sun goes down. Suddenly I drive into snow. I slow down to 50, then 35. I can't see anything. When a bright light appears I discern a tiny grocery store. I pull up not only to find food but to see if there is a hotel in this town.

The lady behind the counter stands less than five feet tall. Her hair is wrapped in a regal braid around her head, like a halo. I have never seen a woman dressed as she is in a very dated cotton dress with a fancy apron over it. She is measuring a pound of dried beans for the woman in front of me. I look around the store and feel like I have stepped back into the 1950s. There are all kinds of nails on one wall, flour, oatmeal and other bags and bottles of foodstuffs on another wall and material on the third. There are no carts, people just bring up purchases, lay them on the counter and pay. Despite the deepening snow, I'm mesmerized. It has an almost indefinable smell, a little hardware, dill pickles and fresh bread. When it is my turn I realize that my hands are empty even though I have every intention of buying something to eat.

"I'm lost," I blurt out. "And, I need to find a hotel before the weather gets worse."

"Well, ma'am, there's no hotel or motel for twenty miles."

I must look a little wild-eyed because she is quiet for a moment before suggesting, "Old Harley's mother's house is empty. I'll give him a call and see if you could stay the night." I'm absurdly grateful and hang on to every word of her side of the conversation. In a few words she conveys the situation then turns to look me over. I don't know what she sees but she says, "Yes, sir, she looks like a respectable woman."

"Tell him I'll pay."

She waves me off and hangs up. "It's just a half mile down "A" then turn on Blueberry Road and go one mile past a big blue barn on your right. It's the next house."

"Thank you!" I'm relieved not to have to drive much further. I turn back, "Key?"

She just smiles. "Door's open. Should be some canned food in the pantry but you'd better stock up with some fresh stuff."

Gratefully I buy cheese, smoked salmon, crackers, eggs, bacon, oranges, tea, coffee, and bananas. She adds two pounds of hamburger, a couple of steaks, milk, and bread to my pile.

"I believe there will be plenty of canned goods in the house because the boys stay there from time to time, but it could be a while before you get plowed out."

Is she implying a couple of days? Don't they have snow plows here? I open my mouth but realize that this is my one choice, this or more driving. I nod gratefully as she urges me out the door.

I drive slowly even though I pass only one other truck. With some effort I spot the blue barn and see a blurry structure in the distance. I plow on afraid to stop for fear of ever getting my car to move forward again. I pull around the side of the house and get stuck. My shoes fill with snow as I struggle to the front door. It is indeed unlocked. Who leaves their doors open these days I muse?

I enter a small foyer with a woven rug where I wipe my wet shoes. I slip them off and look for a thermostat. There is a neat pile of wood next to an old pot bellied stove. Damn. I have never been a Girl Scout. How do you start a fire? Will I burn the place down? I decide to leave the fire for now. I make two more trips through the knee deep snow for my suitcase and the food. I'm plenty warm enough now so I explore. I walk into a sprawling farm kitchen and open a small door to the left. Here is the infamous pantry and indeed it is full of canned food. I pull out the nearest jar, vegetable soup is written neatly on the top with last year's date underneath. A second can is labeled spaghetti sauce while the third is green beans. I send up a prayer to the woman who worked so hard to can all of this food. I tentatively turn on the water; it works.

I find the door to the basement but in the best of situations I don't like old basements so I shut and lock that door; I'll just trust that the furnace is working. The dining room is filled with one long table and a cabinet of knick knacks. I study a collection of depression bowls in a rainbow of colors thinking how pretty they must look in the sunlight. Off the dining room is a small bedroom with a dresser and a free-standing armoire. The bed is neatly made and as I sweep back the covers I inhale the sweet smell of summer on the sheets.

Now I'm hungry so as I put the food away in the old refrigerator I nibble on the smoked salmon. I should have bought some chocolate. I search the drawers in the kitchen and sure enough in a heart-shaped tin is a whole stash of chocolate—chocolate stars, Hershey candy bars, mallow cups. I only hesitate a moment before I snatch up the mallow cups vowing to replace them as soon as I'm able. I savor one slowly then put the tea kettle on. Before it boils I study the pictures on the kitchen walls. I try to guess which one is Old Harley but most of them look to have been taken 20-50 years ago and I guess that Old Harley wasn't Old Harley that long ago. I study women with funny hairdos, buns and bad permanents; men in bib overalls or starched white shirts; strong faces, interesting faces. When the tea kettle whistles I make tea and carry it into the living room. Wrapped in an afghan on the couch I feel fairly toasty. I look around the room. No television but an old floor model radio and an older record player. Looking out the double windows in the back of the house I wonder what the scenery would be like if I weren't in the middle of blizzard.

I vow to tackle the wood stove in the morning. The old bed has an electric blanket so I turn it on high. I slip into my sweats to sleep and my next conscious thought is that I have indeed started the house on fire because I'm sweating. When I realize it is the warmth of the electric blanket I laugh and turn it down. I slip off my sweats and decide to sleep in my underwear and T-shirt. Now I can truly appreciate the worn softness of the sheets and their heady fragrance. I doze but wake to find myself reaching across the bed. Of course, there is no one on the other side. My cheeks are wet with tears and I realize what has awakened me.

I wander into the living room and turn on the radio. It is set to an oldies station. I'm soothed first by Dean Martin, then Tony Bennett and finally Frank Sinatra. I look outside and realize that the snow hasn't let up. An old clock on the night stand says 12:48 a.m. I might as well try to get some sleep.

I wake with a start. There is an imperceptible lightening of the sky. I try to convince my bladder that it wants a few more minutes of sleep but she won't have any of it. Groaning I slide out of bed and gingerly slip my feet into my cold shoes. That damned stove keeps taunting me. Today, surely, today I'll figure it out. After all I have a PhD, I should be able to figure out something that primitive. In lieu of a robe I slip the afghan around my shoulders. I am half way through the living room when I realize there is a body lying on the sofa; it wasn't there when I crawled into bed.

A man sits up and we eye one another. For some reason I'm not afraid here, alone in the middle of nowhere. It reminds me of the time I was driving down the highway and got rear ended. I calmly offered my hand and introduced myself to a mildly crazy driver who kept apologizing. From that same calm space I feel myself smiling.

Today I extend my hand. "Cassie Burns."

"Will Harley." Ah, the Harley clan sent someone to check up on me.

"Glad to meet you, Will. Is this your grandmother's house?"

"Yes. I'm sorry to barge in. Because of the storm I decided to stop instead of trying to make it home. My father said that he had a lady staying here. Really, I'm sorry to impose. I knocked but you were sleeping so soundly I let myself in. I didn't mean to scare you."

"Do I look scared, Will Harley?"

"You sounded scared earlier when you were crying in your sleep."

I look away. "Excuse me." I go into the bathroom and sit for several minutes. When I come out the fire is blazing and I'm amazed at how cozy the little room suddenly feels. I sink into an old leather recliner and stare into the fire. It is several minutes before I realize that I smell bacon cooking in the kitchen but I feel lethargy so strong I just close my eyes.

"Ms. Burns, I have made breakfast, won't you join me?"

Suddenly I can't breathe. I'm trying hard to hold back the ache but a sob breaks through. Why did I think I was strong enough to make this trip by myself? I can barely hold myself together. I must be scaring Will Harley.

"I'll get dressed and be right out," I blubber and slip into my sweats to join him in the kitchen. I'm not sure that I can eat anything but my first forkful of eggs makes me close my eyes in appreciation.

"Are you O.K.?"

"I am, Mr. Harley. Please forgive me. I recently lost my husband and this trip alone was supposed to be my time to heal. Unfortunately, it's not happening as quickly as I had hoped. I'm 300 miles away from home and think maybe I should just give it up and go back."

"What were your plans, Mrs. Burns?" Will asks quietly.

"Please, call me Cassie, Mrs. Burns sounds like my mother–in-law. Initially my destination was Eagle River, but recently I decided I was going to drive until I felt like stopping, then rent a place for a few months, do some writing, and just think. I have a new job starting in September at a college back home."

Will is silent for a long time. I finish eating breakfast while he scrutinizes me. I self-consciously smooth my crazy bed head.

Trying to be social I say, "So, Mr. Harley, will you tell me about yourself?"

He smiles and I notice laugh lines at the corners of his eyes and bracketing his mouth. I revise the age I assigned him when we met upwards to late 40s, early 50s—around my age. Tall and rangy, weather-beaten with an interesting face that looks like it doesn't smile often enough.

"I'm a lawyer by profession, a farmer by choice. I work in Green Bay three days a week and farm seven. I'm trying to care for my father who broke his hip when he flipped a snowmobile on himself trying to keep up with his grandson."

I try to repress a smile. Will sounds disgusted with his father's antics. I picture an old geezer racing around on a snowmobile and break into a grin. I don't know anyone who has ridden on a snowmobile let alone flipped off. I hope I get to meet this rural version of Evil Knievil.

"It is not a funny as it may sound, Old Harley is not a good patient." I try to look properly solemn. He must have caught the glint in my eye because he smiles briefly.

"O.K. it was pretty funny." Together we laugh and the atmosphere lightens.

"Pa has always been a cowboy. Ma was able to control him some when she was alive but since she's been gone, I think he's purposefully reckless. He misses her a lot. They were together more than 50 years and now he is lost without her. He keeps busy with the farm but this close to spring I'm worried about how we're going to get everything plowed and planted let alone keep up the house and feed the working crew. We have two hired hands and a half dozen neighbors who help but Dad is the supervisor of it all and with his limited mobility…" He trails off thoughtfully. "Do you know anything about farming? Nursing?"

"Sorry, I'm a born and bred city slicker. Well, I'm a mother so I do something about nursing."

When he asks, "Do you want an adventure?" I'm taken aback. The old Cassie would have made excuses. I seriously consider it for a few moments before responding.

"Since I owe you a debt for letting me stay here in a snowstorm, I could try." This time he actually grins.

"Old Harley is pretty demanding and can be a pain in the ass," he warns.

"I have taken care of a dying husband, a home, four children and worked. I believe I can take on one elderly pain in the ass."

"Alright, I'll talk to the old man as soon as I get reception on my phone again. Until then do you want to play checkers or cribbage since the storm isn't supposed to let up any time soon?"

He beats me two games of checkers, but I skunk him in cribbage. We talk about important things, his grandmother and my husband and trivial things like the next season for the Packers and the value of reality television shows. We find a stash of Sudoku puzzles and I challenge him to see who will complete theirs first. We choose the hard version. I beat him by a couple of minutes and study him until he looks up.

"So rub it in. PhD trumps lawyer."

"Exactly what I was thinking," I lie.

"So four kids? You must be busy. I have one in college. Plans on coming back to run the farm. Not sure if I should encourage that or not."

"Well, your wife must be worried about you now."

"Ex-wife."

"Sorry."

"Don't be. It was a long time ago, actually another lifetime. We were college sweethearts from different worlds. She hated farming and wanted to leave but farming is in my blood. Lawyering just pays the bills. Jared is the best thing that came out of that sad affair."

Gently I tease him, "Well there must be a long line of women here in…"

"Canton."

"…Canton willing to fill in the gap."

"I can tell you haven't been here long. Three quarters of the town are my relatives and even here we don't allow that kind of in-breeding. And the other quarter, well they'd be mostly neighbors I have known all my life. Slim pickings."

We sit quietly for several minutes.

"And, you?"

I start, "Oh, you mean relationships?" I reflect a minute then smile. "Nary a one. So what would you be doing if you were home?" I ask.

"Checking on the cows and pigs and the sheep. Planning which crops would go in which fields. Arguing with Pa about buying new equipment. Hanging with my brothers. There is a plethora of things to do in Canton, Cassie."

"A plethora, hmm."

"Still doubting that anyone from here would use multi-syllabic words?" His grin is taunting.

"No, I just like the word. Pleth-o-ra." I roll it around my tongue. "I also like the words ephemeral and pithy. They evoke a higher level of images than say frog, minimum, or section. My friend Bailey, he's a poet, and I like to argue about words. Things like forever being more intimate than infinity or sensuality having a higher level of importance than sexiness. Deep, deep thoughts." I make light of our musings. I don't know Will well enough to be this open. I'm an introvert and it usually takes me months or years to form friendships and now in the last 48 hours I have developed three.

"Let me try. Compassion trumps honesty. Disillusionment is too slippery and intimacy pales next to tenderness."

I'm astounded. Nobody catches on to our game. Gordon never did.

I get up. "Teach me how to deal with the fire. I have never even been camping so this is all foreign to me."

"O.K. but you have to tell me what you would be doing if you were home."

"Spending time with my grandkids. I have three. Doing research for my classes this fall. Walking the dog. Going to the symphony or a play. Having friends over. Golfing. I had a good life."

"Had? Surely it's not over yet."

"No. but I'm past the middle and gaining on the end."

Will reflects for a moment. "I guess that could be said of most of us."

He teaches me the basics of fire making and I'm a good student. I promise to make the fire the next morning and he just laughs issuing a challenge, "Come camping with me and I'll show you how you can start a fire without all of these amenities."

"I just might take you up on that, Mr. Harley." I grin back. Although the thought of going camping doesn't thrill me, I love a challenge.

We circle each other with words and with our eyes. I dredge up some distant experience and realize that I'm flirting and he is, too.

I walk around the small living and end up mesmerized by the snow. Silently he comes and stands by my side, together but each alone with our own thoughts. I'm feeling warm and mellow. Will doesn't speak to his feelings but the silence is comfortable. He starts singing a Tony

Bennett song while I hum along. His voice is scratchy like he hasn't sung for a while, then he starts adding moves. First of Dean Martin drinking a martini and smoking and then getting into some crazy Elvis moves. He slips out of the room and intones, "Elvis is leaving the building." We laugh until we're exhausted.

Abruptly, he announces that he is going to check on the cattle in the barn. I didn't know there were cattle in the barn. I open my mouth to ask to come along but he puts on his coat and is gone. What did I say?

Lost, I look around the room and realize that it has been some time since anyone has really cleaned. I find cleaning supplies under the sink and expend a great deal of energy making every surface shine. It seems like a long time until Will returns. I wasn't sure he was coming back.

I turn expectantly as he stomps off the snow.

"It's not done snowing," he announces unnecessarily.

"How are the cows?"

"They are beef cattle. We raise them to be eaten. We don't milk them. The milking cows are over at the big farm." He talks as if he is explaining this to a child.

I nod, expecting some kind of explanation for the sudden exit.

He chooses to ignore the unspoken question. "I think I should try to get my truck out. You can stay until I can get the tractor back here to pull you out—probably tomorrow."

"Are you running away, Will Harley?" I'm surprised at my audacity. I don't like confrontations. Besides, maybe he is just tired of my company.

He shifts uncomfortably from one foot to the other. "I don't know that I can stay."

"Well, it's your house. I'm the one who should be leaving," I say, deliberately misunderstanding his statement.

"That would be foolish. You can't even get out of the driveway and the snow plow hasn't been through. Besides, where would you go?"

"Hotel."

"Closest one is twenty miles north. I can't imagine that the weather is any nicer there."

"Well, Will, tell me what you want me to do."

"Stay."

"Will you stay?"

"Yes, I'm being foolish, even with my four wheel drive I can't get out."

"So let's make dinner."

"But, I made breakfast. It's your turn." His face splits into a slow grin.

I accept the challenge. I find some flour, the pantry is still well stocked, and make biscuits. I warm up a jar of grandma's green beans and broil the steaks. Will is impressed. When we're done I raid the chocolate stash and put three stars artistically on a plate and serve them. I keep three stars for myself.

"And with these we need some fine wine. Grandma always kept some dandelion wine on hand for medicinal purposes. Should we raid her supply?"

The wine is sweet and thick in my mouth. "I love it. It is like drinking silk."

"Be careful, it is more potent than it seems."

We're drinking out of juice glasses and I top mine off. I get the most deliciously floating feeling. I seldom drink so I didn't notice the caution signs—euphoria, liquid muscles, and an overwhelming urge to talk.

Will sits back amused at my constant chatter.

"You're not an experienced drinker I take it?"

"Nope, I get too…" I can't find the word.

"Crazy? Silly? Sleepy? Dopey?" he teases.

I throw my final chocolate star at him; he opens his mouth and catches it.

"You ate my last star!"

He sticks out his tongue with the star on it; then smiles and says, "Why don't you come and get it?"

Suddenly, we're sober. I get up from the table and head for the bathroom.

"It's time for me to go to bed, Will. I'll see you in the morning. It has been a great snow day, one I won't forget. Good night."

There are three other bedrooms upstairs but they have been shut off for so long they are like the inside of a refrigerator. Will chooses to spend another night on the too short couch. I offer him the bed since the couch is better suited to my size but he refuses.

"I bless your grandmother, Will, every time I crawl between the sheets because they smell like summer. I've never hung my sheets on a clothes line. I didn't know what I was missing."

"I hang the sheets on the line, Cassie. I have a theory that if everyone slept on windblown sheets there would be no insomnia and no wars because people wouldn't want to be away from their beds at night."

"And no crime because there are no clothes line sheets in prison. Good night, John Boy."

"Good night, Elizabeth."

"Cassie. Cassie." Someone is talking in my dream. I have a hard time surfacing and when I do it is Will shaking me.

"What?" I'm hanging onto sleep and don't want to be disturbed.

"You were crying. You sound so lonely that it is very hard to listen."

I try to push the dandelion wine cobwebs out of my head. What is he talking about? I can't remember my dream. I don't remember crying. But I do feel lonely.

He sits on the edge of the bed, "Are you O.K.?"

"Yes."

He doesn't move. "What can I do to help?"

I shake my head and keep my eyes closed then say, "Tell me a happy story, Will Harley."

"Once upon a time…"

"Come under the blankets and get warm. You're shivering."

We are lying on our backs, carefully not touching in the little bed. I reach for his hand and he holds mine gently. He continues on with his story, something about a princess and frog but he is giving off so much heat that in minutes I'm asleep. When I wake up in the morning he is gone.

"Hey," I say when I find him sitting at the kitchen table.

"Hey," he replies. We sound like idiots.

"Looks like we'll get plowed out today."

Indeed, I can see a brilliant sun and the snow already melting. I feel a sense of loss—an ending.

"Talked with Dad, he is sending someone around 8 to move the snow and then we can be on our way." Will is talking like he is on some kind of commercial; his cheerfulness forced. I make tea. From the stove I ask if he would like some breakfast. He says no. I tidy up the kitchen.

"Dad's looking forward to meeting you, Cassie."

"Likewise."

I pack up my belongings and wait for the plow. Everything is scrubbed and put away. No one would realize that I had been here. There is something sad about that thought. I say good bye to the little house and follow the plow to Old Harley's place; Will stays behind.

"Hello, Miz Burns. I'm Winston Harley, commonly known as Old Harley." A tall man, at least six foot three with salt and pepper hair, crutches his way to me. His large callused hand swallows mine. He does not look or act like an invalid. He looks me over. I do the same with him. I can see where Will's looks come from. For a man in his seventies he looks fit and faintly dashing.

"What do you know about farmin'?"

"Very little."

"Why're you here?"

"I was passing through. The storm took me by surprise. Thank you for letting me stay in your house."

"You know how to work?"

I look him in the eye. "I do."

"Drive a tractor?"

"No."

"Milk a cow?"

"No."

"Bale hay?"

"No."

"Polka?"

"No….hey you cheated. We were talking farming here."

"Well, do you know how to polka?"

I smile. "Of course, and when you're back on two feet I'll show you. My Dad is German and I learned to polka before I went to school. Where did you learn?"

He grins. "I was born dancing."

"Your poor mother!" I smile, too. Old Harley and I'll get along just fine.

Chapter Four

The weather warms up and the snow begins to melt. After the first day when he wakes me us at 4:30 a.m. and I'm confused until noon, Old Harley and I settle into a routine. I make breakfast of eggs, biscuits, ham with potatoes for Old Harley and his three sons Bart, Colin and usually Will, along with the two hired hands—Manny and Christo. Then I make a full meal at noon—they call it dinner. For supper everyone goes home to their families and I just cook for Old Harley and sometimes Will if he makes it back from the law office. In between, I do laundry, cleaning, some shopping but mostly I plan for the next meal. These guys are big eaters. Plus they love desserts. Pie is a favorite followed by chocolate cake. Although I can't say they are picky, there are never any leftovers.

Life takes on a rhythm. I slip up once in the Piggly Wiggly. I'm in the produce aisle when a young man holding the hand of a little boy, three or so, asks me how to pick out a good watermelon. Without looking up I say, "Hey, Gord, show him your method." When the silence stretches out too long I realize my mistake. The young man eyes me curiously. My stomach clenches. I try to smile.

"My husband used to rap his head and then the watermelon. If the watermelon sounded hollower than his head, he claimed it was a good watermelon."

"Was he right?" thc young man asks softly.

"Most of the time he was. Enjoy your watermelon."

When I get back to the farm Old Harley says, "Today we'll tap the trees." I'm getting used to his declarations so I wait patiently.

"Ever tap trees?"

I shake my head.

"You'll like it then. We do it the old way. No hoses for us. Just muscles and totin' buckets."

Old Harley is college educated so I know his colloquialisms are just for me.

The next day we carry buckets and drill holes all morning. I can't tell one tree from another so I'm glad that I'm given the job of hanging the pails on the trees. By pail number 200 I'm getting a little tired. By pail 500 I'm exhausted. The snow in the woods is still over a foot deep and soft so every step is like wading through mud.

In the afternoon we set up the cooking shack, cleaning the four stainless pans and then balance them over their individual fire pits. When the guys split the wood I stack it under the lean-to. I try splitting wood because I'm tired of carrying and stacking but I can't hit the same spot twice with the axe. It looks easy when Bart or Will or Old Harley do it—one whack and two neat pieces of wood. I just can't find the sweet spot and I take a lot of razzing. There has to be some physics lesson or something that would make the task logical and practical for me. I don't discover the secret so I continue to tote and stack.

By the time we stagger home at 7 p.m. and call for pizza delivery, I'm more tired than hungry so I'm in bed by 8:30 and asleep by 8:35.

I must be getting the hang of this country rhythm because I'm awake by 4:30 a.m. and get breakfast started by 5. A quick shower, jeans and tee shirt and no makeup makes for an easy start to the day. I hear some groaning as the guys pull up their chairs and am glad I'm not the only person with sore muscles.

Every day we check the pails. When the majority is three quarters full, we "pick up" the sap. Old Harley drives the tractor pulling a trailer of milk cans behind. The rest of us disperse into the woods with two five gallon buckets, empty the pails from the trees into the buckets and then carry them to the trail, wait for the tractor, empty the buckets and trudge back into the woods. Picking up takes most of the morning. When it snows we just empty the pails on the ground because the snow dilutes the sap too much to make it worth collecting.

When we have enough sap to fill two pans we start the boil down process. We need forty gallons of sap to get one gallon of maple syrup;

that's a lot of boiling. If the weather is cool enough we just boil until we have to do the other chores and let the fire go out. If the weather is warm the sap needs be boiled down before it goes sour. That means firing up well into the night or staying overnight. When we have all four pans full Old Harley, Will, Bart, his wife Anna and their two sons Aaron, age 14 and Justin age 12, Colin, his wife Sally and I spend the night wrapped in old sleeping bags, eating hot dogs and s'mores we roast over the fire. Old Harley keeps us entertained with stories of his childhood until around 3 a.m. when everyone is asleep but Old Harley, who seemed to need only 4 or 5 hours of sleep a night, and me.

There is something about the wee hours of the morning and the heady smell of cooking sap that encourages a different level of intimacy. A month ago I didn't know these people and now here we are, just the two of us talking about books and movies, politics and religion, and traveling. Old Harley has done quite a lot of traveling in his life time. He is a mesmerizing storyteller and I can envision many of the places he talks about because his stories are so vivid. Each place has some crazy anecdote—they had left the youngest at the Alamo when they were in Texas. In San Francisco, two of the boys were wrestling when Will fell off the bed and broke his arm. In Maine, his wife Lorraine discovered she was allergic to lobster and ended up the Emergency Room.

I watch the sun rise for the first time in years and realize that my chest is no longer tight and that the chronic exhaustion I have felt for so many years is gone. In its place is a good tiredness that comes from physical exhaustion, fresh air and a lack of stress. I don't want this night to end. Even as I think this the rest of the crew is stirring. Anna and I make bacon, coffee and scrambled eggs on two tripods over an open fire. We all smell wonderful, like sweet syrup flavored with smoke; it is a heady perfume. I get to know Anna. She is a quiet woman who runs a computer business and home schools her four children. The girls, Sarah and Angela are with Anna's mother because the ritual of staying overnight at the maple syrup shack requires the children ages to be in the double digits. Anna's and Bart's children and the best-behaved kids I have ever seen. They never whine and I have never heard them beg for toys. They don't have a television in their home and their time on the computer or any electronic gadget is limited to one hour per day. They live just across the road from Old Harley and they all help out on the farm at least two hours every day.

The rest of the gang flow out of the shack and soon the two hired hands are sitting at the picnic table. We try to toast bread on the hot dog skewers but lose most of it in the fire. What we rescue we slather with Grandma's strawberry preserves. Even though I eat like a lumber jack my clothes are getting looser.

I talk to my kids every couple of days. Already I have missed a dance recital and several soccer games. The grandkids regale me with a detailed description of the dance practice, what everyone wore and sing a song about vegetables. I clap; I miss them all. They are dear to my heart and I'm used to being part of their lives. But when they ask me when I'm coming home I hesitate. I don't know, I say honestly. They want to know what I'm doing without them and I try to explain the rhythm of farm and the maple syrup and the animals and the work but words don't do justice to the experiences.

I work virtually every day but it doesn't feel like work. It feels like a natural extension of life. I'm out in the barn when the calves and the lambs are born and am sad when one doesn't make it. 100 baby chicks arrive. We put them in the hen house with two light bulbs burning to keep them warm. Sarah and Angela feed them every day. I have pictures of them carefully holding the fluffy little bundles. I sneak out to the hen house to pick them up myself. It is impossible to be sad or angry when you're cupping a yellow fuzz ball in your hands. Despite all of the peeping going on, the chicken house is the most peaceful place I have ever been. O.K. I admit, I like the calf barn with those little red and white creatures running around for the sheer joy of it; that's my second refuge.

For the first time in many years I sleep hard and wake up without an alarm clock ready for whatever the day might bring.

Suddenly the snow disappears and the sap turns dark and thick. Old Harley decides today is the day to bring in all of the pails and boil down the final batch. Everyone celebrates but I mourn just a little thinking that I may never have this experience again. I have a thing about last experiences. Sometimes you know they are your last, say the last day of high school. But other times…I try to remember the last time Gordon and I made love but I can't find that experience anywhere in my brain. There are other last times I remember vividly—the last breastfeeding of Courtney, the last day before Gordon's diagnosis, the last time I played cards with my Grandmother.

As I fire up for the last time I take deep whiffs of the cooking sap and try to store the heavenly scent in my brain. We spend the entire day cleaning the pails in hot soapy water to remove the stickiness, rinse them in bleach water, and then spread them along the trail to air dry before stacking them in neat piles inside the sap shack. Together, Will and Anna clean the boiling pans like the old pros they are.

On Sunday we have Breakfast in the Woods. Although we have tasted each batch of syrup, this is the first opportunity for the rest of the group to try the fresh syrup. We're expecting at least fifty people, possibly as many as one-hundred so while the guys set up makeshift tables the women are busy cooking. I'm the least competent so I peel fruit and set the table while the rest of the women bake bread, make huge batches of baking powder biscuits, fry bacon and mix up the batter for pancakes. Then we throw everything in the back of the pickup including huge frying pans and bounce out to the woods. The kids are sitting on the tailgate and I can hear them giggling; I wish I were with them.

Old Harley tells me "This ritual started with my grandfather and it grows every year. I never really know how many people will show up, the boys invite whoever they want, but there is always enough food for everybody."

"Kind of like the loaves and fishes?" I ask.

"Exactly like that Cassie Burns," he replies with a laugh.

His eyes sparkle and he looks ten years younger. He is walking with just a cane now. He is a force to be reckoned with and I can picture him as a young man turning the heads of many women. He catches me smiling and I relate my thoughts. He throws back his head and laughs good-naturedly and shifts the conversation to his father. "He was a man with a third grade education who could look at a field and calculate exactly how many pounds of seeds he needed to plant it. He sat on all of the county boards and was liked and respected by his friends and neighbors. This same man's dark side caused him to drink himself to death at the age of 49, leaving his wife to finish raising eight children."

We're quiet for a minute, lost in thought. I wonder what devils chase a man to such a dark ending. We reach the woods and there is no more time for reflection.

At the clearing, the children collect May flowers for centerpieces while the men set up tables to do the cooking. One of the traditions is that each man will wear an apron. Not just any apron, but the silliest, most ruffled and embroidered one they can make or find at Goodwill. They actually have a competition to see whose apron is the wildest and this year Matthew, Old Harley's grandson, a state champion discus thrower, wins. Imagine a 220 pound muscle man wearing an apron that's essentially rows of pink ruffles. I stop eating to laugh each time he struts to the table bringing eggs or pancakes. The syrup is warmed up on the camp stove and it is the best food I have ever eaten.

When everyone is sated the kids start a game of softball. Old Harley umps and Will pitches. Anyone who wants to play can. When four year old Watson picks up the bat, Old Harley shows him how to stand and choke up on the bat. With a little help he hits the ball, Will deliberately fumbles the ball, throws it over the head of the first baseman, Justin, who also takes his time chasing it and Watson makes it to second base. Everyone claps. Watson bows. I get called up to play. I played softball in high school but Will sees me as a powder puff and gently lobs the ball over the plate. I smack it and take everyone by surprise. I run past first base, scoop up Watson at second and waltz him across third and head for home while the outfielders scramble for the ball in the woods. Watson wriggles free and races for home plate ahead of me. I see Will out of the corner of my eye running for home plate and I put on a little speed. He catches the ball and I know I'm in trouble. He should throw the ball to Old Harley but he wants to tag me. I don't want to be tagged. I head into the woods, around the sap shack when Will catches up with me. I'm winded, my knee hurts, and I'm reminded that I'm no longer a teenager. I hide in the outhouse. Too late. Will pounds on the door.

"Just a delaying tactic. You know I'm going to tag you when you come out."

"I'm not coming out," I reply panting.

I peek out the crack. Will is whistling and throwing the ball casually in the air with his back to me. I try to sneak out but Will whirls around as

I try to dance away. He advances with the ball while I backpedal. I trip over a log and go down. Will gently beans me on the head with the ball before offering me a hand up. We're eye to eye for a long moment and then we hear the kids calling.

"Uncle Will, bring the ball back."

He grins and lopes off; I return to help the women clean up. It has been a good day.

Old Harley and I have made a habit of sitting on the porch after supper to talk. Often some of the kids or grandkids join us but tonight it is just the two of us. Originally, Old Harley did most of the talking and I just rocked but, lately I have been challenging him and our conversations have gotten livelier. He has an opinion on everything and I suspect that on occasion he picks the opposite side just for the sake of arguing. Tonight we have discussed the latest political brouhaha, when to plant the corn and now he is waxing philosophical on the role of women in farming. I ask him what role his wife had played.

"She was a better farmer than I am. She grew up here. Knew every inch of land. Kept the books. I miss her every day. But not every woman can be a farmer. Take Will's ex-wife. She hated the dirt and the smells. Wouldn't be caught dead in the barn. But she is still something to look at." He shakes his head as if to clear his head of some memory.

"Farming has got to be in your soul if a marriage is going to work. Lorraine and I nearly didn't make it. When we met I was working at the paper factory and had just been promoted. We moved in here with her folks after we were married and I tried to work here and the plant until she gave me an ultimatum. Either I was a farmer or I wasn't. She didn't want to be married to a 'half-assed' farmer. That's what she called me, half-assed. It was our first big fight. I made the decision then and never looked back. Farming has been good to me. Course I could have retired twenty years ago if I had stayed at the paper mill." He laughs his hearty laugh, and added, "But I can't see myself as a retiree either!"

He reaches over, turns up the oldies station, and starts singing along to an old Dean Martin classic, Standing on the Corner. He is a mellow baritone. I watch the barn cats chase each other around the porch. When the song is over, he pushes out of his chair and heads up to bed. He reads every night—farm journals, philosophy tomes, novels and the Bible. He can navigate all day on just a few hours of sleep and his fifteen minute nap in the afternoon. I envy his constitution.

I remember at the last minute to bring in the bird food. We can't leave it outside because of the raccoons and the rumor of a bear. I'm half way across the yard when I see it—the rumored bear. Not a very big one but I assume that the mama is somewhere close. I freeze when I hear a low growl.

"Back up slowly, Cassie," Will said from behind me, coaching.

I can't move when I see the sow walk up to the bird feeders and effortlessly tear them down. She is huge with rolls of rippling fat, dark fur glistening in the moonlight.

Will's hand is on my shoulder and we begin to back up. She swings her massive head in our direction and we stop moving. Carefully, though, we begin moving again, inching backwards. I can feel the sweat trickling down my back. My left foot accidently bangs the first step. The sow looks up, takes two steps toward us growling and swinging her head. The cub distracts her and we make it up the steps. Instantly, the two animals melt into the shadows.

I'm still shaking. "That's much closer than I want to ever be to a bear. W-w-what were you doing out here?"

"Just listening to you and Pa talk."

"Why didn't you join us?"

"He isn't always so forthcoming when I'm around."

"Next time join us. He has some great stories. Thanks for rescuing me, Will. I might have stayed frozen out there all night."

I move toward the stairs. "I'll see you in the morning, Will."

"Cassie…" I turn toward him thinking that he has more to say.

"Sleep well."

I smile and move up the steep stairs.

The next morning Courtney calls to tell me I have an offer on the house. I'm not even sure I want to sell it. I'd raised the kids there. It is home. If I sell it, where will I go?

"Come home, Mom. We have lots to discuss. If you move into one of those great condos on State Street you will never have to mow the lawn or shovel snow again."

She has my life planned out for me—the life of an old lady who needs to be taken care of. I'm pissed. I count to ten.

"Courtney, I'm not sure that I want to sell. Your Dad and I raised our family in that house. It has been a good house for us." I sense Courtney's impatience. She is not a feeler.

"Mom, you have been gone for what, six, eight weeks? You must be tired of traveling around by now. You belong back here with your family."

"Courtney, I have promised the Harley family to help out until the end of summer. We've just gotten the garden planted and the baby chicks are growing fast. The calves need to be weaned and I'm going to learn to drive tractor so I can help in the fields."

There is ominous silence on the phone. Did I mention Courtney doesn't like her plans to be thwarted? I can picture her rolling her eyes.

"Well, Mother, the Heraldsons want to move in within the month. They are offering full price. You won't get a better offer." She calls me Mother when she thinks I'm being deliberately obtuse.

"Just come home for a few days so we can get this cleared up and you can head back up to farm country if you want to."

"Listen, Court, I'll call you back. Let me think about it. I've got a bunch of hungry people waiting for breakfast."

"Two days."

"Got it. Love you, Sweetie. And I miss you."

She softens a bit. "Okay, Wednesday we will talk again. Do you want me to come up there and pick you up?"

I can't imagine Courtney on the farm, the smells, the dirt, the physical labor.

"No, I drove here and I'll drive back. But Courtney, I'm coming back here for the rest of the summer."

"Whatever, Mom. Got to run. Hugs."

"Problems, Cassie?" Old Harley can move very quietly now that he is using just a cane.

"No, I have an offer on my house; which should be a good thing. That was my daughter trying to talk me into coming home. I'm not sure I'm ready to sell my home for one thing, neither am I ready to go back. I don't want to miss anything here with the planting, the baby chicks..." I trail off, "but mostly it is the rhythm of this place. Already it is in my blood. I want to know what is going to happen tomorrow. I've discovered that I like to work hard and play hard. I want to learn how to plow a field and bale hay. I want to help when you butcher and smoke the hams. I didn't realize what I have been missing all my life."

I feel foolish and exposed. I just can't find the words to explain how the farm had gotten into my soul. I start to cry—for what was and for what would never be again. I cry because Gordon is gone and we will never retire together and I know that he would have enjoyed this experience. I cry for my uncertain future. Old Harley just wraps his arms around me and holds me until I stop crying. He gives me his old red hanky to blow my nose.

"I'll go out and check on the chicks. They may need more water," I say because I need time to compose myself.

I don't suspect anything as I approach the hen house. I open the door and there are no chicks. I realize what is missing is the cacophony of peeping. They must have escaped. I check outside the shed. Nothing. I go back inside and realize that there are bits of yellow fluff and spatters of blood on the floor. I run into Sarah as I back out.

"Honey, please get your Grandpa or Uncle Will."

"What's happened, Miss Cassie?"

"Please, get Grandpa."

Reluctantly she turns to go and I check one more time. No bits of yellow sunshine anywhere.

Old Harley gets to the shed first. He walks around the entire building and stoops to examine a hole.

"Damn skunk or weasel got them." He is quiet for minute. "I don't know if there is time to raise another batch to be ready in the fall."

"They are all gone? It ate every single chick?" I am sick. What kind of crazy world allows some creature to sneak in at night and decimate a whole flock of baby birds? What did those little chicks ever do to that skunk or the weasel? Why is the universe so out of whack?

Old Harley puts his hand on my shoulder. Seeing my shattered expression he softens his voice, "It's O.K., I'll call the feed mill and see how many chicks they have left. Every year somebody doesn't pick up the chicks they ordered. Cassie, it will be O.K."

He pulls out his cell phone and places the call. He hangs up and smiles. "There are 75 unclaimed chicks. We can pick them up today. Come on, you drive and we will pick up some extra feed for them while we're in town."

We get a motley bunch of chicks, some with topknots and some with feathers on their legs. Mr. Andrews explains that the woman who ordered them wasn't looking for fryers like we are, just pretty birds. Old Harley snorts his reaction. We take them all and when they are settled in their new home I feel a renewed sense of hope; it feels like both the chicks and I have been given a second chance.

Old Harley and I spend the rest of the day digging around the entire hen house to put in a protective fence. Then we nail wire over the windows. We have made the chicks as safe as possible.

I have done all of the fetching and bending and most of the digging so I'm exhausted. Supper is a grilled cheese sandwich and a salad. Old Harley and I don't say much. I set bread for the morning and put the dough in the refrigerator. I'm getting better at this but I still have to read the recipe carefully and I don't do any improvising.

I make fry bread in the morning and the crew slathers on Grandma's raspberry jam. There are contented groans when the men get up from the table. They have eaten half my batch of dough and I'll only have enough left for two loaves of bread and they go through that much in a day. I thought I knew how to cook for a family but it didn't prepare me for cooking for a crew of hungry farmers. I'm learning to double and triple every recipe.

Today, I'm going to learn to drive the tractor. When we get to the barn the tractor is attached to a piece of machinery. Christo has backed the tractor out and as I walk around the tractor to get on the seat I'm knocked on to the ground by Old Harley's cane.

"What are you doing?" I ask through gritted teeth.

"You were too close to the PTO."

"The what?"

"The power take off. You were too damned close to the power take off. Ever see the damage it can do to a person if it takes a-hold of your shirttail or scarf?"

I shake my head because I don't trust myself to speak.

"Neighbor kid, Ross's boy, got caught five, six years ago. Pounded his head into the ground for 10 or 15 minutes. Shakes, doesn't talk, will need to be cared for until he dies. Cassie, if anything would have happened to you I'm not fast enough anymore to save you." He closes his eyes and shudders.

I get up and brush myself off. I think he is being melodramatic but I carefully skirt the PTO.

"O.K. Climb up and remember to always give the damned PTO wide berth," he scolds and I nod, chastised. "You said you can drive a stick shift, this is the same concept. Just drive around the field a couple of times to get the feel and then you can start plowing."

The day improves after its shaky start. I do learn to drive the tractor, very slowly and not too smoothly. I do plow the field but don't finish until after 8. The hired men would have been done before dinner. Damn, I forgot about dinner and supper. I drag myself into the house and notice some dishes on the cupboard. I don't stop but go right to the shower. I drop into bed and am sleeping in minutes.

Old Harley is studying some maps when I come down the next morning.

"Planning next year's crops?" I ask curiously.

"No, I'm planning a trip." He looks at me seriously.

"Really? Farmers can actually leave the farm?" I tease.

"This one can. Ever been to Europe?" His eyes are bright and he looks the age of his sons.

"No, is that where you're headed?"

He gets up from the table and says, "You could go with me."

I'm astounded and speechless. Then I remind him that I have a job starting in the fall.

"I'm offering you a permanent position here. The trip is one of the perks."

"Old…" I start.

"My name is Winston."

"Winston," I start but he interrupts, "You don't have to answer me now. I can give you some time to think about it."

I think about my kids and the grandkids—can I move away from them permanently?

"We've got 12 more fields to plow, got to run to town to get a part for the planter, the vegetable garden needs tilling and the apple trees need spraying."

"What are we going to do after lunch?" I tease. He tosses the dog's tennis ball at me; I catch it and send it back. There is something comfortable about Old Harley—Winston, and me. He is an incredibly intelligent, articulate and autocratic man. His posture is military perfect and he works as hard as any of the boys. He senses me studying him and grinning strikes a muscle man pose; he is a handsome specimen.

I shake my head and mutter, "Sexual harassment."

"I'll show you sexual harassment," he threatens then crosses the room and kisses me lightly on the lips.

Oh, crap. What was that? I feel myself flushing.

Winston eyes me seriously and asks, "Was I out of line?"

We sit at the table; It seems that on the farm most of the important discussions take place at the dinner table.

Winston starts, "You're an incredible woman, Cassie. You fit this farm. You have brought it back to life and you have brought me back to life. After my wife died I was marking time. But then you came along and my whole world changed. You soaked up everything and all the day-to-day chores became important again. I wanted to get up in the morning just to experience the farm through your eyes and see the look of triumph when you conquered a new task. When I'm talking to you at night I say a little prayer that the sun doesn't come up and that we'll have a few more minutes together."

I'm quiet for a moment marshalling my thoughts. "You flatter me, Winston. Let me tell you a little about this 'incredible' woman. When my husband died I kept his narcotics and toyed with the idea of ending my own pain. Instead, I left it behind and I ended up here. I'm a woman running away from my responsibilities. I have never told anyone the whole story. I rarely admit it to myself except after 2 a.m." I smile a little. "Winston, right now, I'm not whole. I'm playing at being a farmer. Your lifestyle, your work ethic, your commitment to the land fascinates me. At a time I felt most empty this farm filled me up. This is the first time in my life I have felt such unencumbered freedom. I'll be eternally grateful to you for that.

So, that's a circuitous way of saying I'm in no shape to make a commitment until I resolve a lot of issues in my life. Can we keep the status quo until the end of summer? Or, would you like me to go now?"

He looks sad for a minute and then tells me, "Cassie, I'll take you on your terms. Please stay."

He holds out his hand. "Friends?"

Instead, I hug him. "Better than friends. But we're wasting daylight so let's get some of the chores done or the boss might find out we've been slackin' off."

Later, I am lying in bed thinking about Winston's offer when my cell phone rings. It's Bailey.

"Hey."

"Hey," I reply, "What's up?"

"Georgia left me."

I'm stunned. Georgia has put up with a lot of Bailey's shenanigans, why would she choose to leave now?

"What did you do, Bay?"

"She found someone else. Said she's tired of sharing me." They have had an open marriage for years, so again, what is different?

"And?"

"I got a girl pregnant. It happened the night you left. I got shitfaced and next thing I knew I woke up with Gina."

"Nice going, Bay. Are you nuts?" I'm sitting up now and fully awake. "Georgia is the best thing that has ever happened to you."

He is silent a beat and then says, "You're the best thing that ever happened to me, Cass."

"Bailey Walker, do not go there. We tried—more than once. We weren't good together for the long haul." I lower my voice. "Geez, Bailey, I'll always love you. You taught me about love. You're the craziest person in my otherwise normal life and I cherish that about you. You know my deep, dark secrets and you still love me. But, day after day together," I take a breath, "one of us would be dead."

Bailey snorts.

Reaching for the practical, I switch gears, "So now what are you going to do?"

"I want her back. I'll do anything it takes."

"Have you told her that?"

"She knows."

I repeat myself, "Have you told her, Bailey? Women need to hear it. A lot. Every day. More than once a day."

"She moved her stuff out."

"Find her, Bailey. Beg."

"But Cass…"

I cut him off, "Go find her and do what it takes to get her back. Bailey, you love women. Use your charm to get Georgia back. Call me when you have it figured out." I hang up.

Now I'm too wound up to sleep. I slip out of bed and pad to the front porch. There is someone in the rocker. As I turn to retreat Will speaks softly, "Come and sit down, Cassie. We haven't had much time to talk. I have a big case that's keeping me in Green Bay. Sorry to dump so much of the farm work on you. So, what is keeping you up?"

"Old friend called. His wife just left him. He needed to talk."

"So, what did he do?"

I smile. "What makes you think he did something?"

"Usually the case."

"He got someone, other than his wife, pregnant."

"Smart man?" Will sounded genuinely interested

"Usually smarter than that. Long story. But they have had an open marriage since their wedding day. Both have had some interesting side lines."

"Side lines? What do you think of side lines?"

I think for a minute before I answer. "It works for them, me, not so much. I take…took, my vows seriously."

"So you never …"

"No, I never could figure out how women find the time for kids, work, and school." I laugh. "I guess I wasn't willing to give up my sleep!"

Will continues with his thought, "I slept with a partner in the firm. I felt so guilty I came right home and confessed. Not one of my stellar moments. It was the beginning of the end of my marriage."

I'm a little shocked. Will seems like such a straight arrow. I spend a moment musing about my relationship with Bailey; all things considered, we're pretty intimately committed. I'm uneasy with the thought and return my attention to Will.

"So, on the scale of regrets, where does that one fall? "

"Two," he answers without hesitation. Someday, I'll ask him about number one but tonight is not the night.

He is quiet again. I am comfortable with our silences.

"Cass…" He catches me dozing in the rocker.

"Have a great week if I don't see you. Hope you win the case." I struggle out of the rocker and head for the stairs. He follows me. He hesitates at my door. We look hard at each other for a minute before I enter my room and close the door behind me. I lean my head against the door and hear him breathing on the other side. If I open it...but I don't and then I can hear him move on.

Chapter Five

I get up and make breakfast. After I get the kitchen cleaned and dinner started I pack a small bag. Everyone is in the barn; some powwow to which I have not been invited. They are quiet when they turn to me. I wave my duffle. "I'm off. I plan on being back at the end of the week. Lunch is in the slow cooker and a cake in the 'frig. Oh, and the grocery list is on the desk. Bye." I leave to a chorus of good-byes.

Reversing the trip seems poignant. I change Ms. GPS to French and realize she makes as much sense to me this way as she does in English. I crank up the oldies station and sing along. Two hours south of Green Bay I hear a thud, thud, thud my car pulling to the right; I have a flat tire. By the time I get someone out to bring me a new one and put it on it is after four. I drive until I hit Chicago, switch Ms. GPS to English and I find our way back to the hotel I stayed in just weeks before. This time I don't blink when I pay for one night. Winston paid me and tucked in $500 extra. This time I'm going to enjoy the room.

I take a bath with the incredible smelling bath salts. I wash and condition my hair. I'm putting off the inevitable. I pull on a pair of jeans and a teal colored silk shirt over a cream camisole. It is too late to do anything about my hair, which I haven't had colored in weeks. But it has grown out nicely. It is wavy and almost to my shoulders. In the mirror I still see a middle aged woman with pretty eyes and a decent figure. This farm work has done more for my body than my Pilates DVD ever did. My abs are tighter, my legs firmer and even my butt doesn't seem so saggy. A flick of the mascara wand and some lip gloss and I'm ready.

Bully's is my destination, of course. On this gorgeous summer night there is music in the park and people everywhere. I let the crowd move me. I step close enough to see dancers whirling around the fountain. I begin moving rhythmically hypnotized by the warmth and the sensuous music. A handsome older gentleman bows to me and takes my hand waiting for permission. I grin and he pulls me into the pulsing mass. We dance until I'm exhausted. He bows again, kisses my hand and is gone.

I move light hearted and light footed toward Bully's. I fight my way to a little table in the back, order a margarita and a chicken alfredo pizza. I study the crowd as I wait. There is a couple one table over earnestly discussing mortgages using figures that astound me. There are two young girls holding hands and weeping silently; it looks like a break up. Directly in front of me are two men trying to pick up women half their age. One sounds like a used car salesman but the other one is smoother and at least the blonde girl looks interested. Or maybe she is interested in the hundred dollar bills on the table; I can count six from where I'm sitting.

My pizza arrives and I savor it. It is after 1 and it is time for me to go. I'm not used to being up so late. These days I literally get up with the chickens. I pay my bill; look around one last time and exit. I'm disappointed but feeling philosophical about it. I tested fate; nothing happened. End of story.

As I walk back I scan the cars that pass looking for that odd vintage blue one. It is still a glorious night and the walk back to the hotel goes quickly. I scrub my face, brush my teeth and am in bed within ten minutes. I flip on the television when my phone rings. What are the kids doing calling me at this hour?

"Cassie?"

Well the kids don't call me Cassie. "Yes?"

"Kurt. Why didn't you tell me you were coming back to town?"

Why didn't I? He had left me several voice mail messages; I have his phone number. I don't have an answer; just like I don't know how he knows I'm in Chicago.

"Well, I figured if it was meant to be we would meet up again," I respond slowly.

"So how did you feel when it didn't happen?"

"Sad. Relieved. Philosophical."

His voice softens, “But which one dominated?”

“Sad came first,” I admit.

“Look out your window.”

I see a vintage blue car, the headlights flash.

“Do you want me to come up?”

“Yes, I’m in room 423,” I laugh, “but you know that.”

I want to see if the humming still exists or if I only dreamed it. I hastily redress and I’m waiting for his knock. When he enters even the air in the room changes.

“I chose the Swiss bath salts and the French shampoo for you. They have all been waiting for your return. I didn’t think it would take this long. I’m not generally so patient.”

He is waiting for me to say something, but I have never been in this situation before. Until a year ago I had been a wife and mother virtually all of my adult life. I feel like I have lost my defining landmarks. So another me, one I can barely remember from years ago, turns on the radio, and finds a jazz station. Then I offer him my hand. He pulls me on his lap and the hum is so loud it obliterates the music. I close my eyes to hold onto the moment. He kisses me, I feel the first explosion and I shudder. Already it is better than my dreams.

I see how dark his eyes have become and how intently he is staring at me. I’m confused, not about him, but about my own feelings. We kiss again then he gently tugs at my shirt. I lift my arms. He kisses the warm valley of my breasts. I’m breathless when he pulls off my jeans in one practiced move. Momentarily I hesitate but when his eyes question me I nod that I’m ready. He swiftly pulls off his shirt and jeans and I don’t know where to look. I’m not sure that I still know this dance. But he does. He is slow and deliberate. At first I’m not sure where we are going but after a few minutes I know that I’ll follow him anywhere.

With incredible slowness we practice moves I have only read about. We leave the lights on. We are gentle and kind as the night moves into day. We don’t speak. We don’t sleep. Instead we read each other’s body as if we’re seasoned lovers.

When I stop to catch my breath I’m suddenly aware of the time. It can’t be almost 8! I’m expected home by noon and it is a four hour drive.

“I’ve got to go. I have an appointment to sell my house at noon. If I don't leave now I'll be late."

"So? Let me buy your house. We will call the realtor and complete the transaction over the phone."

I stare at him. Who is this man who can make that kind of offer? I realize that I know very little about him. In my mind I amend that statement, I know very little about his life. I don't even know his real name but I know a great deal about his body.

I take a quick last look. He is handsome in a tousled, devil-may-care way. I have never been attracted to that kind of man. Gordie was stable and dependable. Maybe I'm getting senile. I smile and pray that I'm at least able to keep the memories of this night if my mind is going.

"Thank you, no. I appreciate the offer. But, I'm working on the Cassie Burns plan now."

He frowns. "But we could spend the entire day together. I could show you Chicago. Or we could fly somewhere. You have never even been out of the country. Let me introduce you to Paris or Rome."

"How do you know…oh never mind." I kneel next to the bed. "You're incredible—like magic. Being with you makes my world…" I grope for the appropriate word…"shine is the best I can do. And that doesn't begin to explain the humming." I hesitate then continue, "Please understand that this is a totally new experience for me. I'll be able to live for a very long time on the memories of last night." I feel my mouth curving upwards. "And this morning. But this isn't real. I hardly know if you're real. However, I do have a very real life back home and I need to attend to it. Please don't call. You just confuse me."

Although every fiber in my body is at attention, I don't dare kiss him; I'm not sure that I would be strong enough to leave if he asks me again to stay.

"Thank you, whatever your name is. You have a place in my heart," I say. "Always!"

He just smiles and gives me a languid wave as I shut the door. I think I hear him say, "Soon."

I get into town and just make the appointment at the bank. Courtney eyes me suspiciously. I know I look unkempt and I also suspect that I am glowing. My face is whisker burned and so are other places. I'm not sure how I got home. In my mind I am still back in that hotel room. Then I'm brought back to the present and it hits me; I'm homeless and all of my possessions are in storage. It is a strangely freeing experience.

Courtney wants me to look at townhouses and condos. I plead exhaustion and head over to Mark's place. He is still working so I let myself in. The dogs, Mark has four now, go wild and Lassie circles me three times. I let them out. I play with them for half an hour before I crawl into the swinging bed on the end of the porch. I'm asleep and don't wake until Mark comes home two hours later. We talk for a while and then decide to have a picnic. We call the rest of the kids and start burgers on the grill. It is wonderful to have my family around me. I sit on the ground and let the grandkids crawl all over me. Everyone talks at once and I want to hold onto this moment forever. But it gets dark and one-by-one they leave until it is Mark and me sitting side-by-side on the steps catching up on all that I have missed.

"So how are you doing, Mom?" he asks.

"Really good. Sorting things out. Learning and growing. Making friends. I feel like I'm 18."

"We miss you. It is going to be strange not to be able to go home anymore."

I hold his big hand in mine remembering when his fit into my palm. "And, I miss you, honey. But this time has been so restorative for me. I can't explain how the farm has lifted me up and made me believe in the future."

"We couldn't do that for you, could we?" He sounds wistful.

"Sweetheart, I just couldn't do it for myself in this place. It had nothing to do with you or any of the rest of the kids—totally my issue."

He changes the subject. "Well, how long will you be back?"

"Until the end of the week if it works for you."

"It works for me," he answers with a hug.

The next week goes by in a flurry of activities—dance rehearsals, a political speaker with Courtney, two more picnics and lunch with Lila. Twice we Skype Lucas. The second time he tells us that Cora has broken up with him because of his obsession with his studies. His pain is palpable and I want to hold my little boy in my arms again. But he is strong and determined, at lot like Gordon. It takes my breath away to make the comparisons. I am so proud of all of my children, but Lucas wasn't supposed to survive so looking at him always reminds me of a miracle.

Then I'm ready to go back. Just like that I wake up and wonder if they got the baling done at the Simon farm and if all of the new baby chicks survived.

I have only looked at two condos with Courtney—either one will work. They just won't be home. I stop at the campus and look at my office but I don't move anything in. September is a long way off.

Then I'm heading up north. It's been a glorious week and I feel a bit of melancholy. Home and my family have always been so special to me. Unlike my brother who has lived on three continents, I have never had the urge to explore other places. Is this wanderlust because I no longer have my husband for an anchor?

Fifty miles south of Chicago I see a billboard that says, "Cassie Burns, meet me at the Hotel du Nord in 10 miles" with a picture of a large white house with a veranda on three sides. What? I must be dreaming but no, there is another billboard five miles down the road.

When I pull in fifteen minutes later Kurt is standing beside his car. He is wearing a long sleeved, starched white shirt with the sleeves rolled up and pressed jeans. He looks wonderful. I shake my head but I can't help but smile. He takes my hand and smiles back. My hand feels like it is on fire and he grips it tighter; he feels it, too. We dine outside. It is warm and sunny and I'm half convinced that Kurt has made it so by the force of his will. The food is wonderful. We share a crème brulee. I just want to look at him; he is tanned and relaxed. When I question him, he tells me he's been in the Caribbean.

"You could have been with me, Cassie."

I smile. "I had a wonderful week with my family."

"What made it wonderful? Tell me about it."

I tell him and he looks at me puzzled.

"Does it seem boringly mundane to you?"

"Frankly, compared to the Caribbean, yes."

"How do you spend time with your family?"

"I have no family, I'm an orphan." For a first piece of personal information, this is a jackpot.

"I am sorry," I say and take his hand.

He looks away and tenses but leaves his hand in mine. However, the subject is most definitely closed.

"Let's take a walk." I pull him away from the table and we set off to explore the pond I see in a distance. As we walk he tells me about parasailing and diving, jet skiing and dancing until the sun rises.

"You should have been with me," he repeats.

I smile and shake my head.

"Why not?" he demanded.

"Because we met thirty years too late." Then I laugh. "And thirty years ago I would have been arrested for what we do together." I'm sure that I am blushing.

"I don't understand."

"Well, thirty years ago you would have been a child."

"You know, that's not what I'm questioning. Why couldn't we have gone away together?"

"Honestly, Kurt, I don't often find the kind of peaceful pleasure that I desire now by doing and going. I find it in meaningful dialogue and in meaningful relationships."

"So is ours not a meaningful relationship?"

"Ours is a very passionate relationship but meaningful…"I hesitate, and then shrug.

He frowns but I draw him down in a grove of trees and kiss him passionately. He tastes like coffee and cream. I explore his perfectly shaped lips with my tongue then kiss my way down his chest, opening buttons, as they become obstacles. I'm returning last week's favor. The snap on his pants doesn't stop me and I smile when I notice he is not wearing underwear.

"I am commando because I had high hopes, Cassie."

"Not high enough, I'll bet," I promise recklessly. He shudders as my mouth moves downward.

I continue exploring. There is a lot to explore; his long legs and then, of course, back up again.

I don't know where the ideas come from but I tease him for nearly an hour before he reverses our positions. We make love wantonly. We manage to quiet the hum but never quell it. I'm exhausted but my tired body demands once more. Where does all of this passion come from? I realize that it has been many years since I have been loved so thoroughly.

"You're going to kill me," he pants.

"But what a way to die. So, if we're going to die anyway…" From somewhere I find enough energy to pin him down for one final celebration; he hasn't lost his enthusiasm.

Laying back in the grass, without looking at him, I ask, "So, why me?"

"I beg your pardon?"

"Why me? Why that day, that hour? Why did you pick me out of the crowd?"

"Cassie, when I saw you walking down the street you had this," he looks for the right word, "I don't know, aura, I guess, about you. Other people felt it, too. I saw several men and women turn to look at you as you passed. And then, the other night, when you were dancing with that old guy you moved with a sensuality that took my breath away. Kind of like today." He sat up and smiled, continuing, "Anyway, I was intrigued. I needed to meet you. So I followed you."

"I didn't…"

"Of course not."

He continues his story, "I needed an excuse to talk to you. But then when I touched your arm and I felt," he gropes for a word," I don't know, a buzz… a kind of rush, is the best way to describe it. I felt this buzzing and I didn't want to let go. I wanted it to go on and on. I still want it to go on and on. Come with me, Cassie."

"Do you make it a habit of choosing women off the street?" It's a fair question but he brushes it off.

"Of course not, why would you think that?

"I'm thinking I don't know you. How would I know what typical behavior is for you? Just as important, you don't know me."

He frowns but asks, "What do you want to know about me? I know quite a bit about you."

I ignore the last part and ask, "How do you find women?"

"They usually find me." His grin is sardonic.

I sit up to look him in the eye but he drops his gaze.

"Let me get this straight, you're some kind of chick magnet?

Women just magically track you down?" I'm incredulous.

"Something like that."

"No offense, you aren't bad looking but…what the heck?" I'm only half teasing.

"It is because of who they think I am."

"Who do they think you are…. No, on second thought, don't tell me. I think honesty at this stage might mess things up."

He looks relieved and a little peeved. I don't care, as long as we both know the rules of this game.

"What do you mean honesty might mess this up?"

"You haven't been honest with me since the day we met. I'm not even sure your real name is Kurt. But my point is, we're just building a house of cards and while that's not such a bad thing, at least as far as the sex goes, it's pretty ephemeral. Will you just continue to arbitrarily appear like some apparition?"

"It's never been arbitrary and this feels pretty substantial." His smile is slow and sexy. He draws circles with his finger on my breast. The vibration takes my breath away. I grab his hand.

"Can't handle it?"

I shake my head. "I can't put a label on this, this entanglement. I'm a widowed, mature woman and a touch of your hand turns my insides to mush. Shit and it also makes me talk like some soap opera bimbo."

I turn, red faced to get dressed. I'm acting like a sixteen year old with a crush. I'm disgusted with myself.

"Crap," I mutter.

"I like it when you talk dirty when you're coming." He reaches out to take my hand. I align my hand with his for a minute; then close my eyes.

"I'm memorizing you. Now stop embarrassing me. I haven't thought about myself as a sexual being for a very long time. I guess Gordon's disease emasculated both of us."

"What a waste. And you never thought of altering that circumstance?"

I close my eyes. "Not really." I hesitate, "Well, once in a while in daydreams, maybe." I change the subject; I feel a great need to keep each part of my life separate.

"I need to be getting back," I tell him.

"Why?"

"I made a commitment."

"And you're loyal. It is not a question, it is an observation."

"Yes, I believe in loyalty."

Kurt gives me a look I can't read.

"I'm leaving now."

"Let me walk you."

I wait as he starts to dress.

"Will I see you again?" he asks

"If it is our destiny, then I guess so. I don't mean to be enigmatic. I just don't know where my life is going to take me. And, maybe part of me can't deal with much more disappointment."

"Why do you think I'll disappoint you?"

I don't answer so he continues, "I can make this…"he searches for the appropriate words and ends up with "this hot stuff, our destiny."

I face him. He is handsome and arrogant and so self-assured. "Even you can't force destiny," I point out.

"When I grabbed your arm I chose my destiny."

I eye him for a long moment. He's put on his jeans, but they are not snapped and he is rolling up the sleeves of his shirt. When he goes to tuck in his shirt I look away. He could be on the cover of GQ. He is aware of the affect he has on me and stops to strike a pose. I am miffed; it is too contrived. Suddenly, I'm sure he has successfully used that pose in the past.

"Well, my friend, I haven't yet chosen mine." I leave him standing, which from the look on his face suggests this isn't something he's often experienced.

He catches up to me, saying, "Cassie, I'm sorry, but I'm not sure why. Help me understand what just happened."

"Kurt, you're intruding into my life. I can't let that happen. I think about you. Sometimes you haunt my dreams."

He grins and I continue, "I have dedicated thirty years of my life to other people—my husband, my parents, my children and my grandchildren. I'm not saying that's bad. I would not have chosen a different path. But now, now I am learning about me, Cassie Peck Burns.

What I want. What I feel. You, dear one, are an enigma—an intriguing puzzle. Intuitively I know our paths are only going to intersect for a very short time. You may be Thor, but I'm not Darth. And, I feel like I'm a game to you, one that you will soon tire of. I'm not willing to wait for that day."

"You're wrong about me, Cassie." He is so quiet and earnest at that moment I know that somewhere in his other life he is wildly successful.

I get into the car; turn the key in the ignition before I reply, "Maybe."

Chapter Six

I get to the farm too late for supper. Most of the family and some neighbors are gathered on the porch, eating popcorn. Winston's youngest son, Colin, is strumming his guitar; they are singing a mix of country music and hymns. I sit in the car listening for a few minutes before grabbing my suitcase and joining them in singing "Mama don't let your babies grow up to be cowboys." Winston gets out an accordion and starts playing the Beer Barrel Polka. The kids get up and start swinging each other around on the hard packed dirt in the driveway. Anna, the quiet wife of Winston's second son, starts playing a crazy stick with a pie tin, bell and wire spring attached. I am fascinated anyone can make music from such an unsophisticated, cobbled together instrument.

"Polka stomper," Sarah shouts at me because the noise level is increasing. Old John Calaway from the farm just east has his fiddle out and is tuning it. The man must be 85 years old but the way he is jigging and playing you can imagine the young man he once was. The yard light flickers on and I notice at least fifty people dancing or tapping their toes on the porch, on the steps and milling around in the driveway. Someone has brought a big pitcher of lemonade; there is a plate of fudge and a bottle of something being passed around. When it comes to me in the excitement of the moment I take a big swig. Colin's wife Sally pounds me on the back as I cough to get the fiery liquid out of my throat.

"Moonshine," she whispers, "it's an acquired taste."

When I can breathe again I clap my hands and whistle. Winston passes the accordion to young Matthew who starts to play Roll Out the Barrel. Winston grabs my hand and we whirl around. At first I'm awkward because I'm out of practice, but Winston knows how to dance and soon we move gracefully around the driveway. For a big man his movements are light and practiced. I lean back and enjoy the rhythm. Will cuts in and we move quickly around the yard. He is trying to trip me up so I increase my speed. He responds and adds an extra step. Soon we're whirling so fast that at times my feet don't touch the ground. When the music stops I sink to the grass, gasping. I'm gratified to see that Will is winded, too.

"Nice try," I say when I'm able to talk.

"What?" he asks innocently, but he is smiling.

"You thought you could dance me into the ground, didn't you?"

"For a FIB you're not a bad dancer."

I try to glare at him, but the night is so beautiful and the music so perfect I just smile.

I dance with shy, fourteen year old Aaron next. He has the potential to be a good dancer when he becomes more assertive. Then little Angela and I whirl around in circles. Anna and I make a strong showing for the women. When we get to the chicken dance there is so much posturing and crazy moves by the men we barely get through the dance.

When Winston starts the Circle Two Step, I move to the sidelines; this dance is new to me. Matthew starts out calling, "Everybody two step, everybody dance." Some neighbor I have never met grabs me and drapes me over his large stomach. He is holding me way too close when Matthew says, "Two by two, circle right." We dance a few minutes then he adds, "Ladies, one step ahead. Everybody two step, everybody dance." I get a new partner who expertly swings me around several times before we move on. We whirl through the night. The commands get crazier and crazier. At one point the women go to one side of the driveway facing out and the men to the other side. Then we back up until our butts touch and we turn around to find our next dancing partner. Another time the men hold hands, circle the women and give us a squeeze. Then we turn around, choose a partner and off we dance.

I meet Meredith who owns the farm across the road. I learn that her husband died shortly after they purchased the farm. She is originally from San Francisco and she has two children she raised herself. She was a former model and engineer. The reason we hadn't met earlier was because she had been out east purchasing alpacas. Beef cattle pay the expenses, but alpacas are her retirement, she tells me with a laugh. She is gorgeous, tall and regal looking. Even tonight she is dressed in a beautiful shiny blouse tucked into tight white jeans. Her white hair is coiffed in a perfect bob. If she weren't so nice I would be envious. Instead, I find myself hoping we become friends.

The sky is turning pink when the final dance is called. It is a waltz, Good Night Irene. Winston once again gives up the accordion and together we dance like we have been dancing for years. He gives me a little hug and bows. I squeeze his hand and thank him. I don't want this night to end—it has been so silly and so perfect. I wonder if there will be another. I have seen too much sadness in the last few years to believe that I have a right to more than a few pockets of happiness.

I look around at the people who have been so good to me, who have made me part of their lives and I send up a prayer of thanks. As day breaks people head home and I head upstairs for a quick shower before I start breakfast. My body may be tired but my brain is amazingly alert and active.

"Great dance. Great night. Who makes the moonshine?" I ask Will who smiles but doesn't answer.

"Will Harley! You devil. That stuff almost stopped my breathing. Will you show me the still?"

"Ms. Burns," he says with an exaggerated drawl, "I don't know what you're talking about."

When I turn around he snaps a towel at me and before I can respond, he shuts the bathroom door.

Today, haying is on the agenda. Being the least experienced, I'm directed to the haymow; I suspect it is where I can do the smallest amount of damage. The mow workers get a little break when the hay wagons change places but I feel sorry for the guys on the wagons as they work nonstop. The big barn is for the round bales which require less human labor but the square bales are easier to handle with less waste.

We can't bale until the hay is dry because, as it is explained to me, wet hay can start a barn on fire. There is a lot of discussion on just when the hay is ready to be baled. That's why I'm up here at 11 a.m. wearing long sleeves and jeans with a bandana around my hair. It is already 90 degrees outside. It must be 100 up here. I hear someone climbing up the elevator. I climbed up earlier and it gave me the willies. I hope there is an easier way down.

Will pokes his head in. “Just you and me?”

“Looks that way. What’s the plan?”

Will explains the intricacies of stacking hay so that the bales don’t fall over and we use the space as efficiently as possible. Then the hay bales start coming up the elevator; Will throws them as far as he can towards me and I drag them into neat rows. I get so far behind that from time to time Will stops to help me lay the foundation. Then he hurries back to his position and continues throwing bales to me. Once when I am bent over moving a bale he throws one that hits me in the rump and knocks me down. He shrugs an apology but I’m not sure if it was an accident, so I ignore his hand when he offers to help me up.

Walking on the second layer of hay gets harder. Sometimes I fall into the cracks between the bales and end up sprawled face down. When we get the first wagon stacked we have a few minutes to rest. I’m sweating and my hair is plastered to my head. I take off the bandana to swipe at my face. My bra is already so full of chaff that it pokes at me every time I move. When I fall between the bales the sharp hay pushes up my pants and scratches my legs. Checking my calves I see several little rivulets of blood. I blot them with my all-purpose bandana.

Will has taken off his shirt and I envy him the freedom of feeling a breeze on his bare body.

“Go ahead shake out your shirt. Who’s going to see you up here?” he encourages me.

I move to the farthest corner of the barn, remove my shirt and shake it for a minute. The cloud of dust it produces makes me cough. I consider removing my bra; my shirt is big and baggy enough no one should notice. I glance at Will. He is still sitting in the doorway trying to catch every breeze he can. Quickly I remove the sticky garment and shake it out. When I put my shirt back on I feel immeasurably cooler. But, what to do with my bra? It is underwire so I can’t stick it in my pocket. I don’t want to just leave it here, it’s one of my favorites—dark blue with white lace.

As I am considering the possibilities, Will says, “Why don’t you just hang it on this nail and grab it on the way down?"

"You were looking!" My tone is accusatory.

"Wouldn't have missed it."

"When do men ever grow up?" I grumble.

"We don't," he smirks at me, "And you wouldn't want us to." He pulls me to his hot body. I stumble into one of those darn cracks and I'm eye level with his belt buckle. It is apparent he has something besides baling hay on his mind. I have to roll over to pull myself out of the fissure. Will doesn't offer to help. I'm still holding my bra; I hang it on the nail he indicated earlier.

The elevator starts and we're back to stacking hay. We drink water and lemonade all day but neither of us goes down the elevator until dinner at 1. We unload the last wagon at 8:15. I'm not sure that my legs will carry me down the elevator, but the thought of one more minute in the stifling mow moves my wooden legs. I should have called *uncle* two hours ago but my damn German pride said I could finish. Now I'm exhausted; it is an effort to put one foot in front of the other.

The men are hosing off and playfully spraying each other. Winston's daughter-in-laws have prepared supper. I move past the long table filling up with men. I'm too tired to eat.

"At least drink some water, Cassie." Anna presses a glass on me. I can hear her chastising the men for working me so hard. I smile; we women have to stick together. I take the glass gratefully and head upstairs. Heavens, when did they add so many steps?

In the bathroom I slump against the tub as I turn on the water. When I'm done with my shower I take the clumps of hay out of the drain. My arms are scratched and my legs look like I have been attacked by a mountain lion. I'm too tired to comb out my hair. I trudge to the bedroom. Two minutes later there is a knock. It doesn't seem important enough to open my eyes; nothing seems important enough to pry my eyes open.

"Yes?"

It's Will. "You forgot this."

I open one eye. It is my bra.

"Where would you like it?"

"I can think of a few places, but right now on the dresser will work,"

I mumble.

"You shouldn't go to bed without combing your hair. You'll scare people in the morning."

"Why aren't I scaring you tonight, Will? I'm exhausted. How can you still be moving around and talking and making sense?"

"I've done this all my life, Cassie. I've got some ointment to rub on your muscles so they are not so painful in the morning. Let me rub your shoulders and legs."

He notices my arms. "Let me get something for those scratches."

He is gone and I drift off to sleep. He comes back.

"Cassie?" I moan and move away. He doesn't leave.

"Roll over." He lifts up my pajama top and rubs my shoulders. I sigh. When he moves down to my legs, I melt. Then he puts the salve on my arms and I wake up.

"That stuff is disgusting. What is it?"

"Udder balm."

"Udder balm?"

"You know, for the cows…"

"I know what udders are. I don't want to smell like a cow's udder."

He laughs, "You will thank me in the morning, Ms. Burns."

"Only if you crawl in here with me." Shit, did I say that?

Will sits back on the bed and says, "Interesting proposition."

"I didn't mean it. I'm just grateful for the massage. Women will do anything for a massage," I babble. Now I'm wide awake. Will remains on the bed.

"I'm exhausted, Mr. Harley," I fake a yawn.

He leans over dangerously close.

"You are in my personal space," I complain.

He leans closer; I squirm over toward the wall. He lightly kisses me on the head and is gone.

I slump down. I'm pretty sure it is not disappointment I feel.

The next day we bale hay again—you can only do it when the sun shines. It also seems like the other caveat is that it must be over 100 degrees in the mow. Will is in Green Bay and today, Christo and I work in companionable silence. I think I'm getting a rhythm, pick up, drag, position. My mind is free to wander.

My psychologist always wanted me to examine my feelings. Sad, glad, mad, hurt, happy, anxious, he would ask and I would try to assess where I was. Today the feeling I identify is contentment. I like the way my muscles still work. It is nice to fall asleep every night grateful and humbled and to wake up looking forward to something new.

A little less exhausted the second day I eat supper and listen to the discussion of rotating crops, the price of fuel, and the local baseball team, the Bullfrogs. Then someone mentions swimming and everyone scrambles to finish the dishes and get ready. We load into a couple of trucks and we head down the road a couple of miles to the local swimming hole. Many of neighbors are out swimming so someone strings up a net and a game of water volleyball starts. Competition is strong. Colin and his son Matthew are amazing players and rarely get beaten. It's fun to watch. I just float in the pond. Finally I feel my core temperature drop to less than 100 degrees. I'm almost asleep when twelve year old Justin splashes me. I splash him back and we race around the volleyball net. Will is playing now and when I make the turn he deliberately trips me so Justin can race ahead. I come up sputtering determined to get my retribution. I swim underwater and try to pull Will's feet out from under him, but he is too strong and too quick and soon I'm underwater again. Then we're playing dodge ball with 4 or 5 people throwing balls. We're having so much fun I don't realize when the darkness set in. I have never worked so hard nor played so hard in my life. As we load back into the trucks I reflect that many days I have gone from exhaustion to exhilaration. Farming seems like a life of extremes.

In Illinois I suffered from headaches, acne and sleeplessness. None of these have bothered me since I have been here. The Harleys should bottle the farm air and sell it. I amend that thought, maybe not after we spread manure.

When I get back to my room my cell phone tells me I missed two calls—one from Mark and one from Courtney. I debate saving the calls until morning but my mother guilt jumps in and I call Courtney. Like always, she is short and to the point. "Lucas has been in an accident. They flew him to Central Hospital."

"How bad?"

"We don't know yet, he is in surgery."

"I'm leaving now and will be there as soon as I can. Hold onto him for me, Courtney." She is crying; Courtney never cries.

* * * *

Several hours later, I walk into the now familiar hospital. I'm so frightened I hold myself in check by cursing Gordon for not being with me. It is easier if I am angry. When I find Lucas' room I don't recognize the still body in the bed. There are bandages on his head, his right arm is in a cast and there are tubes running in and out of him. I take a deep breath, and begin talking to him in a slow, soft voice. Over and over I murmur how much I love him, that he has work to do here so he can't give up. I tell him his dad would push him out of heaven because it is not his time yet. Lucas doesn't move. A nurse comes in and tells me he is in a drug induced coma to help his brain heal.

A doctor comes in and gives me percentages and odds while I nod and hold Lucas's hand willing life back into him. Clinical people file in and out, but I don't pay them much attention. Lila comes and starts crying so I encourage her to go home. Courtney and Mark call and I tell them to go to bed; that I'll call if anything happens. I keep a vigil through the night afraid that he will slip away if I close my eyes. When the sun rises I go to the window and pray hard.

A tall, beautiful woman in a white coat slips into the room. I ignore her thinking she is one of the many physicians coming in to poke and prod, until I hear her soft murmurings to Lucas—words of encouragement and hope ending with a prayer. Then she turns to me and introduces herself as Gia, a close friend of Lucas. I study her more closely—wide set brown eyes, long dark hair, solemn and serious.

"I met him here in the hospital. I'm a first year resident and he drove the ambulance. We became friends almost immediately. He may look rough now but he is a very strong man and I know that he will come back."

"He overcame much greater odds when he was born," I tell her relating the story of his birth and his tenacity.

She allows herself a small smile and suddenly she is incredibly lovely. I can see why Lucas would be attracted to her.

"I'm working but I'll slip in as often as I can. Don't worry, Mrs. Burns."

"Call me Cassie," I call out after her. Then Lucas and I are together for another long day. I talk to the kids. Courtney stops by and stares transfixed at her brother. When Mark comes he cries soulfully and then we're all crying. In the middle of it all Lila calls to say that she has a sick child so she won't be coming to the hospital.

Finally we calm down and the kids leave. I must have dozed and was dreaming because suddenly I see Gordon looking the way he looked when we first met in college, unruly black hair, scrawny mustache and an irrepressible grin.

"I need your help here, Gord."

"You're doing fine." He answers.

"Not so fine. I'm afraid for Lucas. I can't lose him."

"He's going to be fine, but you need to take care of yourself."

"What's it like in heaven, Gord?"

"It is impossible to explain," he sighs and I realize that he is fading.

"Don't go, Gordon, please. I miss you." My pleadings go unheeded because now he is gone; I feel his absence.

"Mrs. Burns…"

I turn to Lucas's physician, Dr. Gregory. "Who were you talking to?

"I…" I know I'll sound crazy, but add, "My husband. He died a year ago."

"You need some sleep. I will order something for you. Go to the visitor's bedroom and wait for the nurse to bring you some medication."

"But Lucas…"

"He is in the best possible hands. I'll let you in on a secret, Mrs. Burns: we never give up on one of our own. So sleep and tomorrow will be a different day." As a mother, I'm not pacified. He said different, not better, but I'm in no shape to question him.

I sleep in the visitor's bedroom until noon the next day. The doctors have congregated when I make my way to Lucas's room.

"A good sign, Mrs. Burns, Lucas is breathing more easily. Moving in his sleep. Even saying a few words. Please come here and talk to him."

"Sweetie, please wake up, its mom. You're missing some great summer days. Courtney and Matt were here and are coming back tonight. Lila's littlest, Jesse, has an ear infection so she can't be here."

Lucas moves his left leg restlessly. He licks his lips.

"Mom," he mumbles.

"Lucas, it is time to wake up, honey." I remember a little ditty I sang with all of the kids so I sing to him, "Wake up, wake up, you can't sleep all day. Wake up, wake up, you've only got fourteen hours left to play."

He groans and I lean in to hear him. Laboriously, he says, "That's…embarrassing."

I sing louder.

"Awake. Stop…singing." He groans again.

I move aside as the physicians step in to conduct their examinations. Gia slips in a few minutes after they leave the room. She is smiling. She kneels next to him and holds his hand. She murmurs something too low for me to hear. I see Lucas squeeze her hand.

I move to the back of the room and whisper, "Gordon, he is going to be O.K. You were right, again. Thank you. I love you. Good bye."

Each day, Lucas recovers a little more. He was in great shape before the accident and now youth and resilience are on his side. He doesn't remember the accident. By the start of the eighth day after the accident he is talking about going home. The doctors are cautiously optimistic. He's been making great strides in physical therapy. Gia is taking care of him and I learn that she will be moving in when he goes home.

I go to Mark's house to finally get a good night's sleep. He is still up. Suddenly I remember that he had left me a message two long weeks ago.

"Why did you call me?"

"I didn't call you, Mom," he replies.

"I mean the day of the accident."

He is very quiet for a moment before he answers, "I wanted to tell you that I'm in love and am getting married."

"Wow. Who is the lucky woman? Do I know her?"

"He, Mom, Mickey Dolata. I don't think you have ever met him."

I ruminate a minute, the name sounds familiar. "Sure, high school, I think. Great long distance runner and starter on the basketball team." I close my eyes and continue, "Tall, red hair, loved brownies. Used to come over after practice."

"That's Mickey, Mom. You have quite a memory."

"So tell me about it."

"We met up again a few years ago and have been together ever since. He is in banking."

"A few years? You never said anything."

"The timing was never quite right. Still isn't really with Lucas and the accident but we're having a civil ceremony this weekend. Are you surprised, Mom?"

I think for a moment, am I surprised, but not really. Slowly, I shake my head and ask, "Are you happy?"

"Yes, I'm O.K. alone with my introvertedness, but Mickey adds…" he hesitates a moment to find the right word, "exuberance to my life."

"That's all that matters, honey."

"Would Dad have been disappointed?"

"No, he wants you to be happy, too. Am I invited to the ceremony?"

"Of course and Lucas is my best man. Courtney says she isn't coming. She is against it on principle."

"Lila?" I ask.

"Coming and bringing the kids. I'll be their show-and-tell when they get back to school," he laughs unselfconsciously.

How could I have missed all of this? I wonder what else I have missed.

Saturday dawns as one of those perfect summer days. A simple ceremony is held at Mark's, I guess I should say Mickey's and Mark's, place. It is solemn and touching. Courtney and her husband, Rafe, deign to attend. All of Lila's children are the flower girls; each wears a different color pastel dress and they are heartbreakingly beautiful. Lila's husband isn't with his family. I make a mental note to talk to Lila about his absence. Mark and Mickey are in tuxedos as is Lucas, who is in a wheelchair with Gia close by.

Mickey's parents, two brothers and three sisters attend. There are a handful of friends, several of whom I remember from high school and college. My brother flies in from China and instantly becomes the center of attention.

As Mark and Mickey turn to each other I reach for Gordon's hand.

Self-consciously I pull my hand back. I see Courtney look at me and frown, my judgmental oldest.

Then the ceremony is over and everyone is clapping and hugging. We have a Mexican spread of burritos, tacos, and margaritas under a big tent. Mark doesn't stop smiling. Mickey sits down by me on the steps. "Well, Mrs. B. what would you like me to call you?"

I put my arm around him and respond, "Whatever feels right"

"Well Mark always refers to you as Mom, I refer to my mother as mother, so if you are O.K. with Mom…"

"Perfect!" We hug and he moves on to receive congratulations from the other guests.

Lila drops by next, little Jesse on her hip. We talk about the wedding and then I ask if Anston is working. She looks away and I remember her on her own wedding day, the day after her high school graduation. She couldn't wait to marry the charming Anston Blake; she wasn't even 18. I didn't know that she was three months pregnant until weeks later. Now her blue eyes cloud, she looks like that vulnerable seventeen-year-old again.

"He's sleeping around, Mom."

Although I catch my breath, I'm not really that surprised. For a moment looking at her stricken face I wish Gordy was here to knock some sense into Ashton. Then I remember ruefully that Gordy never hit anyone.

"Aw, Sweetie." I hug Lila and little Jesse pats me on the shoulder and coos. I kiss Jesse's baby fingers and she giggles. I have no words of wisdom so I ask, "What can I do for you?"

"Just be there, like always. I don't know what I'm going to do yet. Thank you for not giving me unsolicited advice. I get plenty from Courtney."

We talk for a few minutes longer before Jesse starts fussing. I hug her fiercely when she gets up to leave and she gives me a tight smile. My brave youngest daughter; in many ways she is stronger than tough talking Courtney. Sandy and Ashley give me good-bye hugs and I marvel again at how much they have grown.

I walk around the house picking up trash and talking to Gordon in my head. We're having a lively debate when Courtney stops me with an uncharacteristic hug. "We're quite a family, aren't we Mom?"

"Actually, I was just thinking how proud your father was of all of you. Thank you for being here for Mark."

She waves me off dismissively.

"What do you think about Lila's news?"

"I'm sad for her. How are you two doing?"

"Lila and me?"

I nod.

"Sometimes she is so gullible I just want to shake her. But she has three of the most gorgeous daughters I have ever seen. And, they are so well-behaved she must be doing something right." Her voice is wistful.

We never talk about why *she* doesn't have children. I wait to see if she will share any more information, but she doesn't. We talk a little about the condo she picked out for me. I'm non-committal.

I seek out Lucas who is looking tired. Gia is hovering. She's been urging him to go home for hours. I hug him carefully. He attempts to give me his old sassy grin but fails. I, too, urge them to leave.

"When are you heading back up north, Mom?"

"Tomorrow or the next day. Depends upon how you're doing. I'll stay as long as you need me."

"Mom, I appreciate your offer, but go back up north. I haven't seen you look this happy for a very long time. I suspect that the farm has a lot to do with that. When I'm feeling better Gia and I'll come for a visit."

"I'd like that, Sweetie. Now scoot."

I hug Mark and Mickey, plead exhaustion and turn in. The party keeps going and I fall asleep to the sound of laughter and jazz.

The next morning after helping Mark and Mickey clean up I'm restless; I've had too much idle time. I mix up a batch of bread. After explaining the intricacies of kneading it and letting it rise, I leave. I stop for a moment to say one last good-bye to Lila who whispers that Anston has returned. I keep my face purposefully blank.

"I love him, Mom."

I smile and hug her again. She will figure it out; she is smart beyond her years. Sandy and I kick the soccer ball around, Justin showed me a few moves and she is impressed.

"Grandma, I saw grandpa."

"Really? What did he have to say?" I ask curiously. Sandy is our dreamer; she's had a number of imaginary friends in her short life time, the last was a blue frog named Elmer.

"That heaven is bea–u-ti-ful."

"I'm sure it is."

"And that he misses us, but he is protecting all of his baby birds."

"He said baby birds?"

"Yup."

I pull her onto my lap and she cuddles in. When our children were little, gathered around the table talking and eating, Gordon would refer to them as baby birds because of the noises they made. Unless Lila talked about it, I don't know where Sandy got the term, unless of course, she really is talking to Gordon. If I do, why does it seem impossible that she does?

"Does it scare you when you talk with grandpa?" She gives me a "why would it" look.

"'Course not, its Grandpa. But he looks different—kinda skinny with a, you know, hair on his lip. And his hair is black. But I know it's grandpa 'cause he calls me his sweetie pie. Do you think there ain't no food in heaven, that's why he is so skinny?"

"Isn't," I correct her. She looks worried about the food situation so I assure her that people in heaven get everything they need.

Then it is nap time and with one more hug, I'm on the road. It makes sense that Gordon would talk to Sandy because as the oldest grandchild they spent a lot of time together. They had an incredible bond and I'm pleased that death did not break it. Sandy will always have her grandfather.

My next stop is Bailey's house. It is a beautiful, new brick two story. His car is in the driveway but he doesn't answer when I knock. I'm worried. Bailey can hit some pretty low points. The front door is open so I go in. I haven't been here often. Bailey's and my relationship lives in its own little world.

"Bailey?"

No answer. I open doors and continue yelling. I finally find him in the bedroom. It smells like a tavern. I shake him. He is drunk. Bailey has always been about extremes. That's one of the reasons we couldn't stay together; he is just too exhausting.

"Come on, get up. You're going to take a shower and I'm going to make you coffee. When did you eat last?"

He mumbles something. I drag him out of bed. I turn the shower to cold. I can't shove him so I climb in and drag his sorry butt into the shower. He slumps against the wall. I adjust the temperature to warm. Eventually he starts groaning. I shake him.

"Bailey."

"Cass. What'er you doin' here?"

"Looking for you. Tell me this drinking is a fluke."

"This drinking is a flu… Tis drinkin' isa fl.. flu.."

"Bailey, finish your shower. I'm going to make some eggs and we're going to talk. And brush your teeth—you smell like a drunk." I check on Bailey in the shower; he is asleep. I turn the water to cold. He yelps and crawls out. I hand him his toothbrush and a robe. Never svelte I see he's gained at least 20 pounds.

In the kitchen there isn't much to work with so I quickly dress and run to the store for eggs, bacon, coffee and bread. When I return Bailey is at the table with his head in his hands. I make breakfast. He eats what I put in front of him but is unusually quiet. I get up and go behind his chair to hug him. He leans against me and I see the anguish in his eyes. The guy looks like a linebacker and has the heart of a child. I rock him back and forth.

"I have missed you, crazy man," I whisper to him. Finally, I sit down next to him and as I hold his hands he lets loose a torrent of words. Today I see the little boy whose father beat him regularly so that he "would become a man." As an adolescent more than once I begged my parents to call the authorities to make the beatings stop, but Bailey's mom always denied there were any problems.

The day I'll never forget is the time Bailey's dad hit me. I was just collateral damage. What happened is this: I was about twelve years old, which would make Bailey eleven and a half (he insisted on remembering those extra 6 months). His dad came home early from his job; he was a psychologist. Bailey and I were building a fort in the backyard. I don't know why we were at Bailey's house because we rarely played there—too risky because we did not want to run into his dad. Anyway, his dad walked into the fort and just punched Bailey. I was stunned. My parents didn't believe in corporal punishment and Bailey's dad had been pretty careful in the past not to be violent in front of other people. Bailey lay on the ground bleeding from a cut on his head so I wound up and punched Bailey's dad with all of my eighty-nine pounds of anger. He backhanded me into a tree like I was a bothersome fly. I lost consciousness, my parents were called and I was taken to the hospital for overnight observation. Something happened between my parents and Bailey's dad that day. Nobody ever talked about it. Even today, Bailey and I never mention the incident.

But since that day I find it hard to believe the adage, what doesn't kill us makes us stronger. While those beatings didn't kill Bailey's body, on days like today I know they did something terrible to his spirit.

Like an over-wound clock, Bailey finally runs down. He is quiet for a moment and I kiss his puffy face. He pulls me out to his shop and shows me his new project—a 1949 dump truck. The front half is painted bright red with a yellow horizontal flame. He explains how he is going to fix up the back end. It is nice to see him animated. When he is like this I just want to bask in his circle of energy.

Looking at him now I see the eighteen year old who went to a Chinese restaurant and started dancing to the music. Lord, it was embarrassing then but retrospectively endearing—the looks on the faces of the other patrons! It makes me smile to think about that night. Kooky, sincere, sensuous, thoughtful, broken, warm—there aren't enough adjectives to describe Bailey.

We talk all night. He is resigned to Georgia's leaving. He is considering selling the house. He just bought another business—pest control. When I ask him what he knows about pest control he just grins and tells me it was such a good deal. He always needs projects. If he is still too long he looks for trouble; for Bailey trouble often comes inside a bottle.

I make him promise not to drink again; that he is to join AA and that he will start writing poetry again. When he is introspective his insights are profound. I have no doubt these last days will be fodder for his next poems.

As I turn to leave, I hug him trying to impart strength into a body at least twice my size.

"Thank you for rescuing me." His eyes are sad.

"I can't think of anyone I would rather rescue. But," I admonish, "don't pull this stunt again."

I soften my voice, "Let's talk more often."

I leave and don't turn around because as a caretaker I could be easily sucked into his abyss. I'll always need strong boundaries with Bailey.

Chapter Seven

Finally, I point my car north. For about 100 miles the scenery is achingly familiar from family drives, picnics and mini vacations. I feel a strong urge to turn around, settle into the Courtney-chosen condo and start the life I once believed was mine. But when over the next few hours the landscape evolves, I can feel myself changing, less mom-like and more adventurous. I take a new route and ignore the GPS. Twice I get lost, but eventually discover a road that gets me where I want to be.

My soon-to-be new boss, Francis Jensen, calls me on my cell. She asks why I haven't been into work; I murmur something about it still being early. She chastises me for not submitting outlines for the four classes I am teaching. Then she reminds me to read the handbook, 'especially the section on sending out department-wide e-mails I haven't approved'. She rambles on about several other breeches that new professors typically make. I tune out. During the interview I related to several professors instantly, but Francis, with her black and white credo, wasn't one of them. One of the newer professors, Suzanne Rango, took me aside and assured me that *Doctor* Jensen was so busy climbing the ladder that she typically couldn't be bothered to harass the peons. For some reason, Dr. Jensen is making the exception with me. I assure her that I'll read the handbook and report to the college two weeks prior to opening day. I must have sounded properly compliant because she wished me a good day. I hung up thinking that I might have made the wrong decision. My actual thought was 'bitch'.

I'm nearly to Green Bay when I remember that Meredith sells alpaca fleece and sweaters at a farmer's market on Saturday mornings. When I pull in it is late morning and am glad to see she is still going strong. She greets me warmly and I help her pack up her things. She's done some bartering and I pack up kettle corn, a bag of vegetables, frozen emu sausage and half dozen pastries from the Too Sweet Bakery. She shares the pastries with me and I impulsively invite her to lunch. She chooses the Green Canary, a tiny hole-in-the-wall that serves fabulous fresh mushroom quesadillas. We talk about our husbands and loneliness, our kids and the future. We talk until the alarm on her phone reminds her that she has to check on one of her pregnant alpacas.

As long as I'm in town I decide to get my hair cut and a facial. I have missed some of these hedonistic pleasures. I get talked into a manicure and pedicure. I stop at the mall and pick up a slightly sexy nightgown, a few new tops and a pair of jeans. I celebrate going down a size with a little jig in the aisle; a willowy brunette shopper smiles and gives me two thumbs up.

After changing into my new clothes I decide against fast food for dinner and go to a supper club—Hawk's Rise. It is on the bay, the seafood is great and I indulge with a glass of wine. Right now I'm between two worlds, my old life and the farm with no responsibilities or accountability to anyone. I don't think I have ever been this free.

A tall, dark haired man approaches and offers to buy me a drink. I turn him down with a smile and return my gaze to the water. He sits down at my table. Startled I turn to him and frown.

"Excuse me."

"You know you don't want to be alone tonight," he says, smiling.

"Oh, but I do," I say politely and firmly, once more turning away.

"Don't turn your back on me." His voice is suddenly cold and low.

Angry, I decide he will not force me to leave. I continue to stare at him.

He reaches for my hand and I jerk away.

"Don't," I say between clenched teeth.

I'm so intent on dealing with the situation I don't see anyone approach the table until the man is yanked out of his chair so quickly I miss what happens next. Shaking I sit down. After a few calming breaths I look up to see Kurt smiling at me, and the dark haired man staggering out of the restaurant.

Kurt's knuckles are split and bleeding; he sits down and wraps his hand in a napkin.

I pick up his good hand, turn it palm up and kiss it. He cups my face. I close my eyes and enjoy the humming. Kurt puts his other hand to my face, draws me to him and kisses me until I feel liquid.

When I open my eyes the waiter is hovering anxiously.

"Crème brulee and two spoons, please." Kurt orders. We stare at each other holding hands across the table. I thought my libido had died, but all I want when I'm around Kurt is to be in bed. Naked. Doing things that take my breath away. We eat the dessert slowly, like foreplay. Over his protests I pay and pull him out the door.

"I have a place not far from here," he says. "Leave your car, we can pick it up another time, or I'll send someone."

I study him in the faint light. "There is a song about the dashboard light by Meatloaf…" I hum a little. Kurt picks up the tune and starts singing; he has an incredibly full voice. He knows all of the words; I chime in when I remember them.

I notice that we're in the old part of town with big, three storey houses. What I see of his house when we run through the kitchen and dining room is that it is very beautiful. Later, I'll stop and examine the pottery and sculpture. Right now there are more important opportunities. The bedroom is maroon and black with a highly polished wooden floor.

I pull out my purchases from earlier in the day. I hold up the midnight blue nightgown. "I could model?"

"Superfluous," Kurt says, grinning.

I drop the nightgown and go to him. We take off our clothes and climb into the high bed. In this half light his eyes are golden, like a cat's; a dangerous cat; a cougar or a lion. He is warm when he pulls me to him and with one more kiss we're ready. Having him poised above me is exciting and feels slightly dangerous. He looks like some kind of Greek god. I keep my eyes open to capture the moment. Making love with Kurt is like a ballet. We don't bump noses, we don't get tangled in the sheets; instead we move together and each time our dance feels brand new.

Kurt is amused at my fervor. Tonight I can't get enough of him. When we finally slow down, I flip on my stomach to better study his classic features; deep set eyes, strong nose, lips that are too full to be on a man. He has a tiny scar by his right eyebrow and longer one on his back that I feel when I hold him. In an attempt to control the humming I move just far enough away so that we're not touching. I don't talk but that seems to be our pattern. We don't need many words to go where we go.

"It's time," I say after what could have been a few minutes or hours. I move to get up but he pulls me back. Like an addict I capitulate to my craving. At 3 a.m. we're sated and Kurt falls asleep. I slip out of bed to shower. I get a cab to take me back to my car. I feel paradoxically drained and as light as air. I think I could bale hay, clean the house and dance all night.

I'm back to the farm by 5 a.m. to find Winston pacing and looking at the sky. He hugs me quickly and explains that threatened rain is making him anxious because there is still a small hay field that needs to be baled. Everyone is busy and he doesn't know when to expect Will.

"Why don't you and I get started then?" We have to wait until the dew burns off so I head to the house to unpack and check the kitchen; it is a mess so I clean until Winston whistles.

We argue over who should be on the wagon. I'm not sure his hip is healed enough to take the heavy labor. I flex my puny muscles and he just laughs. I drive. The field is hilly with a drop off to the river on my right. I'm inexperienced and tentative. I look back and Winston is comfortably balanced on the wagon. He gives me a signal to speed up and points up at the sky. I speed up but overshoot the row and have to backtrack. Winston yells and gives me the speed up signal again. I step on it hanging onto the steering wheel tightly to control the darn thing. When I look back I see I have bounced Winston off the wagon. I stop. He gets up so I know that he is not hurt. I can see his mouth moving. I'm sure he is not happy with me. For a moment I think about gunning the tractor and heading for home. Then I turn to take my tongue lashing but Winston just shakes his head and swings back onto the wagon. We get all of the hay baled and in the barn before it starts to rain. I raise my hand over my head in a gesture of victory and Winston gives me a high five.

Impulsively, Winston asks me if I would like to go into town to eat. He seeks out a tiny building that was once a train station, now cleverly called the Waiting Room. Everybody knows Winston. Old Mr. Wiscow stops to talk about the price of milk, and then hobbles back to his wife who waves timidly. Doc Miller's son, Victor, the owner of the restaurant, steps from the back room to shake Winston's hand and comment on how well he's healed. Widow Milton, beautifully coiffed and made up, spends several minutes flirting with and flattering Winston.

"Looks like you're king around here," I tease.

"I have been here a long time. These people, with their strengths and foibles, are like family. You can't ever take that for granted. In '97 when the tornado came through and upended the big oak putting it through the roof and blowing out windows, I had twenty people in the yard with chainsaws and boards before the siren stopped. And when they were done with us, we all moved on to the next farm. We didn't stop until we knew everybody was safe, dry and accounted for. Sure Billy Tartan drinks too much and Rosie May steps out from time to time and rumor has it there has been some wife swapping going on but..." he stops and grins.

"Really, who? I haven't been hanging out in the right places all of these years." I smile back at him.

"Small town rumors shall never pass these lips." He sits up primly trying to give me a supercilious stare but the twinkle in his eye gives him away.

"You crazy man," I say as I lean over to kiss his cheek. He moves and my lips graze his. He puts his calloused hand over mine.

"Honey," he says softly.

"Sugar bun," I joke to clear the air.

"Baby cakes," he shoots back, taking up the game.

"Hunka-hunka". I waggle my eyebrows.

He sits back and smiles. "I just like being with you, Cassie Burns."

"And Mr. Winston Harley, I like hanging with you, too."

We talk all the way back to the farm. I can see Winston is flagging. I tell him I'm tired so we skip the porch debate tonight. He touches his fingers to an imaginary hat and I curtsey.

In my room I call the kids; Lila first to hear about the swim meet where Sandy came in second and the Ashley's dance practice—she promises to e-mail pictures. I ask about Ashton and find out he is back and being a wonderful father and husband. I send hugs.

I call my parents in Florida—they are well and enjoying their pinochle club as well as Wednesday's pool tournaments. Mom is practicing cooking seafood and Dad is a favorite fix-er-upper for the many widows. I smile at the thought of Dad as a Lothario.

When I call Lucas, Gia answers. Lucas is in bed. He is recovering but still tires easily. He is back in classes and is nearly caught up from the time he was in the hospital. Like a typical mother I ask if he is eating and Gia laughs, a soft tinkling sound, and exclaims over how much he is eating. I thank her for taking care of my son and ring off.

I call Courtney and she tells me about issues at the hospital, an abandoned child, a six car pileup. She is also taking cooking lessons, which amazes me since she's never been interested in domestic duties. Her current assignment is bread, and she explains the intricacies of good bread. I smile and just listen. Perhaps we will find something in common yet. She tells me about a concert she and a friend attended. "Infyniti, new retro band, and Mom, even you would like them. They sing Rat Pack music—40s and 50s—with this whole new dreamy sound. Plus K.C. Troy, the lead singer isn't hard to look at. I think their last gig was up near you. Are you close to Green Bay?"

"Yes, I'm, less than an hour north." I'm getting tired and need to call Mark before I go to bed so I am only half listening.

"Sweetie, I need to call Mark and Mickey so I'd better get going."

"Mom, have you forgotten they are on their honeymoon in Sweden?" I can hear the inflection in her voice when she says *honeymoon*; tonight I choose to ignore it.

"And Mom, Bailey is off the wagon." All of my kids like Bailey. He is the quirky uncle who slipped them a $20 or loaned them a car when they were growing up. So, essentially they are my spies.

"Thanks, hon. I'll touch base with him." I blow out a breath.

"Do you think Georgia is gone for good?" Courtney asks.

"I do." My answer is honest.

"Could you talk to her? I mean, Bailey is losing it. I know what he did was stupid but he's suffered enough."

"You know what he did?" I ask.

"Everybody knows. Bailey's about as transparent as a condom."

"Courtney!" I try to sound mother-like but she catches me by surprise and I laugh out loud.

She sighs. “Mom, save Bailey from Bailey, will you? He seems to listen to you. I’m so glad that you married Dad. Bailey’s a great, crazy uncle but he would have been a hard guy to grow up with, if he ever grows up.”

“When did you get so wise my child? Can I take the credit for it?” I tease.

“A large part, Mom, a large part. But actually, Dad explained Bailey to me years ago.”

“He did? What did he say?”

“That Bailey never got over you.”

I hesitate for a moment and then say softly, “I’ll give Bailey a call. I miss you, darling.”

“I miss you, Mom, and I love you.” Then she is gone, my private, stoic, oldest daughter.

I call Bailey. “Word’s out that you aren’t keeping up your end of the bargain.”

“I tried,” he answers.

“Not hard enough. What am I going to do with you?” I let him hear the frustration in my voice.

“Come back home. We’re both free. Let’s try it one more time,” he asks softly.

“Bailey, can’t happen. I’m not the same person who left.”

“So tell me.”

And I do. I tell him about all of the crazy things that have happened to me in the last weeks, more than my entire life. I tell him how alive I feel. He is quiet for a few minutes before he says softly, “I can’t remember the last time I heard you talk like this. Cass, you’re where you need to be.”

“Oh, Bay, I can’t be truly happy when you’re so miserable. Tell me what you need from me.” I want to help him.

“I don’t know anymore, Cassie. I need to get my act together. I need to grow up. I need to let you go. Good bye, darlin’.”

I try calling back twice but he won’t pick up the phone. I leave a message with Courtney’s answering service to please check on Bailey and call me back.

Now I’m too restless to sleep. I drive to Grandma’s house, the little house beyond the blue barn where my adventure started. I stop at a Quik Trip and pick up some chocolates to replace the ones I ate, some hoarhound candy, and a large red geranium for the front stoop. Then I return to the house to spend several hours cleaning and polishing until I'm sure the grandma I never knew would be pleased.

I sit down for just a minute and fall deeply asleep only to be woken what seems like minutes later.

"Hey, Goldilocks."

I blink to clear my head. "Hey, Will."

"What are you doing here?"

"I thought the house could use a good cleaning."

"In the middle of the night?"

I look at my watch; it is midnight.

"It's been a long couple of weeks."

"Tell me."

So I explain about Lucas and Gia, Mark and Mickey, Lila and Ashton. Then I explain seeing Gordon. I expect some comment but he just nods.

"I talk to Grams pretty often. I was her favorite. She stills gives me advice. Damn good advice."

"So Miss Burns, why do we keep meeting like this?" He is only half teasing and his voice is rough and soft.

"I could ask you, why did you stop here tonight?"

"I had a meeting with my ex-wife."

"Does she want alimony?" I tease. I know she is a very successful executive.

"No, she wants us to try again."

"Really?" I'm trying to keep my tone non-committal, "And…?"

He is quiet so long I think he isn't going to answer. Suddenly he is looking at me so hard I turn away.

"There are a few complications now," his voice is so low I strain to hear him.

"Let's listen to some Dean Martin, he has all of the answers." I reverently put some of Grandma's records on the old turntable. Soon Dean is crooning Innamorata and I stay on the far side of the small living room. Has anyone sung so sensuously since Dean? I feel something low in my gut. Will crosses the room and takes my hand. We dance slowly around the room.

Suddenly, I want to run my hands across his bare chest, feel the length of his body against mine. I draw him down to the sofa and take off his clothes. His smoky blue eyes never leave me. Quickly I remove my own clothes and lay next to him. We don't speak until he tries to roll on top of me and falls off the narrow couch. We laugh and the solemn atmosphere disappears. We run into the bedroom, pull down the covers and inhale the sweet smell of summer on the sheets. We move together with such abandon that I climax immediately which causes him to stop in bewilderment.

"Please...don't... stop." I get out between clenched teeth.

I can feel him smile and then continue. Daylight comes much too early.

I think he is still sleeping when I slip out of bed until he says, "Where are you going?"

"Breakfast at the farm," I whisper.

I turn with a smile but Will is not smiling. Instead, he asks, "So what's next? Are you going to Pa's bed?"

I frown. "I beg your pardon?" I'm sure that I have not heard him right.

He continues, "Well, aren't you playing both of us?"

"Why would you say that?" I struggle to keep my tone controlled.

"I understand Old Harley offered you a permanent position and a trip to Europe."

"He did."

"Are you sleeping with us both to make sure you get a piece of the farm?"

I'm so hurt that I cannot answer him. I take my clothing and leave the room. I'm dressed before he gets out of bed.

"William Winston Harley. That was the cruelest thing anyone has ever said to me. I'm sorry you feel that way about me. But to answer your question, no I'm not sleeping with both of you for a piece of the farm. I..." my voice falters and I turn away to regain control. When I turn back my voice is deliberately hard, "If you remember you're the one who invited me into your world. I was perfectly content to keep driving on to Eagle River. I'll go back to the farm to collect my things and be gone before dinner. What do you want me to tell the rest of the family?" My throat is so constricted I can barely get the last few words out. I blink to keep the tears back.

Will hesitates a long moment studying me. I wonder what he sees, a desperate woman? A conniving bitch?

"Cassie…"

"Just tell me what you want me to say to the rest of the family." I know that my voice is harsh.

"Any damned thing you want. Why don't you try the truth?" he snaps at me.

"O.K., then come with me and we can tell them the truth together."

I drive to the farm and am thankful no one is around. I go to my room and pack. By the time I get back downstairs, Winston and Will are in the driveway talking. I take a deep breath and join them.

"Winston, I have something to tell you. Will and I just came from Grandma's house where we slept together last night. This morning he accused me of sleeping with both of you so that I can get a piece of the farm." Winston closes his eyes for a moment then looks towards the barn. An eagle flies overhead. I hear the drone of a tractor in the field across the road.

I continue, "I'm leaving. Winston, I want you to know that this has been a …" I struggle to find words encompassing enough to describe the way I feel. Then a treacherous tear courses down my cheek. I brush it away as others follow.

"Anyway," I choke out," thank you for everything." I stick out my hand which is shaking. Winston, instead, wraps me in a warm hug and gets out his old red handkerchief. I turn to go but Winston doesn't release me.

"Will, I never thought I raised a fool for a son but today proves me wrong."

"Pa…"

Winston cuts him off. "We all need to reconnoiter. Go to your corners and let's think this through."

"I don't think…" He gives me such a look that I know why he is the king of this particular mountain.

I relent for now and turn to go into the house. "I'll go out to the garden," I mutter without looking at either man.

I change my clothes to old shorts, a tank top and my old garden shoes. That's the thing about the farm; everyone has everyday or barn clothes and special clothes for going to church or town. It is one of those funny quirks that took me a while to understand. But I soon discovered that all of my clothes smell like the barn if I don't keep them separate.

Justin and Sarah are both in the garden already half way down two rows of corn. They smile shyly at me and I smile trying to hold back tears. I attack my row of corn with a vengeance and accidently hoe out one seedling. I feel Sarah and Justin eye me curiously to see how I'm going to handle the mistake. I bend over, dig a hole with my finger, stick the plant upright and move on down the row hoeing more carefully. They look at each other and giggle.

There is something about the rhythm of hoeing that's calming. By the time I reach the end of what seems like an endless row, I'm feeling better. Justin and I talk about his soccer games—they are 0 and 6 but getting better he assures me. Then Sarah tells me about staying over at her friend Katie's and how they had ten Barbies to play with and how they played dress up and she was a princess. Her little face is earnest as she describes the flowing pink dress and tiara. I felt a twinge of homesickness for my granddaughters.

I hug little Sarah and offer to teach her how to play cribbage when we finish our chores. When Justin mentions he doesn't know how to play either I extend the offer to him, too.

On the way out of the garden we check the strawberries; they are ready to be picked so we grab pails and pick for an hour. Now we have a dishpan full of berries to stem. We all sat at the picnic table cleaning the berries and eating the biggest ones. Sarah lines hers up to eat with sugar and cream when Winston swoops in and snatches two. When she chastises him he grabs another handful and runs around the table. She chases him while he crams the strawberries into his mouth. When she catches him his mouth is so full he can't talk. He sits down; she curls up in his lap and kisses his cheek. "I'll stem more for you, Grandpa. There are still lots of big ones left."

He swallows and with glistening eyes he kisses her on the top of her head. "No, let me stem some for you," he said. So he searches through the pile of berries for the littlest, greenest ones he can find which he solemnly presents to her. She seriously searches his face and then she starts eating. Winston throws up his hands and the berries fall into the grass.

"I'm teasing you, pumpkin, here are better ones." He gently picks through the strawberries and stems a half dozen to share with his beloved granddaughter. She snuggles close and I snap a mental picture of the two of them—a sticky faced little girl and her doting grandfather.

While Winston and Sarah are talking, Will sits down at the table and starts stemming berries.

"Uncle Will, could you practice some hoops with me?"

"What about kicking around the soccer ball? Am I too good for you?" Will gets up and makes some fancy soccer moves.

"I'm diversifying," Justin explains.

"Me, too, Uncle Will. I'm diver… divers…" Sarah hesitates and looks to Will for help.

"Diversifying; means you're trying other things, re-thinking things." I feel him looking at me but I'm not ready to look back.

Will and the kids take off to shoot baskets.

I start picking up the berries to take to the kitchen when Winston lays his calloused hand over mine.

"Cassie." I look up. His brown eyes are looking at me with more warmth than I deserve.

"Winston?"

"Do you want to talk?" he asks quietly.

"Does apologizing and admitting to being a schmuck count as talking?" I make a wry face.

"So, what now?" he asks softly. I look at that beautiful, weathered face and reach to push his hair back from his forehead when I pull back realizing that my hands are red and sticky with berry juice. Winston smiles a resigned smile.

"I never meant to hurt you, Winston. You have been nothing but kind to me and I have repaid you with pain. I'm not usually so… I guess callous is as good a word as any. I have no excuse. I need to leave and stop this craziness."

"Will you go home?"

I think for a moment. "Not yet. I'm not ready to return to what was. Nor am I ready to become the old lady my daughter Courtney thinks I am. I need to get my equilibrium back. I've been so busy, I've not spent enough time pondering." I smile at him and qualify the statement, "Good busy. Productive busy. Guess I'm still working on what's to come." And, I add, "Who I want to be in my next life."

Winston is silent which is unlike him. His eyes seem to have lost their focus.

"Winston?" I put down the pan of berries and touch him.

He blinks and looks up at me. "Must have had a senior moment."

"I'll take the berries in and make shortcake. There's probably enough for a batch of jam. Wonder if Anna has time to help me."

Anna does have the time and she teaches me how to make jam and incredibly light shortcake. We get oohs and ahs from the family who eat until they are groaning.

The next week is busy with the haying and preserving. Anna, Sally and I can peas, beans and peaches. Then we make dozens of jars of peach preserves. The temperatures are in the 90s and of course the farmhouse doesn't have air conditioning.

Will and I keep our distance; we have an uneasy peace. No more is said about my leaving but I no longer feel so lighthearted.

On Wednesday I return to Green Bay to pick up chicken feed and groceries. I can't move past melancholy. I stop at the farmer's market and spend a few minutes with Meredith. Business is brisk, but her quick mind doesn't miss the fact that I'm sad. She gives me a quick hug and promises a long talk within the week.

I'm loading the truck when my phone rings. It's Winston; the John Deere needs a part. I drive to the John Deere dealership. There are three farmers, two discussing the corn crop. I'm impatient. I grin ruefully; I haven't felt impatience since I left Illinois. Maybe the magic of farm is waning. Maybe it is the rift between Will and me. Maybe it is time for me to go home or to move on.

I'm bent over carefully placing the $522 part in the bed of the truck, a decidedly unflattering position when I feel the electricity. I close my eyes and straighten up but don't turn. Every hair on my body is standing up straight.

"I've often thought of you bent over like that, an offering of sorts," he whispers in my ear.

Then he continues, "Actually first I would take off that ugly shirt and I'll bet you have on my favorite bra, the one that hooks in the front. Then I would shimmy off those jeans and..."

I turn and Kurt is smiling. I feel my mood lightning.

"Thor."

"Who else talks to you like that?"

"Oh, there is the farmer on Z and the clerk in the dealership mentioned something about showing me his newest disc out back," I tease. "You look gorgeous. What have you been up to?" He leans against the truck a deeply satisfied grin on his face.

"Busy. This and that. Work stuff."

I lean against the truck and ask him to tell me about 'this and that'.

"Wouldn't interest you, Cassie. Boring, boring, boring. Tell me about you. Have you had any dreams about me?"

"No, I'm pretty much locked into reality." But I look away grinning.

"Ah," he pounces, "you *have* been thinking about me. Confess! I take up your every waking moment."

"You're an incorrigible, pompous ass," I retort.

He turns to me, puts his hands on either side of my body and leans in. "Call me an incorrigible pompous ass again, Ms. Burns."

"You are…" then Kurt kisses me long and slow.

When I come up for air I try again, "You are…" I stop, look into his cats' eyes and admit grudgingly, "the sexiest man I know."

He moves away and looks off down the highway. I can feel him withdrawing.

"What did I say? I thought you wanted me to admit I think you're sexy. Oh, let me guess, you hear it so often it bores you. Kurt, talk to me, I don't live in your world. I don't know what I did wrong."

He turns to me with an artificial smile and waves his hand in dismissal.

I take his hand and say softly, "Hey, no more pretending. Tell me what's wrong." Then he does something totally unexpected, he puts his arms around me and starts sobbing. I hold him for few minutes then lead him to the truck. I search frantically for a tissue but he pulls out a pressed and embroidered handkerchief.

"Let me take you back to your place. I need to stop for a minute and drop off this part for the tractor."

Kurt remains uncharacteristically silent during the drive, simply staring out the window.

I stop at the law office expecting to drop off the part and be on my way, but the receptionist waves me to Will's office. I knock on his door and explain what I'm doing. Will doesn't say anything until I turn to go.

"Cassie…"

"I don't have time right now." I know I sound dismissive.

"I see that you have someone in the truck with you. Big date?"

"Friend in trouble."

"You seem to have a lot of those." He is short.

I take a deep breath, "I'll ignore that, Will. It is beneath you."

I drive Kurt to his house and put him to bed.

"Are you going to tell me about it?"

"She died."

"Who died?"

"My wife."

I'm incredulous, "Your wife?"

"Ex-wife. She and the baby died. Something went wrong during the delivery."

I listen quietly as he tells me about Elise. "We met in middle school, two orphans; I had no parents, but Elise had it worse. Her parents were so emotionally distant they weren't even in the same state most days. We were high school sweethearts and got married right out of college. It lasted 4 years and then she left me. Walked out of the apartment and never looked back. I didn't know what I had done so I just waited for her to return. When she filed the divorce papers I spent a year doing drugs and drinking every night. Eduardo pulled me out or one day I would have been found dead in an alley. I worked so hard to be successful so that Elise would realize the mistake she made and come back home. I stayed in the same apartment for three years just waiting. Even when she remarried I knew it wouldn't last. Shit, the guy was a loser, some kind of ag teacher or something. Elise and I belong together." I notice that he is still using the present tense.

He puts his head in his hands. "I knew she was pregnant, I even sent her a crib and a silver spoon. I read about her death this morning in the paper. The bastard didn't have the balls to call me."

"Why would he call you, Kurt?"

"Because I loved her and she loved me."

"But she was married to him, Kurt."

"She was coming back. I know she was coming back. And… now she is never coming back."

His sobs are muffled in his hands.

After a moment's hesitation I crawl in bed and stretch my body out alongside him in an effort to stop his shaking. I spoon him and rock him gently. Gradually I feel him relax and when I'm sure he is asleep I cover him and slip out of the room.

I check the clock, it was nearly supper time. I call the farm and leave a message that I have been detained in town and might be late getting back. I apologize for not calling earlier.

Then I wander to the kitchen; it is well stocked so I make homemade macaroni and cheese and chicken noodle soup, a meal I have made many times to mend small and large heartbreaks.

When I carry the meal to the bedroom, Kurt is sitting up staring out the window. Even though he turns when I enter I'm not sure he registers who I am or what I'm doing here.

"You need to eat," I say in my best mother voice setting the tray on his lap.

"You didn't need to do this, Cassie."

"Do you want to talk some more? " He shakes his head looking forlorn.

"Is there someone I should call? Eduardo?"

"Just sit by me." Then unexpectedly, "How did you cope when your husband died?"

I hesitate for a long moment. Do I want to go there with him? Instead, I give a rather pat answer. "I'm not so sure that I did. I mourned. I cursed God. I gave up. I ran away. Gradually I decided that since I was still alive I had to do something with myself. That's how I ended up here." I'm quiet thinking of the things that have happened since I left

Illinois.

"So, I am not always going to feel like this?"

"I won't promise that. This kind of pain stays in your soul. But, you have already proven you're tough so eventually it will feel more like a scar—covered over but never gone."

"I don't feel tough. I don't know that I'll ever feel tough again. I don't know that I'll ever feel anything again."

"I'm not wise enough to help you there, Kurt."

"Come to bed." I hesitate then take his tray and set it on the dresser. I'm not sure that I want to be a stand-in; maybe that's what I have always been. I try to brush away the thought.

Suddenly his eyes clear and as if he's read my mind and says, "I'm not trying to make you a substitute for Elise. Cassie, I need our humming to warm me up."

I undress quickly and crawl under the covers. He moves to cover me with his body.

"I thought I was warming you," I whisper.

"This is the way you do it best," he says as he enters me. I'm never prepared for the magic of our lovemaking; it is sensuous and engulfing. I try to prolong the moment, until I can't anymore. When I roll him on his back he sighs. I spend the next hour helping him forget.

"Don't leave me tonight." His voice his hoarse and low. "I need to do some writing and I am very prolific when I have been with you..

"Really?" I ask. I am curious, "What do you write? Swashbuckling romance where you're on the cover ripping off the bodice of a raven haired lady? Comics? Penthouse Q and A? Articles for GQ?"

He looks perplexed for a minute then he smiles and shakes his head. "What a wild fantasy life you have. Some days I would just like to live in your head." Then his face changes and he adds, "I write music. Please come here." I crawl out of bed and walk to the desk. Briefly he pulls me to him and buries his face in my warm stomach.

"Please, turn on the sound system." I obey; I find the remote and the room is filled with the warm voice of Bing Cosby.

"I hate to be the one to break it to you but Bing is dead. He can't sing any of your music." I flip the switch and another CD drops into place. I'm mesmerized by the next song; the singer's voice is low and sexy, sounding like a modern day mix of Dean Martin and Frank Sinatra. I listen to two more songs without saying anything. Then I look through the CD cases—Sammy Davis Jr., Dean Martin and Infyniti, with K.C. Troy as the lead singer. The picture of Kurt on the front is so sensuous I catch my breath; he is singing to a dark haired beauty in a canopied bed.

I can feel Kurt looking at me so I turn to him and ask, "You couldn't have told me? I feel like you've punked me. Why couldn't you just be honest?" I am hurt and angry.

Kurt takes my hand. "When we first met I thought it would be a quick one night stand and I have to be careful so I had Eduardo do some checking. Then I realized that you truly didn't know who I am, and I got carried away by the anonymity and frankly by your naiveté."

Stung, I pull my hand away. "You can call it naiveté but I spent the last nine years taking care of my dying husband, away from all things fun and frivolous, especially concerts. " Even to myself I sound like a pompous martyr.

"I'm not being critical, Cassie. You just aren't like the women I know. I have pretty much gotten used to women well, moshing me. I expected to seduce you and move on. But then I touched your hand and it felt like we were exchanging heartbeats. And when you left me, and let me tell you that doesn't happen to me, I had to track you down. I tried to sleep you out of my mind, but my body won't let you go. Since I have met you I have written an entire CD. For me, that's unheard of. In the past it has take me more than a year to write enough songs for a CD. Let me sing this one for you."

He pulls out a keyboard, plays a few notes and hums, "It's called A Forever Tattoo".

"When you kiss me you leave a burning tattoo on my lips.
When you kiss me you, dah, dah I haven't found the right words yet, but I have the melody.
When your body touches mine
I feel a tattoo where your fingers used to be.
Your breasts leave an imprint, permanent and true
Your eyes open to invite me in. They take my breath away.
The age old dance we practice becomes brand new today.

I want you, I need you, I miss you
My everlasting, forever, tattoo.

He pulls me to him, nuzzling my neck and asks, “How can you be angry when I’m writing about you?”

I shake my head. “Kurt, K.C., whatever you name is, I’m not your twenty-one year old groupie. Please don’t use your charming performer persona. It doesn’t work with me. I’ve got to go. But you’re on a roll. You know that you can keep writing. Good luck.” I soften my voice, “I’m very sorry about Elise.”

Chapter Eight

I have an hour to think as I drive back to the farm. I have led a pretty straight-forward life until this time; I don't keep many secrets. I've pretty much been a garden variety wife and mother. I examine my feelings for Kurt. We have an odd, fabulous, sexual relationship. It defies definition. We have nothing in common; I'm older than he is, better educated, he is richer than I could ever imagine, handsome, and we live in totally different worlds. However, when I am with him nothing matters except getting into bed. In bed I am transformed into a sexy goddess. It makes me smile to think about it.

Having always been more readily aroused than Gordon, it feels so wonderful to be appreciated for my sexuality. I marvel that I have discovered this at my age. I speculate about what I been missing; about what is to come. A deer runs in front of the car, then two more so I leave off my musings.

I reach Meredith's driveway and turn in. I find her with her alpacas, Romeo and Juliet, and she hugs me. We go into the house and she pours me a glass of Pino Grigio and hands me the beautiful crystal goblet.

"So, tell me about the mystery man."

I don't ask her how she knows. I tell her about the crazy way we met and the instant connection we had and that I'm confused about the relationship.

She is thoughtful for a minute, and then asks why it is so important to define the relationship. I don't know, I admit, it feels sleazy when I describe it out loud.

"Sleazy to whom?"

"Me," I say, feeling as naïve as Kurt's earlier description of me.

She surprises me by asking if I'm happy. I nod immediately.

We sit quietly for a while then she starts talking about her relationship with Winston. I'm not surprised, two strong people drawn to one another. Then she moves on to her friend in Minnesota who she visits regularly. I'm fascinated by her varied sex life. I think she is subtly giving me permission to act on my own sexuality.

We hug when I leave after a second glass of wine. It's wonderful to have such a close friend after so many years alone. Caretakers, I muse, don't have much time for friendships.

Winston is sitting on the porch when I drive in. I pull up a rocker and he turns down the radio.

"Hard day?"

"Odd day. Friend lost his ex-wife and is struggling." I change the subject, "What happened around here today?"

"Started on the second crop of hay. Manure spreader broke down and took two hours to fix. Burnt the pizza. Missed you."

"I missed you, too, and I am sorry that I was so undependable. That's not like me. I promise I won't slack off again."

"How is it going between you and Will?"

"Ah, Win…" I hesitate, confused.

"Lorraine used to call me Win," he reminisces, his voice soft and low.

He's been leaving me more and more, lately, as we talk in the dark on the old porch. He talks about Lorraine often and sometimes goes back further into his childhood and how hard it is now to be the last surviving sibling. I'm awed when he tells me that at one time he had 46 first cousins. It is almost 10 when he winds down. I kiss his prickly cheek and head up the stairs glad that he's momentarily forgot the Will and Cassie issue because I don't know where we stand right now.

Crap, I've been shirking my duties so I turn around and head to the kitchen. I turn the radio down low and begin mixing bread. The rhythmic kneading puts me into a trance until Will enters the kitchen. The kitchen is my domain; I will wait for him to speak.

"It feels disloyal to talk about it but Ma was never a good cook. She had lots of great traits but cooking and baking weren't among them. We have been eating like kings since you came, Cassie."

"Thank you." I know that I'm not being cordial but let him carry the brunt of the conversation; I was doing fine before he entered.

"It's hard for me to apologize."

"Will, you called it as you saw it." I keep my tone carefully neutral and continue kneading; this will be the most elastic bread in history.

"That's not exactly true. I was scared. Scared about all of the changes that have happened since you came, worried about Pa and to be honest, wondering how we could possibly return to our old life when you go."

I don't say anything so he continues, "And while I know that it is none of my business, how does that other guy fit into the picture?"

I look up and attack. "Will, I don't ask you about your ex-wife or any women in your life, what gives you the right to interfere with mine?" He opens his mouth to speak and like a cop I raise my hand. "Wait, I'm not through." I hesitate and look at him for a moment. "I like you, Will Harley. I like your dad, heck I like your whole family. But, you can't force me into a corner. You can't compel me to make decisions I'm not ready to make. And, pushing me away the way you did was cowardly. There, I feel better. It is your turn to take a shot."

I keep kneading. The way I'm adding flour this bread will feed us for a week. I feel invigorated. Talking to any of the Harleys makes me feel that way. They are passionate, articulate, and stubborn; makes for good discussions. I was getting really tired of all of the people back in Illinois being nice to 'the widow'.

Will stands up. "Are you about done with the bread?"

Reluctantly I place the bread in a greased bowl in the refrigerator and cover it with a damp cloth. I feel more in control punching that bread around.

"Have you ever played poker?" Will asks unexpectedly.

"Nope, only bridge, Crazy Eights, Hearts and War."

"Well, I'll teach you how to play. "

I reach in my pocket and pull out two quarters, three dimes and a nickel.

He smiles. "Big stakes."

We played poker until almost daybreak. I lose my entire fortune but we have some open dialogue and I learn a little about the game.

When Winston awakes we are still playing. He smiles and stands over my shoulder giving me pointers. Will goes upstairs to take a shower because he is working in the law office today. I turn on the oven to bake the bread. I should be exhausted, but the day gets so busy I don't have time to think about it. I work in the garden, pick the strawberries and freeze a batch of jam. The peas are ripe so I pick them and sit on the front porch shelling them, trying to catch a breeze. It is over eighty degrees and my clothes are sticking to me.

I hadn't seen much of Winston during the day, but he comes bounding up the stairs with a bag of ice declaring we will make ice cream to go with the strawberries. He pulls out the old ice cream maker with the recipe taped to the top, which I take to the kitchen to interpret. He points out this is Lorraine's recipe that we will be using. I call Anna who has already heard about the ice cream making and is on her way over. She cooks the eggs, cream, milk, and sugar together, and then adds the vanilla. We cool it in ice water. Winston is in and out of the kitchen every few minutes trying to get us to hurry; his sons and grandchildren are lined up to crank the old machine. There is arguing over how much salt should be sprinkled over the ice and each one admonishes the other to crank the machine at a slow and steady pace. I go back to the kitchen to mash strawberries and get out the dishes. Sarah confides that on ice cream days we don't have to eat real food and that there are special ice cream dishes for the occasion. I find them in the back of the cupboard and take them down to wash.

We're still cranking the ice cream—it takes longer than I thought it would, when Will comes home. In one swift glance he assesses the situation, adds more salt and then sprinkles a little water over the ice—the quintessential oldest taking the lead. He sheds his suit coat, rolls up his sleeves, and takes over the cranking. The brothers continue their friendly bickering about the proportions of ice to salt. When even weightlifter Matthew struggles to make one more turn Winston declares the ice cream turning finished.

Will orders me to "bring a big plate and a couple of spoons. We need to get the dasher out, cover it with a couple of towels, and let it ripen." Everybody groans but we each gets a taste of the ice cream and fight over the melted mess on the plate.

Justin suggests we play charades while we wait. Everybody quickly breaks into teams. I'm on Winston, Bart, Angela and Sally's team. We acted out songs. Angela acts out *Row, Row, Row Your Boat*. The other team guesses it right away. Then they act out *I Walk the Line* and our team guesses correctly. We each get to play three rounds and we stump them on *The Ballad of John and Yoko.* They groan because it is an old people song so nobody would know it. We just strut and brag about winning.

Winston declares the ice cream ripe and ready to eat. It is the best ice cream I have ever eaten. Sarah leans against me and talking with her mouth full regales me with her day. I brush the hair out of her eyes and drop a quick kiss on her head. She grins and I grin back.

In my other life I had never stopped in the middle of the day to eat homemade ice cream and play charades. I was always too busy, too focused, too serious, too responsible. No wonder I'm losing weight, I'm no longer carrying around all of those responsibilities. Bart asks me what I'm smiling about and I just point to the ice cream. He shakes his head and pushes the old porch swing with his foot.

Six year old Angela who is just learning to play pulls out the checker board and challenges her grandfather to a game. They play seriously for several minutes with everyone giving Angela advice until she stops playing, puts her hands on hips and admonishes the crowd to let her play herself. She loses and her little face drops until Winston picks her up, puts her on his shoulders and explaining checker strategy walks her out to peek in on the chickens.

The men head for the barn to check the animals and the women clean up. It's still hot and humid but we're all humming because of our ice cream respite. Sally and I plan our strategy for working in the garden, cooking and preserving. We have over 200 pounds of ripening peaches in the pantry that we will pick through to determine which ones are ripe enough to can.

After we finish our chores Justin, Sarah and I pull out the cribbage board for their first lesson. The game goes too slow for Sarah so she wanders away to play with the kittens. But Justin catches on quickly and we play three rousing games where I just squeak by beating him the first two and with him winning the third. Then Anna calls the kids home and I rock contently on the swing. Will and Winston come back from the barn and we sit companionably for a few minutes before the men start discussing crop rotation and adding to the herd. I say my good nights and slip away, but they barely notice my absence.

I call my children and one by one learn about their week. Mark is building a log cabin for a couple who want to retire to the area; he spends several minutes explaining his eco-friendly additions; solar panels, outdoor log furnace. He complains about Mickey's long work days.

Surprisingly Courtney says very little about work, instead she shares her newest recipe for roasted vegetables and talks excitedly about the herb garden on her deck.

Lila puts each of the girls on the telephone and we talk Barbies, swimming lessons and Jesse's new words—up and no. Lila says nothing about Anston but her voice has a troubled note to it. Lila will let me know when she is ready to talk.

Lucas sounds wonderful. Classes are difficult but he loves the challenges. His life, he tells me, is all work and studying. I ask about Gia and his voice changes, taking on a reverence when he talks about her. I listen to his praises about her for several minutes before he winds down and whispers that she is making faces at him. "Ouch, and now she is throwing pillows at me, an invalid, unable to defend my poor self." I laugh and after a few more minutes of bantering I hang up.

I save Bailey for last. "Hey, sweet man."

"Cassie." I love the way he says my name, even when we have an argument he says my name with love and respect.

"How're doing? I have spies everywhere so tell me the truth."

"Georgia's really gone."

"Yes, she is, so what are you going to do next?"

He is silent for so long I prompt him, "I, Bailey, am…."

"A manic alcoholic. A loser. Exactly what my father told me I was every day of my life when he wasn't beating the shit out of me."

I feel the familiar tug to fix it, to tell him he is wrong, that he isn't a loser, but I want him to come to that conclusion himself so I wait. This is a new strategy for me and I have to rock back and forth to keep my mouth shut.

"You don't love me any me anymore, either?" he asks plaintively.

I sigh. "Dumb question, sweetheart, you know that I'll always love you."

"But you're not here for me and I am hurting."

"I know Bay, and I'm so sorry. But tell me what you're going to do next?'

"Drink a pint of vodka and find a nubile 21 year old?"

"You must be feeling better if you're going down that road. If you won't be serious tell me how your new business is going." For the next twenty minutes Bailey talks about his new business and he sounds nearly like his old self. I ring off feeling pretty good about my family and friend.

I sleep hard and wake before dawn. I look out the window for a few minutes watching the farm come to life—the roosters crowing, the cows complaining, noises from inside the house. I dress in jeans and a tee shirt. Already it is hot so I turn on all the fans. Blueberry pancakes, raw fries, and bacon today with juice and coffee. I make a triple batch of pancakes but there are only two left for Sally and me when she comes over 10 minutes after the men clear out.

Canning peaches is a big project. We wash the jars, heat the lids, make the syrup, fill the canner with water, and put it on the stove to heat up. Surely it is easier and cheaper to buy them in a tin can I muse but Sally is a diehard traditionalist so I keep my thoughts to myself.

Sally puts ice and water in a large bowl heats up another in the microwave and gives me instructions. Drop the peaches in the boiling water for one minute, then into the ice water so that the skin slips off. It takes me several batches of either over cooking the peaches or not leaving them in the boiling water long enough so I end up peeling the peaches. Sally is patient. The day gets hotter and hotter. I run upstairs and exchange my jeans for shorts. The men come in an out looking for lemonade and ice water. Mostly they get in the way.

We've got two batches of peaches in the canner and still there are about a million peaches sitting on the countertop. It is easily 100 degrees in the kitchen so I run back upstairs and look for a tank top, the only thing cool enough is a wispy little hot pink camisole I usually wear under a shirt. I pull it on as I hear the buzzer on the stove and race back down the stairs. The men are crowded in the kitchen as Sally tries to shoo them out.

Will winks and says, "I can't wait to see how much smaller your next ensemble will be. C'mon heat!" I smile sheepishly; in my hometown this camisole wouldn't have engendered a second look. Here, I have opened myself up to more razzing. I push him out the door so we can finish the peaches.

Sally reminds me that they will be back in an hour for dinner so we hurriedly fry chicken, and put potatoes on the stove to boil. I peel and slice early tomatoes and kohlrabi.

"If they wouldn't have to eat every few hours we could get something done," I mumble under my breath.

Sally just laughs and says, "It is the ebb and flow of farm life, Cassie. Everybody works hard, plays hard, and eats regularly."

We take a second to sit down with ice water to talk. She explains, "I grew up in a military family, always moving, strict parents, and very little love. When I fell in love with Colin I felt like I had come home. Colin is so centered and committed to the farm and his family. I know this sounds sexist but I enjoy having four men take care of me."

She is silent a moment before she tells me, "I had three miscarriages and one stillbirth between Matthew and Watson. But you know these guys rallied around me and kept me from sliding into depression. I credit the farm and this crazy, loving, family with keeping me sane."

"They love big, Cassie. And once you're a part of the family, you're never alone again." I give her a quick hug before we set the table and mix up another batch of lemonade.

Eventually all of the peaches get canned, two cans don't seal so we put them in the refrigerator to make pie or cobbler. Sally runs back across the street to her family and I make subs for supper for Winston, Will and me. Winston and Will get to arguing about diversifying so I go for a walk. Meredith has a car in her driveway…her Minnesota friend? I decide to walk down the road. Mrs. Bieber drives by on the tractor and waves. I have got to ask Winston about that. Candy Jackson, the 16 year old from two houses north, stops and chats about her new cat and speculates on which movie she should see.

Finally, I'm alone with my thoughts. They are not very deep. I admire the gorgeous sunset; pinks, yellows, and purples then reluctantly turn around and head back. I'm still afraid of running into the bear, although plenty of people have told me that she is more afraid of me that I am of her but they are wrong; she scares the bejesus out of me.

I feel a presence but this one doesn't frighten me. "Gord?"

"Hey, honey, how are you doing?"

"I'm O.K., how about you? "

"The best." He used to say that even on the hard days.

"I miss you." I say

"M-m-m . The kids are doing well. I like Gia, she is good for Lucas."

"I worry about Lila."

"She is a tough woman, like her mother; give her time to figure out what she wants to do."

"You couldn't smite Anston, could you?" I ask only half kidding.

He laughs and I remember how that laugh could ease my fears; it still does.

"Sorry, I don't have any smiting power. Maybe I'll get that at the next level. I'm watching over you and the kids, Cassie, so don't worry."

"Gord, how do you feel about what's happening in my life. I mean the new job, Kurt and Will, I guess. I mean, Gord…" There is no answer and I know he is gone. The night feels empty and I'm suddenly tired.

I get back to the farm, unscathed, and check the chickens. They are fine, so I fill the water container and the feeder. Next, I head out to the barn to check the calves. I pick a handful of strawberries to eat along the way. I count the new calves and everyone is accounted for. I sit on a bale of hay and make a mental list of tomorrow's plans; laundry, shopping, picks peas and beans to can or freeze, pickle the kohlrabi per Sally and…I must have drifted off.

"Hey, is the bed so uncomfortable you decided to sleep in the barn? Most of our guests choose the house."

"Please be quiet, I'm dreaming." I recognize Will's voice and don't open my eyes. I'm not ready to surface.

"What about?"

"Pickling kohlrabi."

"You're getting boring, Ms. Burns, when you start dreaming of vegetables."

I laugh and so does he; perhaps our standoff is easing.

"I have just the solution for boredom, I'll take you to Friendly's tavern and beat you at a game of pool."

"Isn't it late?" I no longer wear a watch. There is a natural rhythm to my days that defies increments.

"Only if you consider 8:30 late."

"You don't go to Green Bay tomorrow?"

"Nope. Case is over. Nothing until Monday."

I consider a moment then decide, "Let me go in and change my clothes."

"You look fine."

"I look like I have been working in a hot kitchen all day. I do not look fine. It will take me two minutes."

Ten minutes later I have combed my hair, put a shirt over my camisole, added black capris and gold slides.

Will whistles; I blush. We jump in the old truck and talk about what the weather will do to the crops and if there will be any money in corn this year. Friendly's is surprisingly busy for a weeknight. Neighbors stop us to talk farming for a few minutes. Will puts a dollar on the pool table and soon it is our turn. I'm rusty not having had many opportunities to shoot pool in recent years, but soon I remember the physics of the game and give him a run for his money. But, when he calls the corner pocket and easily banks in the eight ball I admit defeat. However, there is an air hockey table in the corner and I put my dollar down and challenge Will to a game. I love air hockey and used to be good at it from accepting the challenges the kids threw at me. I take off my over shirt so nothing gets in my way.

"Getting serious are you?"

"Damn right." I grin at him.

I put in the first two pucks before he realizes that I have played before. He straightens up and smiles at me when I stay bent over protecting my goal. He shoots the next puck so fast I don't have time to react. Now it is two to one. He is not going to beat me two games tonight. We play hard and fast and pretty soon we each have a cheering section. I'm too focused on winning to play to the audience and finally with one grand slam I win. Cheers go up in the bar and I bow. I get several challenges from young guys which I accept and win them all. It is my night.

I wipe my face on my shirt. When you play air hockey you expend a lot of energy. I gulp a cranberry juice and suggest we head home.

Will drives right past the farm and we end up at Lee Lake.

"A nice night for wading," I suggest.

"If that's what you want. I'm going swimming." And with that he skims out of his clothes and dives in.

He comes up for air and just floats. My capris are feeling heavy from the humidity and even with my over shirt off, the breeze isn't cooling me down. I kick off my shoes, take off my clothes, and neatly fold them. At first the water is cold and then as my body adjusts it feels like a caress. I'm tired and hot and feel like I could just float on the water all night. When Will grabs my foot and pulls me under I momentarily panic until I realize I can touch the sandy bottom. I pop out of the water, but Will stays under and brushes his lips across my stomach. It contracts and I catch my breath. He disappears for a moment and I go back to floating. He pulls my feet down until I'm standing in water up to my neck. He is kissing me and then works his way down my body. It feels like we're in a silky, black world of our own. He comes up for air, kisses me, and dives under.

"Stop," I whisper and I'm glad when he doesn't hear me. Suddenly there are headlights coming down the long dirt road. Will comes up sputtering. I race for the shore and my clothes.

Ray, Cy and Dan walk down to the pier where I'm waiting, wet and mostly dressed. Will calmly treads water. A few sly remarks are passed around; Will bounces them back. Ray brings out a six pack and hands the cold Bud around. Soon the stories move onto farming and crops and I doze.

"C'mon, Sleeping Beauty, time to get you home."

"Before I turn into a pumpkin," I murmur. I fall asleep on the five minute ride back to the farm. I sleep walk to my bedroom and decide that sleep trumps brushing teeth and don't remember crawling into bed.

I hear a rooster crowing and I squint at the alarm clock: 7:00! I slept until 7? Sally and Colin are the only ones in the kitchen after I finally get showered and my teeth brushed. They are kissing and whispering when I walk in. I apologize for disturbing them but they just smile continuing to hold hands. They make a great looking couple, she is tall and blond and he is tall and dark haired. She is organized and proper; he is dreamy and silly. One day while we were working in the garden he started serenading her with "You are my Special Angel" with Watson mimicking his dad's every move. The next thing you know Will and Bart are singing backup with the bebop moves, snapping their fingers like they'd been rehearsing for this for days. What a crazy family.

It's raining so some of the outside work gets delayed, well my outside work; the men still have the cows and fixing that has to get done. It seems to me that the machinery is always breaking down and I'm continually surprised that one or the other of the men is able to fix almost anything. When I mention this to Winston he just grins and says that all farmers have to be mechanics, veterinarians, builders, accountants, and meteorologists. He would have added to the list but I laugh and put up my hands in surrender.

"I get it," I said, "farmers are almost perfect."

"No almost," he says grinning slyly. I whack him with the rolled up newspaper I picked up to throw in the trash. He rolls up another section of newspaper and we have a lively newspaper sword fight interspersed with "ahas" and "got yas". Justin and Sarah come in and join the fray. We knock over a few glasses and break a candle before we stop fooling around. Sarah snuggles up to me and whispers that grandpa has been much more fun since I came. So I dance her around the kitchen table and then I grab Justin who surprises me with several minutes of graceful waltzing before he pulls away, embarrassed.

"Where'd you learn those moves, Justin?"

"I learned them from watching Gramps."

"Well, you have a great teacher. You're going to break some girl's heart, handsome guy."

"I already have a girlfriend," he reveals shyly.

"What's her name?" we ask simultaneously.

"Dierdra."

"A beautiful name."

"She lives on Willow Road. Sometimes we ride our bikes together."

Sarah pipes up, "Does mom know?"

Justin shifts from foot to foot, blushing.

"I'm telling. I'm telling mom." Sarah darts out the front door with Justin chasing her threatening bodily harm.

Winston and I sit back enjoying the few minutes of silence when I ask, "Do you miss those crazy times when the kids were wrestling or crying or threatening each other?"

He is quiet for a long time before he says, "It seems like only yesterday when the boys were that age."

I put my hand over his. "Yeah, time flies when you're busy."

"Where has all of the time gone, Lorraine?"

"I'm Cassie, Winston," I answer softly.

His eyes refocus and he says gruffly, "Of course you are." He is up and out the door without another word.

I shake myself out of my reverie. Rain or no rain I've got work to do and I have already slept away half the morning. I'm bound to get a teasing about that.

Chapter Nine

After lunch, I'm finishing writing out the grocery list when my phone rings.

"Cassie?"

"Hi Kurt."

"Can I pick you up and go for a ride or something?" Although his words are innocuous enough, his tone is suggestive.

"Is that like coming over to see your etchings?" I ask jokingly.

"I have missed your odd sense of humor, Cassie. It could be but I've got something to talk to you about."

"I was planning on coming into town to do some shopping this afternoon, what if I stop by your place later?"

"What time?" his tone is demanding so I'm quiet for a moment. "Sorry, I know, I know you're not one my twenty year old fans. Let me try this again, what time works for you?"

"Late afternoon."

"Thank you," his voice softens, "but hurry".

A bunch of errands slow me down, besides the grocery store I stop at the hardware store, the John Deere implement store and Younker's to get a gift for Angela's birthday.

It is after six before I pull into Kurt's driveway. When I knock on the door there is no answer. So I ring the doorbell; still no Kurt. I push open the door and say, "Hey, I'm not that late."

Someone puts a blindfold on me but before I can react, Kurt whispers, "It's O.K. I just want your total concentration". He leads me to the bedroom where I sit on the edge of the bed. Kurt leaves and I wait a few minutes before he reenters. He starts singing; it is the song about the tattoo he started when I was here last time, but now the band in the background adding richness and depth. He croons, there is no other term for it, and despite the blindfold I close my eyes so that I can concentrate on the words and the emotions they evoke. There is a warm, heavy spot in my gut. He changed one of the lines from 'look into her eyes' to 'when I'm between her thighs'. I smile and the warmth I felt earlier radiates further down.

He continues singing while he tugs at my shirt; I help him remove it and then my shorts. Then my underwear and bra are off and he starts kissing his way down my body. I realize that I'm not breathing and take a big gulp of air. I can feel a flush moving from my face down my naked body and I'm so warm and wet when Kurt enters me, still singing, I climax immediately and Kurt follows seconds behind me. As my shuddering stops and I attempt to remove my blindfold, he restrains my hand and whispers, "There is a third verse."

It is after ten when I leave the house in Park Place. Kurt is busy scribbling and playing on the piano. I'm sore, satisfied, and ravenous. I drive the hour back to the farm in a warm haze.

Will, Winston and Bart are on the porch talking as I unload the car. All three men offer to help but Will waves them off and starts grabbing bags. "Long grocery list?" he asks wryly. Without looking him in the eye I say, "Something like that." I know I look a mess, so I run my fingers through my hair. I catch a glimpse of myself in the mirror as I put the shampoo away in the bathroom; I'm still flushed and bright-eyed. Sex is so invigorating; had I forgotten that or is this different from what I experienced with Gordon? Will is talking so I jerk myself back to the present. "I beg your pardon?"

"I was just commenting that rainy days seem to suit you."

"Don't you like the downtime they give you?"

"It depends upon how you spend that downtime."

"Let me help you," I tease, "you could sleep in". He snorts but I continue, "read a book, watch a movie, learn to whittle, paint the kitchen, practice a new dance step. There, I have given you lots of ideas."

"You didn't say anything about the way you spend a rainy day.

The groceries are put away so I sit down and face him, "Hmm, well

I like to daydream, write, talk to my family and friends, bake something, play cards, go to a museum. Sometimes I like to take a nap."

"So it must have been the County Museum that made you so flushed. What was the exhibit? The causes of pollution? Native fishes? Trapping in Northern Wisconsin?"

"Let me think, ah yes, the trapping exhibit is very titillating."

"That was last fall."

"I must have read about it in the paper then. Even retrospectively, trapping is exciting." I'm egging him on.

He is quiet and I see he is puzzling me out. I study him from his salt and pepper hair, down his broad chest to his slim hips and long legs; interesting face; strong, assertive nose, a nice smile when he deigns to bother with it, but, overall serious, too serious. He favors Lee jeans and tee shirts but looks rough hewn and handsome in a suit and tie.

I must have stared too long because he asks, "Do I pass muster?"

"Winston did tell me that farmers are just about perfect, so who am I to quibble?" I ask, and then settle back into the old rocker allowing myself to re-experience the evening. I feel like a sinuous creature, a cat maybe, or a deer. I don't remember ever feeling this way at sixteen or twenty-five. I wonder if this is how beautiful people feel all of the time.

Will rouses me from my musing, "Sally called to remind you that she will pick you up at 6:15 to head for Sturgeon Bay to pick cherries. She is taking the van so we can squeeze in a lot of pickers. If we get back in time we need to get the hay off the field behind Wilsons. Pa said you're getting good at driving the tractor now." He smirks. My face turns red remembering how I knocked Winston off the wagon with my bad driving.

"I'll go up in the mow, thank you."

"I thought that you didn't like the mow, especially climbing up the elevator. We're taking bets on how you were going to get out of it."

"Can't aggravate me tonight, Mr. Harley." I wink at him and sashay out of the room.

Thursday dawns hot and humid. I rush through breakfast and we pile into the van and play word games on the two hour trip. It is just a little after 8 when we pull into the Kennedy Cherry Center in Door County. We all hop out. There are already four cars ahead of us. Sarah snatches a piece of binder twine off the railing and shows me how to use it as a belt for my pail so that I can pick with both hands.

"Follow me, follow me Cassie," her tiny warm hand tugs me into the grove. Watson is trying to catch up yelling, "Me, too."

We pass what seem to be perfectly ripe cherries to move further among the trees. Finally Sarah declares we're at the right tree and she settles down to serious picking. I follow her lead. In 20 minutes she's picked a pail of cherries. She carefully sets the pail out of the sun and starts on her second pail. I realize that I have got to stop tasting every other cherry and put my mind to picking. The heat and the ripe fruit combine to create a heavenly aroma. My forearms are sticky from picking the cherries over my head. I'm a pail behind Sarah when Sally rounds us all up. We count and together we have 25 pails of cherries. Inwardly I groan. While picking cherries was fun, I have a feeling that the next phase is pitting, and then canning them in this ridiculously hot weather.

We rinse off our sticky hands at the outside faucet, shake them dry, and pile back into the hot van. After ten minutes the cool air finally reaches me in the back seat. Winston starts singing a hymn, *The Old Rugged Cross,* and the rest of the voices chime in. Sarah and I each nestle up to Winston as he carries the tune through three verses. He is such a rock. I think about the force he must have been in his younger years. I feel a flash of envy for Lorraine who knew him then; was a part of his orbit. He switches gears and launches into Tony Bennett's *Wrap Your Troubles in Dreams.* The kids get impatient so he switches to 'name a food that starts with all of the letters of the alphabet'. The sun is warm on my face and I doze.

Sarah shakes me awake and whispers, "Its pitting time." She is excited. I would rather bale hay. Damn, I'm not getting out of this. I help line the picnic tables with newspapers, realizing that I haven't read them in weeks. When did gas prices start rising again? I catch a glimpse of a grainy picture of Infyniti and I study Kurt's face.

"Hey, you're slacking here," Will says as he dumps a pail of cherries in front of me, making the band disappear.

"Yes massa," I reply as I pick up a hair pin to start on what looks like a mountain of cherries. First we see who can pit the fastest but that loses it glamour after 10 minutes. Then we try it in teams, still way past tedious. Juice is running down my elbows and I stick to the newspaper when I raise my arms. I have eaten enough cherries to feel slightly sick. Finally, we're down to three pails which will be made into cherry bounce—it seems pretty silly to give drunks cherries with pits, but I'm just glad that we can call it quits. I try to rise but humidity and cherry juice have literally stuck me to the seat. Will chivalrously offers to help me up but first he put his sticky hands on my face. I pull myself free and chase him with the kids joining in. Colin grabs Will and we each get to put our sticky hands on his person. I run mine through his hair. Winston declares an end to the foolishness, loads us into a couple of vehicles and we go down to the swimming hole where we all jump in with our clothes on; first time I have been non-sticky in hours.

Winston is the first to notice a crack of thunder and the men argue about finishing up the hay baling. Winston wins and we hurry back to the farm. We change into jeans and long sleeved shirts which are miserable in this heat and humidity. Within ten minutes my clothes are damp and heavy. Will and I are up in the mow again. Justin and Sarah join us. They play hide and seek among the bales as we wait for the first wagonload. Will and I talk quietly.

"Keeping all of your clothes on this time?" he teases as he pulls off his shirt. I look away and move slightly; he is radiating heat. The thick pelt on his chest is mostly gray. I notice that his jeans ride dangerously low on his hips.

"There are kids up here," I admonish.

"They have seen me shirtless before. See, Justin beat me. He already has his shirt off. You're the only one who is uncomfortable. And you have seen me with more than my shirt off, Cassie," his voice drops on the last sentence.

"I'm not uncomfortable," I protest. Gordon always wore shorts and a tee shirt to bed. Maybe I'm uncomfortable. Lord, I'm a prude. I think back to yesterday, O.K., so maybe not a prude.

"You're smiling your Mona Lisa smile again."

"I'm just happy."

"Are you?"

"More than I have been in many years."

Will stares intently at me for a moment "You had some dark times." It is s statement, not a question.

"I wouldn't wish them on my worst enemy. Cancer takes away a lot, your dignity, your freedom and eventually, your soul." Although I'm not cold I wrap my arms around my knees, suddenly transported back to the long dark days and nights. I rock back and forth trying to drive the memories away. These feelings wash over me at the most unexpected times and when they do I'm helpless in the grip of their intensity.

"Cassie?"

I shake my head. If he touches me now I'll lose all control. Gradually I come back. Where did that outburst come from? I have been feeling good for such a long time.

To bring us back from that precipice I ask a little too loudly, "So tell me, Will Harley, what is your biggest regret? Once, you told me that your second biggest regret was sleeping with your law partner." I hear Sarah giggle and I apologize, "Sorry, I forgot the kids were playing in the back. We can pick this up some other time."

"Where did that come from?"

"I've been wondering, is all." He is saved from further discussion when we hear the wagon rumble up.

"Here comes the hay. Take up your positions," Justin commands. "I'm with Uncle Will and the girls, um, woman and girl get to stack."

Sarah protests, but I whisper that we will be so fast we can spend most of our time sitting around. I end up being right because something happens to the baler twine and every third bale breaks so Justin and Will expend extra energy throwing the broken bales to one side. Sarah and I take advantage of the free time to sit on a bale of hay pretending to paint our nails. Justin stomps his foot in frustration but Will laughs and pats his shoulder. After making our point, Sarah and I help move the broken bales closer to the chute to be used first.

It is after ten when we finish and the threatened storm never materializes. Sarah is still chattering when Will and Justin tell us we're finished.

I shower and dig for the ointment and udder balm. Ah, relief! Will is standing outside the bathroom door as I exit.

"Ah, the aroma of udder balm. I seem to remember someone saying, 'oh, that stinks'."

"Stinks, but works. You were right."

"I can't hear you, what did you say?" he teases.

"You're right, so rub it in. Please let me pass. I'm exhausted. All I want to do now is sleep."

"Well, you invited me to rub it in…"

"What? What? Oh, you are…"I stutter.

"Sexy, irresistible, a hunk, your dream?" There is a smug smile playing on Will's lips.

"I'm going to bed, Will Harley. My brain is too tired to play games with you."

"Well, I wasn't thinking of playing with your brain, Ms. Burns."

"Good night, Will." I brush past him to slip into my room when he stops me again.

"Guys have got a poker game going. Now that you know how to play, are you interested?"

"Thank you for the invitation, but I'll pass. See you in the morning."

He touches my shoulder and I look up. He kisses me very carefully for five seconds and then he steps back.

"Friends?"

"Of course."

"Forgiven?"

I think for a moment before I answer honestly. "I'm working on it." But I smile to let him know that we're over the worst part.

I'm sleeping so hard that when my phone rings I turn off the alarm. It can't be 5 a. m. already? When I finally find my phone I'm wide awake, afraid that something has happened to the children.

"Cassie."

My brain takes a few minutes to make the connection. "Kurt?"

"Did I wake you?" I look at the clock, it is 3:30.

"Yes. Actually I thought something had happened to my children. I usually don't get calls at 3:30 in the morning. What's up Kurt?"

"I'm writing a new song called Sassy Cassie."

I smile at his enthusiasm. "So sing it to me as long as I'm already awake."

"I want you to hear it at rehearsal with the band."

"When is it?"

"Tonight, starts at 10, that's when my band and I are at our best."

"10 p.m.?" I ask stupidly. Most nights I'm in bed by that time.

"Yes." His voice is warm and teasing and, as if he's read my mind, he asks, "Past you bed time? I can send a car."

I think of all of the complications of being picked up at the farm and tell him I'll meet him at the studio.

"Sending you a hug …and other things." His voice is serious and sexy now.

"Good night, Kurt."

"Tomorrow, Cassie."

Now I can't sleep. I toss and I turn and finally give up and dress to go downstairs. The poker game is still going. Don't farmers ever sleep?

I stand behind one of the neighbors, Stanley Wilson, and study his strategy. It doesn't appear that he has one; he throws in his money and seems surprised when someone tells him he has won. Even my sleepy brain recognizes that I can play as well as he does.

Then I put on the coffee and start mixing biscuits. I take the sausage out of the freezer for the gravy and shred the potatoes for hash browns. I'm sure that they will be hungry. Farmers expect to eat all of the time I grumble to myself once again.

The day goes by swiftly because there are so many chores, five loads of laundry to be hung on the line, picking the strawberries and peas both of which I end up freezing. Finally, I get all of the clothes folded and the beds made when it is time to make supper. After cleaning the kitchen and setting bread, I shower. I fix my hair and dress in my best jeans and a pretty blouse. I view myself critically then shake my head dismissively. Kurt has invited me. He's seen me, well, less pulled together.

I arrive at the studio ten minutes early. The technicians let me in and I wander around. People start showing up about 10:30. Trina, twenty years old, size 0, with long blond hair and big blue eyes introduces herself first. She eyes me up and down and I feel like the grandmother I am. I introduce myself but don't know how to explain why I'm at the studio so I say lamely that Kurt invited me.

"So are you like his relative or something?"

“No, just a friend.”

“So how did you meet him?”

“Chicago.”

Kurt enters and I’m spared the effort of trying to explain our relationship. Trina runs to him, wraps her arms around him and kisses him deeply.

Kurt ends the kiss and comes over to me, smiling. “Thank you for coming.” Even in an old tee shirt and ratty jeans he exudes a sexiness that makes me look away. He kisses me lightly and hugs me before Trina pulls him away to discuss some music details. The band sets up. Everybody seems to have a role but me. I’m in a roomful of indifferent strangers, most of them young enough to be my children.

The drummer struts over and sits by me. He lights up what I know is not a cigarette. “So, you sleepin’ with Kurt, too?”

“Excuse me?”

“You sleeping with super stud?” He gestures to Kurt.

“I’m not going to answer that.”

“Means yes. Just want to warn you, he can’t keep his dick in his pants. Makes him feel like the king when he has a hole in every town.”

I get up to walk away when he grabs my arm. “Listen, you remind me of my mother. Thought I could save you some time and heartache.”

I pull my arm away and say coldly, “Thank you.” There is no place to go so I walk around the building. I’m shaking, chiding myself for being as naïve as Kurt has pointed out. Kurt finds me leaning against the car.

“What did Beezer tell you?”

“You mean the drummer? Just that you sleep around,” I say flatly.

Kurt is quiet for a few seconds before he pulls me close and kisses me with passion—no denial, just charm.

“Come back in, we’re starting in a few minutes. I really want you to hear this new set.”

Three giggly teenage girls rush him as we start for the studio door. He graciously signs autographs when one tiny blond, jumps up and wraps her arms around him. She kisses him with such fervor that I blush. Kurt disengages himself, gives the girls a wink, and waves them off.

I go back into the studio and take an old recliner in the corner. Kurt goes into the back and is gone for what seems like a long time while the band practices. When he comes out his eyes are overly bright and he starts directing everyone. The band runs through the first song quickly but the second song they quibble over what seems like every other note.

My eyelids start to droop. I have been going since 3:30 in the morning and now it is past midnight. Finally, they agree to the changes on the second song. The third song is Sassy Cassie. The melody is catchy but the words are appropriate for a sixteen year old. When Kurt looks over I just smile and wave. The fourth song is an incredible remake of *Love Me Tender*. When they get to Forever Tattoo, I let the song wash over me; I recognize subtle changes that make it even better than the last time I heard it. Kurt is watching me and I blush remembering the first time he sang it to me.

Somewhere during the arguing about phrasing I fall asleep. When the music stops I wake up feeling foolish. Everyone else is chatting and laughing but I just feel tired and lonely. Beezer asks if I'm bored. I ignore him. Trina is all over Kurt, congratulating him on the changes and improvements, making plans for the next rehearsals. They decide to head over to the Bongos, the all night restaurant on the east side of town. I slip out and get into my car. Kurt ducks his head into the car window, "You're coming with us, right?"

"No thanks, Kurt."

"But we have got to talk."

"About?"

"The next gig. I'll be gone at least three months." By this time he's folded himself into my car. I turn to him and say sincerely, "I'll miss you."

"Then come with me."

"Excuse me?"

"You will see things you have never seen. We would have half the day to sightsee. You have missed so much."

"Thank you for pointing that out," I say dryly, "but I have family and responsibilities and commitments. Besides, I'm earning a living."

"So I'll triple your pay or ....What's eight times? I'll octo something your salary."

"Stop it, Midas."

"Who?"

I study him for a minute. Lord, we're just too many generations apart; he doesn't know Midas?

"I can't."

"You won't, you mean."

"What I mean is thank you. It is the most glamorous offer I have ever received. But can you really see me spending ninety days with your friends?"

He has the grace to look away, but says, "We wouldn't be spending all of our time with them. It could be just you and me. We would have time to talk."

"Kurt, we don't talk, we have sex."

"And it is great sex." He reaches over and cups my breast.

"And is great sex," I agree. "But unfortunately or fortunately, there is more to life than sex."

"So you're turning me down?" He is incredulous. He looks like a little boy who is disappointed on Christmas morning. Then he turns away.

I rest my hand on his neck, which is a mistake; the jolt goes right to my soul.

He hesitates a minute then shrugs off my hand and gets out of the car.

"I am so sorry." I'm not sure why I am apologizing; because I disappointed him? Because I'm too old for this silliness? Because part of me wishes I was adventurous enough to take this chance?

He leans back in. "Trina wants to get married."

I try to muster a smile. "What do you want?"

He looks at me hard for a moment, "Everything," he answers then turns on his heel and walks away.

Chapter Ten

The drive back to the farm is incredibly long. I know that everyone will be stirring in less than an hour but when I get into bed sleep won't come. I replay the evening. There is no other possible ending.

The thought of living with Kurt's entourage for three months makes me shudder. I know I have made the only possible decision I can make so why do I feel so empty?

The next few days I go into mourning. While intellectually I know it isn't possible to live in Kurt's world, the thought of never seeing him again, never having wonton, glorious sex with him makes me deeply sad. Then I hear Sassy Cassie on the radio and the announcer speculating on who the song is about. "Could it be the tiny blonde he was seen with at Othello's on Friday, AND again dancing in the streets on Tuesday?" No, that would be Trina, I respond to the announcer.

While I complete my chores, I know I'm barely sleepwalking. I overhear Winston and Will discussing me when I enter the kitchen one morning later in the week.

"Pa and I think we have been working you too hard. We think you should take a vacation."

"This is my vacation."

"We thought backpacking might be good for you."

"Really? I've never been backpacking."

"Well, the McCormick Wilderness is just a few hours from here and it is beautiful. Crystal Falls will take your breath away."

"All of us?"

"No, just you and me."

"Winston, what do you think of this idea?"

"I think it is a great plan, Cass. You've not been yourself for a while."

"I'm sorry, Win, I've got a lot on my mind." I hug him quickly and search his face for answers. What I see is a wonderful heart reflected in kind eyes.

"O.K.," I say without much enthusiasm.

The next day Will loads up the two backpacks and barks commands like he is some kind of drill sergeant.

"Can you carry fifty pounds?" he asks. "I'll carry the tent and the wine."

"Yeah, sure. I guess," I answer until he straps the pack on my back. I stagger backwards and slam into the refrigerator. He adjusts the straps and I feel a bit more balanced. Still I walk around the kitchen in an awkward, bent over position.

"Have you put rocks in here?" Will thinks this is a rhetorical question.

"Stand up," he commands and I straighten but still feel off balance. "Walk around with it for a while and then add your clothes."

Oh, crap. I thought it was already full. So I tuck my clothes in the nooks and crannies. I decide against carrying another pair of shoes because I'm afraid I'll collapse under the weight. I even eye my extra underwear suspiciously.

Then we each unroll an entire roll of toilet paper and stick clumps into all of our pockets and any remaining crevices. I've borrowed one of Winston's ammo shirts; it comes to my knees but oh, the pockets.

We leave at three the next morning. I sleep most of the trip. When the car stops, Will begins his lecture: if you see a moose don't provoke him (like I'm going to taunt him? How the hell does someone tease a moose?), remember all food, including gum and toothpaste goes into the plastic bag tied on a clothesline between two trees because of bears. Keep the topo map in my right front pocket at all times (why? I still can't read the darn thing), and try to keep up. He has irritated me with that last comment. Actually I feel rather irritated at all of his commands. I should have stayed home I grumble to myself.

The first two miles of hiking are clear trail; not too bad. I can do this, I think to myself. We see several day hikers who, unencumbered, pass us. An older couple keeps pace with us and while the men discuss hiking strategies, Maria and I talk about kids and books we've both enjoyed. She whispers to me that the secret of backpacking is to always offer food from your backpack so that you keep lightening your load. I thank her for the tip. I'm sorry when they stay in the opening to picnic while Will and I move further into the woods.

There are no trails. Three young, tough looking men pass us about a mile into the woods. They make a disparaging remark about old people hiking and I finger my Swiss Army knife sure that it will take me at least thirty seconds to pry out its 2 inch knife; basically, I'll be useless in a fight and with this backpack I won't be able to run. Guess I had better just let them talk smack and keep my thoughts to myself that way all that's likely to get wounded is my pride.

Soon there is no sound but Will and me crunching in the leaves, and well, me panting. Of course, I'm taking two steps to his one and I have to go around downed trees that he can step over and damn, I'm still out of shape. Where are my hay baling muscles? What about all that hoeing and weeding?

I trip over a tree root, lean too far back and go down on my butt. The second time I fall I realize that I can't roll over and I can't unbuckle the backpack straps. This must be what a turtle feels like when she gets flipped over onto her shell.

"Ah, so you have fallen and you can't get up," Will smugly intones.

"I need a hand here."

"And the magic word is..."

"Please give me your damned hand."

Will pulls me up and I prop myself against the nearest tree. I'm exhausted; my knees ache and I'm sure my back is permanently damaged.

"How many miles into the woods are we? Six? Eight?

"Maybe a mile and a half."

"No!" I protest. He pulls out the topo map and shows me. Less than an inch? All that walking and we've moved less than an inch! I scan the map and can't even begin to estimate how many inches we will be walking.

Will easily pulls off his pack and props it against the tree. He helps me out of mine and I stagger. I can tell now that we should have packed more wine. Somebody must make wine pouches with little stick-in straws like the juice pouches for kids. If not, that will be my next project. Now is definitely the time for a little imbibing.

Will interrupts my rambling thoughts. “Now looks like a good time to eat.”

“Let’s eat out of my pack,” I offer.

Will smiles and I know that he, too, knows the number one rule of backpacking.

We make small talk but Will is anxious to get to our first campsite before nightfall. He picks up the pace. He talks, I listen. I don’t have enough energy to talk and lift my legs. Soon I’m in a zone; pick up one foot, then the other. Will walks to the top of a small hill for the view. I lean against a tree and rest. Then I sit down on a ground hornet’s nest. I get up fast and even with the backpack I move pretty quickly, but not fast enough to avoid a sting on my right eyelid and three to my left hand. Will asks if I need anything for the stings. I say no. We walk in silence for a long time after that, at least an inch.

Then we cross a stream using a big old log. The stream isn’t big, probably less than ten feet across. Will maneuvers across in three steps. I fall in and get water in both my boots. I take a minute to catch my breath then clamber up the river bank on my own. Now I’m dirty and wet.

“Want to make camp here?” Will asks.

“Nope, I can make it to the campsite,” I say as my soaked socks squish with every step eventually ending bunched up under my insole. And we march on. The sun is slowly setting. I distract myself by daydreaming about home, the hammock, a can of Monster.

When Will announces that we’re at the campsite it looks like every other hilly, open spot. While Will sets up the tent, I collect fire wood. Then he shows me how to find two trees growing close together to insert my wood to break it into useable pieces. In ten minutes I have a respectable stack. Will says we need more. I gather and break enough wood to build an outbuilding. Will just smiles. I do not smile back. Will collects rocks to make a fire ring. I neatly stack six sticks in the center and throw on a match. I try it two more times before Will pulls the pile apart and builds a little tepee. Then he peels the dry bark off several dead birch trees, shreds it and lays a pile in the middle of the wood fort. He adds several small twigs. Carefully he lights the bark in several places and when that starts he starts feeding twigs until he has a fire.

"Take off your shoes and socks and we will put them over the fire to dry." He sounds bossy, but I'm grateful to get the wet boots off of my feet. Since I did not bring another pair of shoes I hop around in my only other pair of socks. Will carefully rigs a clothes line over the fire while I dig around in the backpacks for food. Twenty packages of ramen noodles, hmm obviously the main course. I slice smoked turkey and cheese. I'm starving so the meal tastes like a feast. This is the first real rest we've had since we started down the trail. I doze leaning against a tree. But we still have to wash the dishes and put the food in the garbage bag in the tree. We brush our teeth and walk away from the camp to spit. O.K., it must be time for bed now.

"What time is it, Will?"

"8:15."

"Really? It feels like midnight." I walk away from the camp to find a place to use as a bathroom. I hum *You Are My Sunshine* loudly, to scare away the bears.

"Well, did you see any?"

"See any what?"

"Bears?"

"No." I flush. I'm tired of the stupid bear jokes.

"*You Are My Sunshine* must work then."

He is teasing me and I don't have much of a sense of humor right now so I say crossly, "It does."

"Why are you taking a stick in the tent?" he asks as I get ready for bed, which entails simply crawling into the sleeping bag fully clothed.

"It's my bear club."

"Hmm, I see."

"Don't laugh at me, Will Harley. This is the first time I've been camping and the club makes me feel kind of safe."

"The Swiss Army knife, too?"

I finger the knife through my pants pocket. "Yes," I answer him.

"If you're going to bed, put your socks and boots on."

"In my sleeping bag?" I don't like the thought of putting those cold wet boots back on.

"They will be dry in the morning if you wear them in your sleeping bag," he explains.

Reluctantly I put them back on. The socks are only damp but it is still not a pleasant feeling. I crawl into the tent and climb into my sleeping bag with all of my clothes on. I'm asleep within minutes.

I wake up to growls and hoots, footfalls and snuffling, aware that only a canvas, or whatever tents are made of now, stands between and the creatures out there. And, now I have to go to the bathroom. I try to convince myself I can wait until morning except it is probably only midnight and I'll never fall back to sleep.

"Will, I have to go to the bathroom."

"Hmm, O.K. Flashlight's to the left of the tent door."

"Will? What should I do if I run into any animals?"

"Sing *You Are My Sunshine*. That'll scare them away."

"Funny." I gather my courage, grab my bear club and my make sure that my knife is still in my pocket. It is really dark out here. I can see maybe three feet in front of me. The moon is under the clouds and I can still hear all of the night noises but now they are magnified.

"You have to go at least ten feet away from the tent," Will yells. He did not have to raise his voice. I'm still clutching the tent flap.

Lord, ten feet! I can disappear and never be heard from again in ten feet. Then Will would be sorry. They'll find my bones in the belly of some big bear and I'll be identified by Dr. Kip, my dentist. Making as much noise as possible and swinging my club from side to side I make ten steps, pull toilet paper out of my pocket and hurry through. I dive through the tent flap and crawl into my sleeping bag, shivering. Shit, I left my bear club outside. I pull out my trusty knife and try to decide if I should pull out the knife tool so I'm ready, or if there is a bigger chance I'll roll over on it in my sleep and stab myself. Before I make that decision I fall asleep and it is morning.

And what a glorious morning it is. The birds are singing. I smell coffee. I stretch out and damn, if Will wasn't right; my socks and boots are no longer wet and clammy. How odd that they dried in my sleeping bag. Before I can think it through Will announces breakfast. Breakfast is

Tang and oatmeal with raisins. I hate oatmeal. I choke down as much as I can and snitch extra raisins as I wash dishes. Obviously I should have done the grocery shopping. We break up camp, re-distribute the stones from the fire ring, and carry our garbage with us. No one will ever know we have been here, a comforting and disconcerting fact.

Crystal Falls is our next destination. Will pulls out the topo map and instructs me to do the leading. O.K. I'll give it a shot. Confidently I start out. Will whistles, not given to idle conversation, and that's fine with me. I am busy studying the map. I need to keep the large hills to my right and the water on my left. Up and down we go, always another hill. We see a deer and a bald eagle. The day grows hotter and more humid. The pack gets heavier. Will brought his camera so he frequently stops to snap a particularly interesting flower or moss or leaf. Initially, I take this time to lean against a tree to rest but by mid-morning I began to pick out interesting rocks or a particularly well-framed scene. When we scare up a turkey, I marvel at the beauty and grace of the bird. We stop a few minutes to listen to the drumming of a partridge.

"We're making better time today," Will observes.

"Really?" Time has become fluid. Without a watch the day is a free form without structure or constraints.

"You haven't asked me what time it is yet."

"Don't care."

"Hmm, you're no longer a woman on a mission?"

"I didn't say that. I...I'm just enjoying the moment."

"How does it feel?"

I reflect a moment. "Light," I say finally.

Will nods to show he understands. He seems to have shed ten years.

"What are you looking for, Cassie?"

"You mean today or forever?" I don't wait for his answer. "In either case the answer is the same. Nothing concrete, Will. Maybe a little peace. Happiness. A few crazy adventures."

"What about you, Will?"

"We were talking about you."

"Now we're not. Now we're talking about you. Share," I command.

He is quiet for a long time.

"I want to raise the best beef cattle in Wisconsin. I want my son to grow up to be a kind and balanced man. I want to be a grandfather some day. I want my Dad to live forever. I want my Mother back for one more hug. I want to be a better man than I have been. I want the farm to be able to support all of us." He picks up a blade of grass and chews on it, looking somewhere over my head.

Interesting answer and awfully deep for this beautiful morning. I change my tactics.

"So what's the dumbest thing you have ever done?"

"We don't have enough time. We need to get to the Falls before it is dark."

"We can walk and talk. O.K., I'll start. I went skydiving and broke my ankle and I had three little kids to care for. Bailey talked me into it. Gordon was mad at me for a long time for that one. I left Gordon once for three days when he had an affair. I kissed my Philosophy professor and I actually went home with him but left before anything could happen."

"Wow, a lot of action lingers under that Pollyanna exterior."

"You can't distract me and you can't put it off any longer so spill."

"I crippled a man—a husband and father with two kids. I was seventeen, trying marijuana and driving my first motorcycle when I hit him. He was driving home from the night shift at the hospital. He was a janitor there for twenty-two years before I ended life as he knew it. There was enough evidence to suggest that he may have fallen asleep and crossed the center line, but I know it was my fault."

Will stops moving and looks directly at me and I can see the seventeen year old boy he had been and read in his eyes that the accident is as real to him today as it was 30 plus years ago. I touch his hand but he neither recoils nor responds. We are standing quietly when without warning lightning splits the sky. Will is brought out of his reverie.

"We've got to find some place to wait out the storm. Come on." The air is suddenly electric as we run awkwardly with our packs to a medium sized pine tree. Well, at least I run awkwardly, Will with his long legs looks much more graceful. We lay flat, pretty well protected from the driving rain. It's a intimate position which reminds me that we haven't showered for two days and we have been wearing our clothes for the same length of time. My hair is squashed flat under an unflattering camo hat. Will hasn't shaved for two days and he is wearing a sweat-stained cowboy hat.

Will is lying on one side of the tree and I am on the opposite side of the trunk. He pulls his hat over his face so I assume he is going to nap. During the quiet waiting I reflect on our first two days and realize that we haven't seen one human being. I try to capture the flavor of our days so I can share with the kids. I wake to Will shaking me.

"Ten more minutes, please," I mumble.

"If we're going to camp by the Falls, we have to start moving."

I shrug back into my pack and adjust it myself. We trudge the remaining miles to the Falls in silence, each of us wrapped in our own thoughts. Will is quieter than usual. I wonder if he regrets his confession. He is a complex man, part cowboy, part sophisticated lawyer, occasionally playful and always driven.

"Why do you call your father, Pa?" I ask out of idle curiosity.

Will grins before he answers. "When Bart was a kid he thought Pa looked like the father, Michael Landon, on Little House on the Prairie. It stuck."

"What was he like when you were growing up?"

"He was strict. He's a pussy cat now. He made us work hard. We were only allowed to sign up for one sport because we were needed on the farm. Sometimes I thought he was just ornery until I had my own son. I disappointed him. He wanted me to be a veterinarian or a physician because I've always been good with fixing things, animals and such, but I didn't want to leave the farm for that long. We quarreled and I left for a year. I learned a lot in that year about myself and I began to understand my father a little better. I came back, took a lot of biology classes, genetics interests me, and completed a double major in political science and biology. You know the rest of the story."

We continue walking but now I begin to see the beauty that Will has been talking about; the way the sun comes through the trees; a shimmering green-black crow's feather; a spider web shiny with rain drops. I'm a little more adept at climbing over fallen logs and up steep hills. The pack feels lighter. We reach Crystal Falls by mid-afternoon; it is breath-taking. The temperature has been in the 80s all day and the water is inviting. I shed my pack and my clothes in record time. I dig out the soap and spend the next ten minutes scrubbing. Clean never felt so good. Will floats by and nabs the soap.

When I lay on a rock to dry I really notice for the first time a mass of bruises from my waist to my ankles; the trees and sticks and falls have taken their toll. Oh well, they are a badge of honest effort. When Will climbs up onto the rock he whistles. "You look like you've been wrestling with a bear and lost."

"Think they're going to eventually hurt?"

"Yes."

"Why didn't I notice them earlier? I mean we have been wearing our clothes non-stop for two and half days but you would think I would feel something this…massive."

"Adrenalin, the novelty of the experience, my charming presence," Will offers.

After a few minutes of silence I say, "There is an elephant here that needs to be addressed." I turn to face Will. "Do you really think my goal is to wheedle the farm away from your family with my 'feminine wiles'?"

He looks at me steadily. "I think you're a lost soul looking for a place to roost."

"I'll grant you that when I first came to the farm I was looking for something, but it wasn't a place to roost. I have family and friends in Illinois who care about me and want me to come back. You see my children want me to settle down and act like a grandmother. My friends want me to come back and play bridge and take bus tours. So many people are trying to define poor widow Cassie. But, from now on, I am going to do the defining." I lay back, flushed and agitated. I flip over to my stomach and groan. The bruises are making their presence known.

"So where do I fit into that picture?"

"I don't know, Will. We barely know each other."

His hand cups my butt and he smiles. "I know you."

I lean in, "But you don't know my middle name or who I voted for or my dreams or my secrets."

"Didn't we just trade secrets?"

I turn away and murmur, "Not all of them."

"So which ones have I missed? Let me guess. Hmm… you dress up in men's underwear? No. You're a hoarder—you have every scrap of clothing your children ever wore? You're not really gray; you dye your hair to look more mature?" He is smiling as he lies on his back.

I look at him long and hard before I admit, "I killed my husband," He looks at me waiting expectantly. I sit up and look at Will repeating myself. "I killed my husband. I looked up a recipe for a fatal narcotic cocktail on the intranet and killed him. He had been in pain that nothing could touch for a week. We had agreed at the start of his illness that I wouldn't let him suffer. He called in his chip. I mixed up the concoction, gave it to him then crawled in bed and held him until he died. So you see, Will, you didn't know my darkest secret." I lay back, spent.

I've never told anyone this secret, not Bailey, not my girlfriends, and certainly not the kids. Do I regret that night? No, I would do it again for Gordon. I know that he would have done it for me. If I were in that situation now, who would I turn to I wonder? Morbid thoughts on such a beautiful day.

I don't look at Will but dress quickly, saying, "We have work to do. I'll collect the wood and start the fire today—my turn to cook."

He is quiet as we set up camp. We're planning on staying in this beautiful place for a couple of days so I gather and break a large stack of wood. I carefully make the fire ring as Will had shown me earlier. I stand back to admire my work. I start the fire then boil water for our dried entrée, beef stew. This meal is many steps up from ramen noodles. We drink our first bottle of wine. I'm in charge of the chocolate and pass out three stars to Will. I balance my three stars on the edge of my plate.

"It started with wine and chocolate, if you will remember."

We are each leaning against a tree, talking across the fire. Camping is such an intimate endeavor; we know what each other is doing virtually every minute of the day. We have not been separated by more than the distance it takes to have a private moment. I have developed a new respect for Will. I admire his vast knowledge about the outdoors. I wonder what he feels about me. I know that initially I didn't want to go on this camping adventure, and I was not the best of companions. I feel differently now.

We have been treating each other asexually; even his playful groping of my butt earlier didn't feel like a come-on. I wonder what that's about. I think Will is attracted to me, physically. I know I'm attracted to him but I'm not sure that either of us is ready to move our relationship to a different level. I also know that he is still in contact with his ex-wife.

Part of my hesitation is that my mind still turns to Kurt, ten or twenty times a day. I replay each encounter in living color, uncensored, minute by minute. The beautiful sunrise yesterday reminded me of the drive back to the farm after he had told me about Elise. I wonder if he married Trina. My heart does a funny little flip at the thought. I try to close the door on those feelings but it won't stay shut.

I rise to put more wood on the fire. The night is turning cooler, what a relief. We wash the dishes, brush our teeth and put all of the food high in the tree. But tonight I don't want to turn in early. I want to marvel at the full moon. I want to have another long discussion. I want to hold this special moment to me just a little longer. I pull on a sweatshirt and scoot closer to the fire. Will identifies the sounds of the night; an owl, a raccoon, a deer. I listen raptly until he moves on to a cougar, a zebra and a dinosaur. I throw a stick at him in disgust.

"Sure you don't want to keep this as a bear stick?" he asks holding up the twig.

"I was just thinking how much I appreciate your intellect and your varied knowledge of the outdoors and now you have blown it, mister."

"And here I believed it was my charm, charisma and fine character. To say nothing about this fabulous body you have been eying up."

"In your dreams, Harley."

Will chews on a piece of grass and looks at me soberly.

"So what is next, Cassie? What happens when fall comes?"

"I'm practicing the one-day-at-a-time school of thought."

"We haven't finished this day yet so what is next?"

"This is it, I'm doing it—nothing. Looking at the stars. Enjoying the night. I'm thinking about how I can get an extra chocolate star out of the pack when you aren't looking. And you, cowboy?"

He is up in one lithe move. He bends down until our faces are inches apart. Will tentatively kisses me. My return kiss isn't as tentative. Will pulls me close. I close my eyes and surrender to the wave that engulfs me. Then I'm hungrily kissing his face, down his prickly neck and opening his shirt. When my cold hands touch him he jumps. I kiss his hairy chest, enjoying the silky feel and the unique Will smell. Will moves directly to my jeans and pushes them down to my ankles. I let out a pathetic yelp when my butt encounters pine needles. Will pulls back and hastily manipulates his sleeping bag under me and we wriggle around until I'm comfortable and Will is covered. When he lowers himself into me I watch his face, unmasked and gentle. His tenderness is unsettling and I begin to cry. He stops and without words I indicate that I want to continue. The tears persist. When his eyes question me I pull him fiercely to me, raising my hips to meet his thrusts. I'm not sure how long we move together. Time stops; there is just the two of us oblivious to the cold and the dark night.

When he rolls off I feel lonely…bereft. We are too entangled for me to pull up my jeans. Instead we cuddle close, heart to heart. Will's hand slips between us and in a warm, lazy haze he teases me to arousal. This time our lovemaking is rougher, insistent. When Will collapses on me all six feet, 190 pounds, the breath is temporarily squeezed out of me. I let out an unladylike huff. He levers himself to his elbows to give me a little space. I admire the muscles in his chest and arms when he looks down at me with a slow grin. He hasn't lost his hat so with his beard and weathered features he looks like a classic cowboy.

"Backpacking is odd foreplay, Will."

"Not so odd, it worked."

I groan, "Tell me this wasn't your reason for backpacking, Harley"

He rolls onto his back and continues, "Actually I come up here as often as I can. It restores my soul. Some of the people I deal with for my job take away my belief in goodness and humanity. Hiking in this Wilderness gives it back."

We pull Will's sleeping bag back into the tent and zip it up with mine. We sleep hard, but I wake up early and sneak out of the tent to get dressed and make breakfast. The sunrise is spectacular as I walk down a trail to the Falls to collect water for washing and for cooking. There are multiple sets of tracks on the small beach and I make a mental note to ask Will about them.

It only takes me three matches to start a fire—wahoo! At this rate I'll have the water boiling in no time. Just as Will sticks his head out of the tent, I swing around too quickly and knock the kettle into the fire, effectively dousing it. Will opens his mouth, then shuts it and ducks back into the tent; wise man. Although I'm sure that I hear chuckling.

I start all over re-building the fire. It takes longer when the fuel is wet. I go back to the beach to collect more water and finally get the fire going for a second time.

I struggle but finally pull the food out of the tree. Great, more oatmeal. Oh, here are three cream of wheat, double yuck. I dig a little further. Here is a bag called biscuit mix. I mix it with instant milk and water, add a little butter to our pan and throw the big patty on to cook. I slice cheese with my trusty Swiss Army knife; finally it has become a useful tool.

I almost lose the biscuit patty trying to flip it. A little done, well black actually on this side. We can cut that off. Will is making his way back from the beach when I put 2/3 of the patty on his plate with a couple of slices of cheese. I pour him a glass of Tang and we dig in. O.K. so one side is burnt and one side is still doughy. Will eats his without a word. I do, too. Then I search the pack for raisins; they kind of help take the taste out of my mouth. I offer some to Will and he takes a big handful. He cleans up and we're ready for another day.

"Oh, what are all those tracks by the beach?"

He looks intently at me. "Animals drinking at night."

"I get that, but what kind of animals?"

"Looks like raccoon, some smaller animals probably fox or weasels."

"And, the bigger prints?"

"Bear."

"Bear? There were lots of big prints." I look around and realize that the trail I have been using to get to the beach is probably the one they are using to get to the beach. The trail is less than five feet from the tent.

"Looks like we're on a bear trail," I observe.

"Looks like it."

"Think we should move the tent?"

"Probably a wise move."

So we pack up and move a couple of hundred yards down the beach. I think I'm getting the hang of this backpacking; there is no timetable.

We take all morning to find another spot for the tent. We eat cheese and chocolate stars for lunch. Will goes off to take pictures. I lie on my back and marvel at the clouds, something I haven't taken the time to do for years. I think of Gordie without too much pain. Tentatively, I talk out loud to him but he isn't answering. I swim in the pool at the base of the Falls. I lie naked on the rocks to dry off and then I doze.

In my dreams every worry and concern falls out of my head; the bears will either eat me or not. Lila can deal with Anston. She will either forgive him or leave him; I don't impact her decision. Lucas and Gia will determine if they want to be together for the long haul. Bailey, well Bailey will continue to be Bailey, and some day he may self destruct. Perhaps I can delay the inevitable but I can't stop that particular train. And then I allow my mind to move to Kurt; I probe my feelings for him like a sore tooth my tongue can't leave alone. I wonder if we have a relationship by any definition other than sexual. I wonder if he is happy and realize that the devil in me wants him to miss me and what we had. I want him to compare our pleasure in bed to what he has with Trina. I want to believe that ours would be hard to top. Then I let him go. Just like that, I wish him a long and happy life and relegate him to the box of happy memories; the one that includes my junior prom, my first kiss, the birth of my children and the completion my Ph.D.

In a sleepy fog my thoughts turn to Will and like an apparition he drops down beside me.

"So is your next vacation going to be in a nudist colony?"

"Could be, Harley. On a day like today, anything is possible. How about you? Did you get some good pictures?"

"Let me show you," he says as he enthusiastically explains his intent and his framing as he shows them to me. I admire his technique and the rest of the afternoon sneaks by as we argue the relative merits of each of the pictures.

After supper, gazing into the fire, I offer, "I feel balanced enough to go back to the farm, Will."

"What changed?"

"All this thinking time."

"And?" he prompts.

"I'm not sure, but I believe that my perspective is back. To repeat a cliché, what will be, will be."

I think a minute. "No, what I really mean is whatever happens from now on, I believe that I can cope with it. When you're holding hands when the man you believed was your life partner as he dies, you simultaneously lose a part of yourself and find traits within you that hadn't previously been tested. Before I made it to the farm I was certain I had flunked the test. But now I give myself a C for surviving."

"What part of yourself do you feel that you lost, Cassie?" Will asks quietly.

"Innocence. Optimism. Did you know that I was a high school cheerleader? The mighty, mighty Falcons lost seventy percent of our football games, but I could make the crowd believe that this time things would go differently; that we were poised on the brink of winning. It doesn't work so well with cancer."

I change the subject. "So, what do you want, Will? Are you ready to return to civilization or should we continue our hedonistic pleasures? Oh, that brings me to the next important question, are you hoarding any chocolate?"

He grins and reaches into his backpack pulling out a whole bag of Mallo Cups. "Just waiting for you to ask."

"Do you have any steak in there? Or a Whopper? I swear I'll never look at another ramen noodle as long as I live. They are disgusting."

"Sorry, no real food other than chocolate in here. What I would like to do is spend one more night here then leisurely make our way back. I know a great restaurant we can hit on our way out."

While we keep the fire going, we decide to eat food that doesn't have to be cooked; cheese, jerky, granola and Mallo Cups. Yup, I decide, I want to be buried with a dozen of these sickeningly sweet morsels. I voice these thoughts to Will who only grins at me.

The night is beautiful and we sit in comfortable quiet. I see a shooting star and give the wish away to my kids, then selfishly wish for their health and happiness. Too soon it is time for bed, but I'm unwilling to end my last night in the woods.

"We could sleep out under the stars tonight, if you're game," Will suggests.

"Have you done that before?" I whisper because somehow the night seems sacred and talking in my normal voice is intruding on the magic.

"I don't usually pack a tent when I'm out here."

"Really? What's the worst thing that could happen?"

"Well, so far the worst thing that happened to me was that a bird shit on my head."

I begin to laugh and can't stop. The picture in my head is so funny. Will joins me and we hoot until we can't laugh anymore.

"Come on bird," I say as I crawl into our exposed sleeping bags, shivering. I feel a delightful sense of adventure tinged with fear; adventure wins. It has been winning a lot lately is the last thought I have before it is morning.

Will is taking pictures when I crawl out of the warm sleeping bags. I stand next to him as he frames the Falls and I take my own mental snapshot. I throw off my clothes and dive in. The cold takes my breath away.

We swim until my core temperature drops and I'm sure that it will at least be several miles before I'm sweating through my tee shirt. Will takes us on a short cut on the way back, more inland, away from the lake. The walking is harder; the mosquitoes are fierce. I find three wood ticks crawling up my pants leg. Will pulls them off but for the rest of the morning I can feel them everywhere.

Will gets annoyed with my paranoia and having to look in my hair or on my back for the non-existent ticks.

"They are not going to kill you, Cassie. Get over it. I'll check you when we get back to the car. If we don't pick up our pace we won't get out of the woods before it is pitch dark."

We only rest a few minutes to eat lunch out of our packs—cheese and granola.

I'm crabby because Will has been so short with me. I move forward quickly to signal my anger. I'm heading down a hill when I realize that Will is not behind me. I hastily head back up the hill to find Will leaning against a tree and sweating. I unbuckle his pack and grab it but the weight brings me to my knees. I help Will to a sitting position. In this filtered light he looks pale. I dig for his water bottle and offer it to him but he pushes it away. He hasn't said a word.

"Just one drink, Will. When was the last time you had something to drink?" I stop to think; maybe he is dehydrated. Maybe it is something worse.

"Will, talk to me." I cast around for ideas. "Have you peed lately?"

He doesn't answer.

"Drink, Will." I force the bottle into his hand then help him bring it to his lips.

He drinks but a large amount of water just runs out the side of his mouth.

"Will Harley, snap out of it." I take him by the shoulders and shake hard. Finally, I take my bottle of water and pour it over his head. I unbutton his shirt and wipe the water across his chest. I break off a branch and fan him. I begin to shake. Control yourself, Burns. We don't need two incoherent backpackers; I admonish myself out loud.

"Not funny, Will. You're not going to leave me in the woods as bear food." In a whirl of energy I pull off his boots, unzip his jeans and pull them down.

I pull out the topo map; which squiggly line are we on? Tears swim in my eyes and I smear them away angrily. Damn, not one more person is going to die on my watch. O.K. so it looks like there might be a stream two hills over. Can I leave Will by himself? Can I make it across those two hills and find my way back?

"Cassie."

"Geez, Will where did you go? How are you feeling? What is wrong with you?"

"I don't know what happened. One minute I was walking across the hilltop and the next thing I know you're pulling down my pants. Funny time to get amorous." He is still pale and seems breathless just sitting still.

"I was trying to cool you down, idiot. No, really, Will what's going on? You just stood still with your eyes closed."

"My heart's racing. Might be this heat, the exertion, I don't know…" his voice trails off.

"No, Will, concentrate. Can you move? It looks like there is a stream just over those hills. Can you make it that far?"

Obviously he can't manage his pack, do I leave it? Do I try to carry both packs? Am I crazy? For one long moment my mind goes blank.

Then I start to scream. I can't stop until I stuff my dirty fist in my mouth. I rock for a few minutes before I control myself, get up and study the topo map again.

"You scared the shit out of me, Cass," Will mumbles

"Me too, I thought I was really going over the edge," I answer honestly. I force him to drink more water and help him put his clothes back on. He is weak and leans on me.

Then he pulls himself up and says, "I can make it to the stream."

I find him a walking stick, put my pack on my back and start dragging Will's pack.

"That's an expensive pack," he protests weakly.

"Sorry," I say shortly, "it is dragging or leaving it behind, your call."

We move at this snail's pace for what seems like hours. We make it to the stream. Will lays in it, letting the cool water wash over him.

I dip my head in the stream and get my hair and tee shirt wet. I soak my arms. When Will is ready we start walking again. I take off my pack and stuff everything that matters, food, my jacket and toothpaste into my pack. It is too heavy for me to carry. I go through it again and take out the toothpaste, extra clothes and, unfortunately, the Mallo cups. I stuff two into my shirt pockets. We eat a little cheese and granola. I force Will to drink and then I rehydrate myself. I pack everything I can't carry into Will's pack, wrap it in a garbage bag and tie it between two trees. We had better not get lost. We are traveling really light now. I've got just our water, some jerky and two chunks of cheese. I study the topo map to determine where we are so someone can come back to get the pack. I ask Will for help and he stares at it a long time before he points to a spot. I spit on my finger, wipe it in the dirt then mark the map. We start hiking again. Lord, this is my greatest nightmare, getting lost. My brain goes into overdrive and I imagine large, angry animals behind every tree. I pick up a heavy stick and start swinging it back and forth through the underbrush making as much noise as I can.

Will is concentrating on walking, I'm trying to lead and make sure that he follows. It is dark when we make it back to the clearing. There is no one camping at the site. I take a deep breath and blow it out slowly. I was so sure we would find someone in the clearing. I choke back my fears. We still have two miles of hiking to get to the car. Will is silent. I help him sit and dig the last of our food out of the pack.

"Will, we can either camp here for the night," I glance around and note that there are not many dead branches lying around, "or we can walk the two miles to the car. What are your thoughts?" No matter how he answers I'm not sure that we should stay here in the condition he is in; I just desperately want to shift the decision-making out of my realm.

"I. Can. Walk." His voice is low.

"O.K. let's move it." I pull him up and he sways slightly. I find his walking stick and hand it to him. He waits for me to lead. It takes us over an hour to get back to the car. I throw the pack in the trunk, get out the old blanket to cover Will and race for the highway. Ms. GPS gets us to the Community Hospital in 35 minutes. We wait an hour and a half in the ER before Will is seen. The ER doctor doesn't find anything after a battery of tests but gives him an IV bag of fluids. Then he tells Will to follow up with his regular doctor when he gets home.

It is midnight when we're allowed to leave. While pale, Will looks better. Now that the crisis has passed I'm starved. Not much is open in this small town at 12:30 but a few bars. One offers food so we stop. I order two hamburgers and two beers. Will eats his solitary hamburger slowly and drinks only water. I need the two beers.

Next we need to find a hotel, motel, bed and breakfast—any place with a bed. The bartender directs us to the next town—ten more miles of driving. I pound on the door for five minutes before an old man in a tee shirt and pajama pants lets us in. He rents us the last unit. Will staggers to the bed and I help him undress. I take a quick shower and join him.

I call Will's brother, Colin, to let him know what happened. He offers to hike into the Wilderness and pick up Will's pack. I explain that Will doesn't want to worry his father. Colin agrees.

Will feels better the next day. We get back to the farm and everyone gathers on the porch wanting to talk about the trip. You would have thought we had been gone for weeks.

"You should have seen Cassie when she played turtle," Will starts.

I roll my eyes. Sarah puts her hand in mine and whispers, "I would have helped you up."

"I know you would have pumpkin. Uncle Will likes teasing, doesn't he?"

"What about the bears?" Justin asks, "The McCormick Wilderness has one of the largest bear populations in the state."

"I'll let Cassie answer that."

"Well, we just happened to set up our tent…"

"Pitch, you pitch a tent, Cassie," Will butts in.

I start over, "As I was saying before I was so rudely interrupted, we happened to pitch our tent on a bear trail."

Bart asks, "You mean the one next to the Falls? That trail has been there for years."

"Really?" I look at Will who shrugs.

"Didn't you pull that one on Justin, Will?"

"Uncle Will got me, too," Matt pipes up.

"Then let Uncle Will tell you about the puma, zebra and dinosaur we heard."

"It's a cougar, Cassie," Aaron corrects me.

"It looks like the camping trip was one big joke on me," I say glaring at Will.

Winston interrupts, "Don't take it to heart, Cassie, the initiation just means that now you're officially part of the family."

With the family still talking I take Will aside and ask him sarcastically, "Was the sex part of the initiation, too?" I leave before he can respond.

Chapter Eleven

My phone rings when I'm feeding the calves with Sarah. I check; it is a number I don't recognize.

"Hello?" I'm harried and want to finish this chore so I can move into the house to make supper.

"Cassie Burns?"

"Yes." I answer impatiently, "Who is this?"

"This is Eduardo Rico."

"Yes," I say again distractedly although the voice rings a bell.

"Kurt's friend."

"Oh, how are you?"

"I'm fine. How are you?"

"I'm doing well, thank you. Excuse me. Sarah, honey, you can run into the house. I'll be in shortly." She waves, a little princess hand movement, and runs off.

"Sorry, Eduardo; what can I do for you?"

"Kurt wants to see you."

"He can't call himself? What's up Ed?"

There is no sound for several long seconds, then, "He is a busy man, Cassie."

"So he married her," I say quietly, confirming what my heart already knows.

"He wants to see you."

"He's married Eduardo. Acting as his pimp isn't up to your standards." I'm breathing hard. I'm angry and sad and I want to take it out on someone.

"Please tell him I hope he lives happily ever after." I hang up and sit down heavily on the nearest hay bale. So my few minutes of fantasy living are over; no more surprise visits, no more hours in bed, no more feeling pampered and cared for. I'm surprised by the emptiness I feel. I knew it wasn't forever. I guess I had hoped for a little more time, or at least one more time.

My phone rings again and I pick it up. "Hello?"

"Cassie, please just listen. One more meeting that's all he wants. There are some things he wants to say. "

"Ed, the first night I met you I thought we could be friends. Please don't dilute those pleasant feelings for this. I'm hanging up again. Please don't call. And, Ed, please tell Kurt I wish him and Trina well."

I hear Sassy Cassie on the radio the next day. I'm in the midst of heavy cleaning but I stop to listen. The announcer's patter sparks my attention, "And Mr. Troy just isn't saying who the Cassie is in this song. Only that she also inspired The Forever Tattoo. He says it is not his new wife, the former Ms. Trina Weston. Well, every man is entitled to his secrets."

"So, do you think that's true, Cass?" Winston asks. I didn't even hear him enter the kitchen.

"Only if it extends to women, Win," I tease.

"Women are all about secrets."

"How do you know about women when you raised all boys?"

"Do you remember when I told you farmers were just about perfect?" I grin and nod. "Well that extends to knowing their way around women."

"You are so full of…"

"Don't say it. I would hate to think that my family has unduly affected your speech."

"Well, you have unduly influenced the rest of me so why not my speech?" I throw the dust rag at him. He wings it back at me as he heads out the door.

Lila calls to tell me Anston has left her and the girls. She sounds tired. "Want me to come back, sweetie?" I ask.

"Mom, he's been doing this for years." She is quiet for a moment and then asks, "Did Dad ever cheat on you?"

I hesitate but she's old enough to know the truth, "Once with his secretary. The four of you were little when it happened. I left him for three days; we moved in with Grandma and Grandpa. He apologized and told me it would never happen again. I believed him and took him back."

"It hurts so much, Mom." I can hear her soft sobs and my heart breaks.

"Where are the girls, honey?"

"They are spending the night at Chrissy's house."

"I can be on your porch before midnight, Lila."

"Oh mom, you can't fix it for me."

"What? I've lost my magic touch?" I stop teasing and say softly, "I used to be able to fix most anything."

"Just knowing you're always here for me is close enough to fixing this time. I'm going to call Colleen and Joy and see if they want to have a girls' night out. It isn't often that I have time for myself."

"All you have to do is call and I'll come back."

"I know mom, I love you."

"I love you, too, Littlest." The nickname Mark bestowed upon her—the irksome youngest sister who adored him.

Lila laughs softly and hangs up.

I check outside to see if there is anything I should be doing but Winston is on the porch reading and writing. I hover over his shoulder and ask, "What are you doing?"

He looks up briefly and smiles. "I'm writing in the margins."

"Why? I was never allowed to write in books."

"Well, these are my books and I write in the margins so when I re-read them I know what I was thinking. And, I want to know if I have gotten any wiser so I compare my thoughts with what I'm feeling now. Sometimes I find that I disagree with the assessment of my younger self. Often I just build on my ideas. Not every book is worthy of being re-read, thus being written in, but the Bible and this one," he holds it up, "Atlas Shrugged, I plan to read many more times."

"You're so darned smart. If I just sit next to you can I get some of it through osmosis?"

"Why don't you try?" he says winking and moving over.

"Actually, I don't want to be any competition."

“Dream on you young whippersnapper,” Winston says imitating an old man’s quavering voice. I laugh.

“I need to clear my head, oh wise one, so I’m going for a quick walk. I’ll be back in an hour or so.”

“Watch out for the bears,” he intones. The whole clan likes to tease me about my aversion to bears. I stick out my tongue.

Chapter Twelve

My destination is a little creek—only here it is pronounced crick—about a mile down the road. Sarah waves but I just walk on, I know that she is disappointed because we often walk together, but today I need to think so I don't invite her to come along.

It is quiet and cool in the shade of a big oak tree. I have a long list of problems to chew on today; the kids, the teaching job, Bailey, Will and Kurt. As if my thoughts have conjured him up, I look up to see Kurt walking across the field. At first I catch my breath, then I watch critically as he walks toward me; perfect hair, pressed jeans, a plaid shirt; must be his idea of how to dress for a visit to the farm. He sits down close to me but not touching.

"Hello, K.C."

"Hello, Cassie."

"How is your tour going?"

"Long, too long. I'm flying back to catch up with the guys tonight. I miss you." He looks like an eager teenager.

I don't say anything, just look at him expectantly. Then I shake my head and ask, "Trina?"

"It was a mistake. She knows it, too. Already she is making noises about alimony."

"I'm sorry. I had hoped that you two would be happy."

"I'm not. I haven't written anything. The guys are driving me crazy with their women and their drugs. They are my best friends and I don't feel like a part of them anymore. And suddenly the women all have interchangeable bodies that never satisfy me. What have you done to me?" He gets up and paces.

"That's quite a problem," I acknowledge dryly. Kurt doesn't hear, or maybe he doesn't get my sarcasm because he continues, "I've worked so hard to get away from those feelings of insecurity and restlessness, and most of the time I can beat them back, but it's been different since you left."

"I didn't leave you, Kurt. If you remember, you left me. I'm still in the same place. I'm still the same woman. And you got married."

He waves his hand at me dismissively, as if his marriage is a moot point.

"Why are you here, Kurt?"

"I don't know, Cassie. No, that's not true; I want to return to what was."

"You can't re-wind that particular tape," I remind him quietly.

"But I can," he explains eagerly. "I'll pay Trina off and we can go back to where we were."

"Where were we, Kurt?"

"We were together. Enjoying each other. We were happy together. We were very happy when we were in bed." He grins then adds, "Or in the field or in the car or…"

He stands over me and I get up.

"Please don't touch me, Kurt."

"What are you afraid of?"

"Starting all over. Letting you in again. Having you leave. Take your pick."

"That's the future and no one knows what it holds. Why can't you live in the moment?" he asks.

"Because I am not thirty-five."

"Dumb answer," he says reaching out to touch my face.

I stand still, willing myself not to react. He pulls me gently to him and whispers in my hair, "Just hold me one more time, and if you tell me the humming is gone, I won't bother you again."

I wrap my arms around him one last time. He stretches his body out against mine and pins me to the tree. He nuzzles my neck but when I don't respond he pulls back.

"It's gone?" he asks.

I gently disengage myself and move away. Looking him in the eye, I say, "Nothing."

"You shivered."

"I'm cold."

"You're lying."

"Kurt, K.C., Tom whoever, let me say it straight, no more buzzing. It's over. It has been a good time, but now we both need to move on. I wish you well. And Trina, too. Try to make it work. Marriage is…" I struggle for an appropriate word and end up with a cliché, "sacred."

He lifts his hand as if to touch me again, but I move out of reach.

"Good bye, Kurt."

His eyes search my face for what seems like a long time. I struggle to keep it open and guileless.

I watch as he swiftly crosses the field, gets into his car and roars away. He never looked back, which is a good thing because he would have seen me on the ground, crying. It took a lot of effort to disguise the affects of the humming, to pull back when I feel like a moth being drawn to a deadly flame.

Dusk is falling before I am able to uncurl myself and walk the mile back to the farm.

Chapter Thirteen

"Since I'm gone, who is going to miss you?
Since I'm gone, who the hell cares?
Since I'm gone, who is going to kiss you?
Since I was the answer to all of your prayers."

I am in the kitchen making breakfast when I hear the end of the song that I recognize immediately as a new one by KC and Infyniti. I can hear the anger in the song, yet I flinch when I hear the title, *Bitch*. I listen to the announcer's speculations. "Looks like Infyniti's got another hit. Mr. Troy is no longer with the lovely Ms. Trina but he's on a European tour. Sources close to him say that he is writing prolifically. Sources also say that he's been seen at all of the clubs with a different lady every night. If this latest song is any indication, he has a lot of angst to work through. In the mean time, Ms. Trina, who says the breakup was amicable, has been seen with Infyniti drummer, Carmine "Beezer" Able.

Winston finds me sitting at the old table, lost in thought.

"Hey, sunshine."

"Winston."

"I'm thinking we should have a party, shoot off some fireworks, roast a pig; celebrate."

"What are we celebrating, Mr. Harley?"

"I am turning the farm over to the boys and retiring."

"You're too young to retire. Besides, what would you do all day?' I ask.

"Eat bonbons, watch soaps, travel."

"What do the boys think of this?"

"I haven't told them yet. I will during the celebration."

"So it is a secret?"

"Until the celebration. So I would appreciate it if you would keep it to yourself until then."

"So, you have chosen a date?"

"Saturday."

"This Saturday. Two days from now? How are we going to pull it all together in two days?"

"Anna and Sally will pitch in. We've done this in the past. It's no big deal, Cassie."

"How many people are you inviting, Winston?"

"Well, the whole neighborhood. That's the way we do it here. We all celebrate together, and we all mourn together. It's only fitting."

I call Sally and Anna and we start the preparations for the party. Winston is like a little kid, in and out, throwing in his two cents until we push him out the door so we can get some work done.

"What about invitations?" I ask.

Sally laughs, "Winston put up at flyer at the Piggly Wiggly, at Friendly's and at the bank. Everyone in town goes to one, if not all of those establishments."

With every hand on deck the old farm house begins to sparkle; windows are washed, floors are scrubbed; the flower beds are weeded. Cooking goes on well into the middle of the night: pies, cakes, cookies, and salads. Kent Johnson, an old farmer from the other side of town, is coming in early tomorrow to roast the pig on an outside spit. I'm just glad that's not part of my assignment and I'm equally glad that the pig isn't coming from the farm. Our pigs aren't big enough to butcher yet and frankly, I'm not sure I would ever be ready to eat them since my favorites have names; Othello and Caesar.

After everyone leaves on Friday night Winston and I sit on the porch and talk. His excitement is palpable and he talks like someone has wound him up. I begin to realize how the solitary farmer's life can be difficult for an extrovert like Winston. I question him about other celebrations, and he reminisces about his wedding here on the farm, the births and graduations and finally he is talking about Lorraine's death and how the community gathered to pay their last respects. He is quiet for several long minutes and I leave him alone with his thoughts.

Will drives up. It was his day to be working in Green Bay, and the three of us review the work that needs to be done in the morning. I kiss Winston's cheek and note that he is moving more slowly than usual tonight.

"Need some udder balm?" I tease.

"No smart remarks from the peanut gallery." He tosses back.

Will hugs his dad, something I have noticed is new between them; and then he and I walk up the stairs, arguing about what drinks to serve and where to put the card tables. He gives me a quick hug and I crawl into bed knowing there isn't much time for sleeping.

I'm awakened at 3:30 by some strange noise. I look out the window and see Will and Kent setting up the spit. I lie back down and close my eyes for a minute and the next thing I know it is quarter to 5. I dress quickly hoping I have time for a shower and make up later in the day, before the guests start arriving. Now I have to get the bread set, 10 loaves this morning. I'm exhausted; my shoulders and arms sore from the extra kneading. I cover the bread, set it on the back of the stove, and go to the sink to wash when Will sticks his head in the front door, "Seen Pa?"

"He's not out by you? Sorry, dumb question. Barn? He's been worried about the new calf not suckling."

He withdraws his head and I go back to the sink where I realize there are no breakfast dishes. Winston always makes coffee and takes a cup with him and at least makes toast leaving a trail of crumbs. I find empty coffee cups all over the farm; sometimes I have to track them down to have enough for the next meal.

Maybe he's in the bathroom. "Win? Come on, It's your party. Snap to it. Are you going to make everyone else do the work?" I rap on the door as I go by but it opens easily, no one is in the bathroom.

I walk down the hall. His bedroom is behind the dining room. I rattle the door knob. "Winston!" I only go into his room to clean and change the bedding. Sally told me that it looks exactly the way it did when Lorraine died.

"Winston, are you decent?" I stick my head in the room expecting to see him in front of the mirror wearing his best jeans and the new plaid shirt with the pearl snaps he bought for the day. He is not standing in front of the mirror. My next thought is that he must be in the barn or out in the field. And then I look down. He is laying on the floor, all dressed up, one hand reaching. I drop to my knees and feel his chest. No movement. I put my shaking fingers on his carotid artery; I feel nothing. He is cold. I rip open those pearl snaps and start compressing. Then I stop to give two breaths. Back to compressions, one and two and three and four… My mind goes blank but my body keeps moving, breaths and compressions, breaths and compressions.

Sometime later Bart finds us, me breathing and compressing, Winston cold and unresponsive. He calls for Will. Will puts two fingers on Winston's neck. He shakes his head.

"Stop pumping, Cassie," he commands.

I can't stop. I continue moving from his head to his chest, counting.

"Damn it, Cassie, he's gone. Stop doing CPR."

"Not until the ambulance, one and two, comes. They will, three and four, take over. Five and six and…"

Will grabs me by the shoulders and pulls me away.

"No, no, NO," I scream. "He's not dead. This is his party. He's going to retire and travel and….eat….bonbons." I am sobbing.

"Take her out of here, Bart," Will commands coldly and Bart pulls me from the room. I collapse on the dining room floor, my face in my hands.

Anna, Matthew, Watson, Sally and little Sarah are working in the kitchen. I hear Bart explaining what has happened. Matthew swears and his mother rebukes him. I hear someone keening. I should get up and comfort them but I can't find the energy or the will to move.

Will comes out of the bedroom and grabs me by the shoulders and shakes hard. "Look at me Cassie. You're making this harder for everyone. Pull yourself together."

He walks into the kitchen and in low tones calms everyone down. I can hear his words but my mind isn't translating them. Anna comes in and slips her arms around me, rocking gently. Sarah comes in and joins the group hug. I pull away, unable to be comforted or to give comfort. I climb the stairs and go to my room.

I stare at the ceiling, I don't know how long, not moving, trying not to think. Someone knocks on the door but I don't want company. My lack of response doesn't deter Meredith who strides across the room, grabs my arms and sits me up on the side of the bed.

"You need to come downstairs, Cassie. They all need you now."

"I can't do it again, Meredith. I lost another one."

"What did you lose?" she asks quizzically.

"A life, I lost another life."

"You're not that powerful, Cassie. Give it up. Come downstairs and do your duty as a comforter to this family who has so graciously taken you in."

"I can't. I have got nothing to give anyone. I don't belong here."

"Coward. I'm disappointed in you. You came in here and made us all love you and now you're going to walk away. In my book that's the definition of a coward."

I look up confused by her anger and tone of voice.

"Alright, I'm done playing bad cop." She takes my hand. "Please come downstairs. Do this for Winston." Her voice falters but then becomes stoic again. "Take a shower first; Will's ex-wife is in the kitchen looking like something out of a magazine. Listen, I have something perfect for you to wear. Take that shower, wash your hair and I'll be back with the outfit."

She waits until I get up from the chair and then follows me to the bathroom.

I take my time washing and conditioning my hair. When I step out of the shower, hanging on a door handle is a long full skirt in blues and greens and a white peasant top with embroidered peacocks. Winston would have loved it.

I don't put on makeup, afraid that I'll cry it off. Let Will's ex-wife win the imaginary most-beautiful-woman contest; I don't want to compete. Everyone is talking quietly when I enter the kitchen. Little Watson takes my hand and my stomach clenches as I fight back tears.

Everyone seems to be looking at me expectantly, probably a little fearfully. I have not measured up they seem to be saying with their eyes.

Meredith loops her arm in mine, pulling me towards the only two strangers in the room. The infamous ex-wife and a young man, obviously

Will's son. Meredith's appraisal is accurate. Caroline is stunning in a short, black wrap dress. And she is tall, not much more than a few inches shorter than Will, exactly the same height as her son. Her hair is a shiny black bob. Her makeup is flawless. Her eyes, huge dark pools.

"Cassie Burns, this is Caroline DeMarch." Caroline's eyes narrow slightly taking in my bare face and messy hair before extending her hand. "Ah, the housekeeper. It looks like you have done a good job of taking care of the Harleys. Thank you." She dismisses me with a wave of her hand and turns back to Will.

Housekeeper? Well yes, I guess I am. But for her to dismiss me so cavalierly puts my back up. "Excuse…"

Meredith intercedes quickly turning to the young man. "And this is Will and Caroline's son, Jared. Currently a student at U of M. Studying vet sciences if I remember right?"

"Like you ever forget anything, Meredith." He flashes her Will's smile and I'm enchanted. However, when he turns back to me he is scowling. "Hello, Mrs. Burns," he said, then he, too, turns away. Stung I wait for Will to say something, but he and Caroline are deep in conversation, his arm lightly around her shoulders. They look good together.

I move away from the cozy scene and choose a seat next to Angela. Watson crawls up on my lap and then so does Angela. The two kids snuggle in, seeking comfort, aware of the undercurrent in the room. I offer to read them a story, and they both race off to pick their favorite book. I look around the kitchen; the brothers are each standing in pairs with their wives, ex-wife in Will's case. Everyone looks comfortable, as if they've been here hundreds of times in the past. I'm keenly aware that I'm really just an outsider.

The kids come back with books and we go into the quieter living room to read. Half way through the burping chicken book that Watson chose, they start arguing. Then Angela hits Watson who bursts into loud sobs and Angela, aware that she's made a mistake, joins the chorus. Soon both mothers come in and claim their tired children to take home.

Again I'm alone. Meredith comes in to say her good-byes. She hugs me tightly and offers a bed at her house. I decline her offer. I won't be able to sleep tonight and I want to be able to wander around without disturbing her. She understands and promises to return in the morning.

I survey the kitchen. Caroline is alone with the brothers and Billy and Sam, two of Winston's oldest friends. I listen at the door to their reminiscing for a few minutes before I slip out.

"Cassie?" I turn to Will as he continues, "We've decided to have Pa's funeral tomorrow and use all of the food we made for the gathering after the service. All of the same people will be attending."

"O.K.," I say. I can't stay here one more minute. Winston lingers in every corner; his ratty slippers are next to his recliner. His Bible is open on the end table. There are two half empty coffee cups on the floor. I pick them up and hold them to my chest, trying to channel Winston's energy, but all I feel is sadness. I can't go back into the kitchen so I take the cups with me out the door. For a minute I sit on the old swing, waiting expectantly but of course Winston doesn't show up so I move on down the stairs.

I spend several minutes looking into the window at the chickens,but tonight I can't find any solace here. Restlessly, I move to the calf pens. Superstitiously, I count the small animals; I'm one short. I count again; still one short. I study them one by one. The one missing is the sick one Winston was worried about, thc one we talked about just last night. I race through the barn; sometimes sick animals are put in the back pen. The pen is empty. Reluctantly, I go around to the back of the barn. There she is, on the manure pile to be buried. She looks so tiny and so perfect that a fresh wave of grief overwhelms me. I lean against the barn while sobs wrack my body so savagely my stomach hurts. I sink to the ground, trying to catch my breath. Finally, exhausted, I stare blindly into the woods. My mind refuses to make plans; my body refuses to move. I wish the bear would come tonight. Then I would have something tangible on which to unleash my fury.

Finally, I straighten up and go back to the house. Only Will and Caroline are still in the kitchen talking. I want to avoid everyone so I go around to the back door and head up the stairs. When I open the door to my room I'm surprised to see Jared.

"Are you looking for something?"

"This is my room." He is surly.

I look around. The closet door is open, as is one of the dresser drawers.

"Did you find anything interesting?" I ask.

"You don't belong here."

I remain silent, waiting for him to say more. I stay by the door, wanting a way out if his anger explodes.

"My mom and dad are getting back together." When I don't respond he switches tactics, "You're not family. This is family time."

My silence is irritating him. "You're a bitch. You come in here, upsetting everyone. Nobody knows anything about you. Maybe you even killed Old Pa."

"Please leave this room. I'll be gone after the funeral tomorrow. You have nothing to worry about." He strides past me, his mouth set in a hard line and slams the door. "And I didn't kill your grandpa," I whisper to the closed door.

I wait a few minutes then go to the bathroom to brush my teeth. The door is locked so I lean against the wall to wait. Caroline comes out, dressed in a tiny black negligee. "Oh, it's you," she says dismissively and slips into Will's room.

I lie on the old sagging bed for the last time and can't sleep. I review memories from the last few months; cooking sap, driving the tractor, baling hay, swimming in the creek, making ice cream. The ringing phone breaks my reverie.

"Mom, its Courtney."

"Hi sweetie, what's up?"

"I left Rafe."

"Excuse me?" I'm addled; I did not see this coming. I wait for an explanation.

"I'm not happy, Mom. I haven't been for a long time. Rafe and I… just don't have anything in common anymore. And my job, I just don't want to work seventy hours a week. Mom, I'm so tired. It feels like I haven't really slept in years."

"What are you going to do?"

"I have over 400 hours of vacation coming; ten weeks. I'm going to take it all and travel. Then when I get back I'll look for a different job."

"Where are you living now?" Ever the mother I want to know that she is safe.

"I found a condo on the east side. I'm not too far from Lila and the girls. All three girls stayed over one night and we had a great time. Mom, I have missed so much. I love these little girls so much it hurts. When Sandy and I were playing cribbage one night she told me that she talks to Dad. She described him the way he looked on your wedding picture. She must have been going through some old albums."

I just murmur something non-committal and don't tell her that I, too, talk to Gordon.

"So how are you, Mom?"

"I'm O.K., honey." I hesitate, and then add, "Winston died yesterday."

"Winston?" I hear her trying to place the name. "Oh, the old guy with the broken hip that you've been taking care of. I'm sorry." She pauses for a breath, "Does that mean you're coming home?"

Before I can answer, she says, "It's Sandy texting me. She is one bright little girl. Got to go. Love you, Mom, bye."

"I miss you, too," I say to the dial tone and hang up.

Fully awake I slip down the stair to sit on the old porch swing.

"I was hoping that you would come down here tonight," Will says from the rocking chair. I notice that he is not sitting in Winston's chair. I'm glad. I could not have handled that intrusion tonight.

"How are you doing?"

"I'm O.K."

"What about you, Will?"

"I can't believe he's gone. He's been such a force in my life; it is like I have lost my compass."

I nod, although I know that he can't see me in the dark. I can't trust my voice.

He continues, "We have so many decisions to make now."

We sit quietly for a few minutes. I push the swing with my foot, trying to find a way to soothe my soul. It resists soothing so I rock harder.

"I had hoped for a few more years. I knew his heart wasn't good. He came through his hip surgery so well, I guess, I thought he was invincible."

"Me, too," I say quietly, but Will continues to speak.

"Now he is with Ma. He's missed her so much these last years. I can just see them dancing. Pa used to lift her off the ground and swing her around until she demanded he put her down. He loved to tease her and since she was such a tiny thing he used to just sit her on his lap and kiss her until he had her laughing again. He was such a tough old bird in so many ways but with her, he was so tender..." His voice trails away as he sits with his thoughts.

"Good night, Will." Tonight I can't listen to him reminisce, especially since he sounds so much like Winston.

"Good night, Cassie."

I must have fallen asleep sometime after midnight because I hear the old grandfather clock chime. I'm awakened shortly after by arguing voices and a slamming door, but soon I manage to fall asleep again.

I wake early and make breakfast: waffles and maple syrup, biscuits and gravy, hash browns. Even on the day of a funeral there are still chores to be done.

I clean up and head over to Meredith's to borrow a black dress. She explains why she owns seven black dresses, "At my age, dear, I attend a lot of funerals, sometimes more than one in a week."

She is tall and willowy and I can be generously described as lush. I try on the first three and we laugh so hard I tell her I might end up with my black jeans and a poncho. It feels good to laugh.

The fourth dress is a floaty chiffon number I want to dismiss out of hand, but Meredith insists, so reluctantly I try it on. This one is full enough across the bust that we can belt it with a sliver of gold. She puts my hair in a French twist and adds a tortoise shell comb. I glance briefly in the mirror; grudgingly I admit I look presentable. Meredith does my makeup and adds waterproof mascara.

We walk across the road together, and she looks stunning in a red dress. "It was Winston's favorite," she confides. There is so much I don't know about this woman. Since I'm leaving I may never find out.

We cram into several vans to ride to the Methodist church. Even though we're early, the church is nearly full. The first voice I hear is Watson, walking around the church, saying, "Where is Papa? I can't find Papa." He runs to me and I pick him up.

"Sassie, where is Papa?" Cassie was a foreign word to him so he's called me Sassie since we first met.

"Papa had to go away," I say, knowing that is a poor answer. I try to distract him. "Let's go outside and I'll race you to the mailbox."

"I want to see in the box," he declares suddenly pointing to the casket.

"Hey, Sweetie, "I whisper in his ear.

"No, no, no. I want to see." He wriggles away from me and heads to the casket.

His mother intercepts him. "We've talked about this, Watson. Let's go find a cookie."

"No, Papa, save me. I want to ride off into sumset." It was his standard cry when one of his parents was trying to make him mind. Often, Winston would swoop down, pick him up, place him on his shoulders, and ride off into the sunset or at least around the farmhouse. By the time they rounded the corner, whatever instigated the skirmish had passed. Now everyone stops talking, casting around for words of comfort.

Suddenly, Will strides over, picks up the squalling child, places him on his shoulders and leaves the funeral home. I don't realize that I'm crying until Meredith slips me one of her mock orange scented handkerchiefs and whispers, "He is so like his father."

All three sons give the eulogy. Quiet Colin sings Amazing Grace with Matthew playing the accordion. Bart talks about his father as a community leader and role model. Will talks about his father as a man: "My father wasn't always easy to get along with. Those of you who disagreed with him know what I'm talking about." When the soft laughter dies down, he continues, "But he was always a man of principle. He was vocal when we disappointed him, but he was always cheering us on.

"My father had a hard life growing up with a brilliant, alcoholic father so he knew early on the kind of father he didn't want to be. He could be so stubborn and absolute." More laughter. "But when he was on your side, you didn't need anyone else. As a boy I thought he walked on water. Then when I became a teenager, I thought I walked on water and that's when the trouble started. We butted heads more times than I care to remember, but I never once doubted that he would always be there for me.

"But now he won't be. For the first time in my life I have to get up in the morning and make decisions without the benefit of his wisdom. My goal, heck the goal of my brothers and me, is to be half the man our Pa was. Thank you for coming."

Several neighbors get up to talk about how Winston had helped out when they were in need; Rosa Jansen relates how a half a hog showed up on her porch when her husband was laid off; Peter Millet about how the Harley boys baled his hay when he broke his leg. Some stories are funny; Mr. Burton talks about Winston as a teenager who had stayed up too late, fell asleep and tipped out of the church pew; Millie Petrie shares a story about she and Winston getting chased by a bull and spending half a day stuck in the haymow.

Matthew plays a lively polka as the casket is wheeled out. Everyone rises and starts clapping. The mood changes from mourning to celebration.

Several hundred people come back to the farmhouse and we're busy serving until after three when Anna, Sally and I finally sit down to eat. This is my opportunity to thank the women who had so graciously taken me in and taught me the art of being a farm worker. I had spent most of the night writing thank you notes and it is fitting that I share my gratitude with them first.

Then I track down each of the kids, give them a hug and share a thank you note. I drew a picture with a heart for Watson; for Sarah I made a picture of us walking down the lane; Angela I show playing checkers with her Grandfather. For Justin and Aaron there is a note about their softball playing prowess and in Matthew's I promise not to place a picture of him in his frilly apron on Facebook.

I find Bart and Collin in the barn doing chores and thank them for their patience. Will's note I place in his barn jacket, fairly certain that Caroline will not find it there.

Then I walk to the cemetery to say a final, private good-bye to Winston. "I already miss you, Old Harley. I know that you're happy with Lorraine, but today I'm feeling selfish and want one more porch conversation. I'm so thankful for that snowstorm, Win. And for you taking me in and helping me heal. Thank you for being you—proud, stubborn, brilliant and kind. But, Winston, now it is time for me to move on. I may never learn to thresh oats, butcher or smoke meat, but all that you have taught me will hold me in good stead. May you and Lorraine never stop dancing."

I'm already packed so when I get back to the house, I change into jeans and a tee shirt for traveling. I track Will to the mow throwing down hay. One last time I climb the old elevator; today it no longer seems scary.

"Hey."

Will puts down the pitchfork and wipes his brow with his shirt sleeve.

"I've come to say good-bye. It has been a great summer and I appreciate you taking a chance on me."

Will just looks at me steadily. I have no idea what he is thinking behind those shuttered eyes. "You don't have to go, Cassie," he says finally.

"But I do, Will. You and your family have to figure out what is next."

I hold out my hand, but he pulls me into a rough hug. He murmurs something into my hair but when I pull back to question him he simply says hoarsely, "So long, Cassie."

I get all of my stuff in the car in two trips. Somehow most everyone ends up on the porch and I take a moment to memorize the kind faces solemnly watching me drive away. Because her car wasn't in the driveway when I got up, I realize it must have been Caroline who left late last night. But now a movement catches my eye and it is Caroline moving to the front, placing her hand possessively through Will's arm.

I still haven't decided where I'm going; left means picking up my original plan and going to Eagle River. Right starts me on the path back home.

I drive until 8:30, with the radio turned up, singing along when I know the words, making them up when I don't. My cell phone rings and I hesitate when I see Winston's name; anyone can be calling from the phone at the farm. I turn off the ringer and put the phone in the glove compartment.

I find *Al's Burgers and Beer* just off the highway and pull in. I sit in the corner. Already there are two men drinking and shaking dice across the U-shaped bar; three women dressed to attract attention huddled around the jukebox and an old man is sleeping at a table by the window.

I order Al's Special Burger and a beer from the bartender who looks like an aging Sam Malone from Cheers. I check out the décor; nice backbar with a beautiful mirror covered with the requisite jokes and profound sayings. There is a small wooden dance floor to my right and a few scattered tables. The bar starts to fill up just as the bartender brings my supper. He sets it at a small table with a flourish so I vacate my barstool and move to the table. I'm entertained while I eat by the three women who were in the bar when I came in as they spread their charms among their appreciative audience; dancing and laughing.

"Haven't I taught you anything?"

"Excuse…"

"Your purse. You left it lying carelessly on the chair." He clucks his tongue in disapproval.

"Kurt! What are you doing here? O.K. I learned my lesson. Please return my purse."

"A dance, that's the cost to have your purse returned."

He touches my back and the buzzing starts. When I'm in his arms even my core is humming.

"You lied. You said you didn't feel anything."

I look at him steadily. His voice softens, "I have missed this. And, I have missed you. I've thought about you every day." He leads me back to the table and takes a bite of my hamburger. He sits across the table from me, silent.

I take his hands and say, "Yes."

"I didn't ask you yet."

"It doesn't matter, the answer is yes."

"Will you follow me to …"

"Yes," I say smiling. I can't stop smiling. I'm sitting across from a man who makes me happy just looking at him.

"What about your family? I figured you're heading home."

"I was."

"But you've changed your mind?"

Kurt gets down on one knee and demands, "Say it again." The bar is quiet and while I don't look up I can feel eyes on me.

"Yes." I murmur.

He turns to the bar and says, "You heard her? She said yes." The Sam Malone lookalike whoops.

When he offers me his hand I take it. We walk out the front door and I don't look back.

Chapter Fourteen

Our first month together is glorious; we can't get enough of each other. We make love everywhere; the counter, the shower, each of the guest rooms, the deck, the attic, the basement. We see nobody. The maid discreetly cleans and leaves meals in the refrigerator which we often forget to eat.

We deliberately leave our phones on the front hall table and for thirty-two days do not answer them or check messages.

On day thirty-three Eduardo walks in on us as we're getting out of the shower together. Kurt looks at him steadily and says softly, "Hey man, we need a little privacy here."

"When you didn't answer your phone Beezer called me and I used my magic key." He holds it up and shrugs. "I thought you might be going through a bad time."

"No, Eduardo, I'm not."

"Now I can see that." He looks steadily at me with no expression. "The band needs to practice and the awards show is, "he checks his watch, "in ten weeks."

"Shit, I…" Kurt looks at me and shrugs. I smile and shrug, too. Naked except for a towel, he looks gorgeous.

Finally a smile crosses his face and he says with enthusiasm, "Well, let's get going, Ed."

Punching in the numbers, Ed says, "I'll let the guys know that you can be at the studio in an hour, since you've already completed your ablutions." For the first time Ed looks at me. He isn't smiling and I'm taken aback at the coldness in his eyes.

"Well, we knew it had to end," I say as we walk into the bedroom, but Kurt is already pulling on jeans and a tee shirt, his eyes bright with anticipation and I feel a sudden cold breeze.

"I'm sorry, babe, but duty calls." He looks at me for a second and says, "You will need a dress, I'll have Ed call someone. Tasha will come in to fix your hair and I'll call my trainer to come in every day. We've got just about two months to buff it." I smile at him and wonder how anyone can improve on perfection. Then I realize that he is talking about me and I frown. I didn't sign on for the public side of K.C.

"But…" I start my protest. Kurt takes me in his arms and kisses me passionately, "I'm going to miss you every minute, Cass." And then he is gone.

When I enter the living room I'm surprised to see Eduardo with a drink in his hand waiting for me.

I look at him steadily, waiting for him to make the first move. It doesn't take him long.

"Kurt lost a million five this last month he was with you."

I'm startled by the figure but wait for him to go on; he obviously has more to say.

"That's not good for anybody." It was good for us I think but keep my face blank as I listen to him. "Kurt is an empire. The livelihood of over 100 people is dependent upon him. While he was here with you we had to cover with the media, cancel engagements, and still keep his image in the front of everyone's mind."

He is silent awaiting my response.

"Come on, Eduardo, you called me if you remember. This is Kurt we're talking about, an adult who can make up his own mind."

"You don't understand…"

"Then help me, I'm not stupid." I snap.

"It would be best if you left."

"I. Beg. Your. Pardon? I'm not Trina, Ed. Don't play games with me. I'll leave when Kurt and I make that decision. You're not part of the equation."

He changes tact, "It's what is best for Kurt."

"Again, adult. Old enough to make decisions."

"Don't take advantage of him, Cassie. After Elise and then Trina, he is vulnerable. Sometimes he's just a kid in a man's body."

"Does Kurt know we're having this conversation? Did he set you up to this?" Suddenly I'm feeling more than a little sick.

"No."

"Then have it with him; I'll go when he tells me to leave."

"Do you want money?" I'm so furious I want to hit him. But I don't hit people. I pace a moment to give myself time to carefully choose my words.

"I'm sorry you feel that way about me. Please leave. We have nothing more to say to one another. "

I stare out the window for a long time after Eduardo leaves. The big oak tree hides the house from the street and me from the world outside. I carefully make the bed and pick up the bathroom. The house is suddenly big and empty and for the first time in a month I'm alone. I pick up my phone and reluctantly reconnect with the outside world. Lila chastises me gently then begs for details. I'm shy about sharing so I keep my plans general and vague. I talk to the girls who have lots of stories to tell. Courtney's answering machine says that she is out of the country. Mark is working and Lucas is at school so I leave messages on their answering machines promising to call back and explain tonight.

Bailey is home. "Hey, Bay, what's new?"

"Georgia's back!"

"Really? Well how did you do that?"

"She showed up one day and said that she missed me. We're going to take it slow."

"You're amazing, Bailey, I would have said she was gone for good. I'm really happy for you."

"And, I'm giving up drinking, Cassie. I'm back in counseling and light therapy. And, I have lost eight pounds."

"I'm happy for you, Bay."

"What about you?" His voice softens, "Are you happy?"

I reflect a moment, "I am."

"That's it?" He is indignant. "No details? No wild stories? There are rumors, you know, about you. There was even a picture of you in one of the rags."

"I wasn't aware of any pictures, Bay."

"Didn't look like you were. Looked as if you two were attached at the hip."

"I don't remember that. Was it embarrassing?"

"Well, you looked awfully moony. Actually, you looked happy—happier than I have seen you in a long time. What happened at the farm?"

I sighed. Five of the voice mail messages were from Will. "It is a long story. I'll tell you when I see you."

"When will that be?"

"Soon, I miss you. I'll call you with a date. Now go take care of Georgia. Love you."

I dial the farm and a woman's voice I don't recognize answers. I hang up. Too complicated. Too late.

The day stretches on. I talk with Annie, the maid, for a few minutes before she scurries out. I try to read but nothing interests me. It is only three o'clock. I have never had this much free time. I drive around the city and drive past a technical college and a two year college. I make a mental note to go on line to see if there are any job openings. I go into shops but don't buy anything. I return to the big empty house at six. I call the boys. Mark talks excitedly about the house he is working on and asks few questions. Lucas is at the library Gia informs me. We speak for a few minutes before her pager goes off. I think about calling Meredith but don't know what to say. How do I explain running away?

I exercise for an hour and still it is only 8 o'clock. This is ridiculous. I put in an old western—Kurt has a ton of them. I watch two Dirty Harrys where Clint Eastwood looks about twenty-one.

At midnight, I fall into a restless sleep. I'm used to making love then snuggling close to Kurt's warm body and having him hold me. Now the bed is too big and too cold.

"Hey, babe!" Kurt bounces onto the bed smelling like sweat, booze and something sweet; something I don't immediately recognize. "I missed you." His kiss is long and deep. Before I can respond he launches into a description of his day. "It was amazing. We polished an old song *Wish I Were Dreaming*, started two new ones, they will be incredible. One is going to be a duet with Foxy. I have tried duets before, but they just never felt right but, Foxy, she can harmonize like an angel." He hums a bit, then pulls me to him, closes his eyes and sighs, "I'm so happy, Cassie. Thank you."

"You're most welcome, Mr. Troy. I'm at your service." I wink. He takes me at my word.

When he falls asleep I crawl out of bed and roam the house. It's 1 p.m. and I assume Kurt will sleep until evening. What will I do with all this time? If this is going to be a typical day, I need to figure out how I want to spend it.

I pull out the laptop and update my resume. I check addresses and send it off to the two colleges. It is 2:30. I find a music magazine and page through it. The afternoon drags on.

At 5 p.m. Kurt appears, wiping the sleep out of his eyes. Beautiful. He snuggles up to me and I hold his warm body. I kiss his sweet face. He snoozes while I watch him, I feel an incredible peace. I remember watching my children sleep and having a similar feeling.

When he awakes at 7, I pad to the kitchen to find dinner. Kurt trails after me and sprawls on a stool. I throw him the lettuce and he puts up his hands intoning seriously, "These hands are golden."

I walk over to him, take his face in my hands, and kiss him deeply and then I intone in an equally serious voice, "Those lips are golden and they still work." He laughs; I snuggle for a few minutes then get up to warm up the rest of meal while he tears up the lettuce.

When he is done I pick up one hand to inspect it, "Doesn't look overworked to me," I note.

"Ah, but they could be doing much more serious work."

"Such as?"

He grabs me by the waist, runs his hands up my ribs and settles on my breasts. I lean into him contentedly.

"I see," I whisper.

"Not yet you don't." He breathes into my ear.

"Dinner?"

"Not hungry."

"All that lovely lettuce." I pout. This is what I have been missing all day—this easy, warm, sensuous playfulness.

He scootches me up on the marble island and I'm at the perfect height; dinner is forgotten. This is the easiest diet I have ever been on.

I awake at midnight when Kurt jumps out of bed humming. "Wha…?"

"The song, Midnight. The melody is coming to me and I have to get it down. I'm going to the studio." He kisses me as he slips into his jeans and he is gone.

So becomes the rhythm of our days and nights. He either works here or he goes to the recording studio. He sometimes goes for hours without sleeping. I suspect he is using drugs, but when he sleeps he can be out for hours. Sometimes he is too wired to sleep so he paces. I just watch him, fascinated; he looks like a caged leopard. Often he will jump in his car or motorcycle and speed off, forgetting I'm even in his world.

When the entire band comes over I make myself scarce. We have an uneasy peace and I try to stay out of their way. The alcohol and drugs scare me. Tonight, Tyler and Kenny get into a fight; I stay in the suite and turn up the music. When Kurt enters our bedroom he is so wired and his eyes are bloodshot so I move away from him.

"Not like this," I say as I move out of his reach.

"Yes, like this." He grabs me by the robe. When I struggle to pull away he kisses me hard, holding my face. He smells like booze and something else.

"No." I back away feeling an odd emotion—fear?

He pushes me onto the couch and I struggle when he holds my hands over my head. With his free hand he pushes up my nightgown.

"Cass," he is slurring his words, "you like this."

I try to pull up my knees to use as a weapon but he sweeps them apart with his own legs. I look away from him when he enters me. I can't believe this is Kurt. When I start crying, he stops.

"Oh, Cassie…" I take advantage of his change of mood and push him to the floor. Then I gather my robe and go into the bathroom, locking the door behind me.

What just happened? Did Kurt try to rape me? I pull myself together. Now I'm mad. I storm out of the bathroom. Kurt lies semi-conscious on the floor.

I dress quickly, find my purse and keys and head for the front door. Kyle and Jake are snoring in the living room. Kenny and a girl I have never seen are having sex on one of the couches. Beezer is in the kitchen, eating.

"'bout time. Thought you would never split. You're such a bitch. Kurt's been a yahoo since you came. Did inspire old Golden Eyes to write some decent shit, I'll give ya that. Don't let the door hit you in the ass on your way out." His laughter follows me down the driveway.

I register at the first hotel I find. I'm glad that anger is the emotion that rules me now. I pace the floor and kick the garbage can. I try to relax with a bath but my emotions make me climb out after twenty minutes. I stare out the window for I don't know how long but I notice night giving way to daylight.

Finally I dig my cell phone out of my purse. "Hi Meredith this is Cassie Burns. How are you doing?"

"I'm glad to hear from you, Cassie. What's going on? You left very suddenly."

"I didn't feel welcome after Will's ex showed up. And, god, I miss Winston." I try to choke back a little sob.

"Well, Ms. Perfect Plastic is gone. Left right after the funeral. With Winston gone the boys are at a loss. Will quit the law firm to run the farm full time. There has been a lot of scrapping."

I feel a smile lift the corner of my mouth. "Will can be downright dictatorial."

"William at his best," she adds with a soft chuckle.

"So what is up? Where have you been? There are rumors that you ran off with a guy."

I swallow hard and answer, "Well, that's not exactly what happened, but it's fairly accurate. I was heading home and stopped for supper…dinner whatever, the last meal of the day and Kurt walked in. We danced. He invited me home and that's where I have been for the last month until today."

"What happened today?"

"He got high on something and tried to rape me."

"Shit. Are you O.K.?"

"Yes, I left and I'm staying at a hotel. M-Meredith, I was so scared of a man I have been making love to for the past month. It…it was like he…I don't know, it was like he had changed into some kind of animal. I didn't recognize him." I begin to shake so I walk around the room. It is ten and half paces from the head of the bed to the door.

I straighten up and make my voice stronger, "But I'm O.K. now."

"What are you going to do?

I stop pacing to think. "I don't have a plan yet."

"Are you safe?"

"Yes, I think he will sleep it off and be sorry. I don't know, I have never seen him like this. I just know that the man I left today is not the man I know. Meredith, I have to go, someone is knocking on the door."

"Cassie, don't open it."

"I'm looking out the window. It's a florist with a big bouquet. Don't worry, Meredith, I won't do anything stupid. Good bye."

I open the door as far as the chain will allow.

A bored voice asks if I'm Cassie Burns.

"I am but please don't leave the flowers. Take off the card and throw it away then take the flowers to the lobby and leave them there."

"But…"

I interrupt, enunciating clearly, "I do not want them. Please take them away."

I shut the door and my phone is ringing. I glance at it to make sure the kids aren't calling. When I recognize the number I ignore it.

Someone knocks again. I open the door to tell off the delivery guy only to see Kurt. His eyes are bloodshot, but he's taken a shower and brushed his teeth. He shouldn't look this good after what he went through last night.

"Please let me in Cassie."

"No."

"I'm so sorry."

I eye him levelly and say, "So am I."

"Please forgive me."

When I move to shut the door he gets down on his knees, "I'm groveling, Cassie. Please just let's talk."

I open the door and let him in. The room suddenly shrinks and I note the stained carpet and the messy bed. I sit on the only chair in the room and he sits on the end of the bed. I stare at him until he puts his head in his hands.

"Do you hate me?"

"I could never hate you," I say honestly. "But you scared me, Kurt. I trusted you and you took advantage of that trust. It is broken. Irretrievably."

He crosses to me, gets on his knees and puts his head on my lap. He is crying, his shoulders shaking. I don't want to touch him but my hands move of their own volition to his hair. Even as angry and hurt as I am, I'm drawn to this man. He takes my hand and kisses it then he straightens up and carefully, tenderly, kisses me. When his kiss deepens I moan, part in anguish, part with desire. Then he rises gracefully drawing me to him, enfolding me in his arms and I feel the familiar passion rising. I put my hands on his chest and push him away.

"Please," I say shakily, "I can't do this." I turn and happen to be facing the full length mirror. Catching my eye Kurt comes up behind me, so close I can feel the heat emanating from his body. "I love you, Cassie. I would never hurt you." He takes a deep breath, "When I'm writing all night I take a few pills to stay on track. I promise I won't ever do that again. I promise. Please give me one more chance. You know that you hurt me when you lied to me under the oak tree but I came back because I know that we're good together. Let's try one more time. Please, please let me hold you."

Every fiber of my being, except my heart, is screaming no and still I find myself back in his arms, the buzzing louder than ever. I'm crying in frustration and hurt but I just can't walk away. He leads me to the bed and tenderly rocks me humming some song I can't quite make out. I hate being this weak-willed woman. I hate being a cliché.

My phone rings; I'm sure it is someone trying to talk some sense into me. Without checking the number I turn off the ringer.

"So you will come back with me?"

I hesitate for what feels like a long time. Maybe if we weren't touching I could think clearly. I move toward the window. There is someone sitting in Kurt's car---it's Eduardo. I walk out the door and put up my hand as a signal that Kurt shouldn't follow me.

I motion for Eduardo to open the window. I bend down and without preamble, I say, "I could leave today. You have made it clear enough that I'm not wanted. What do you want from me?" I can hear the weariness in my voice; I haven't slept for more than 24 hours.

I feel his presence before he speaks, "I want you to stay, Cassie. It doesn't matter what the guys want. I want you with me." Kurt lays a possessive arm around my shoulders

"O.K.," I say quietly. I'm sure that I have ceded something just now, my pride or my future, but I'm too tired to think so crawl into the backseat with Kurt.

When we get back to the house the place is clean and everyone is gone.

"Let me do it right, Cassie. Let me show you how I really feel about you." He pulls me to him and gently begins foreplay. My body betrays me by responding immediately. He begins to sing and I am swept away by his voice and his passion.

"Am I forgiven?" he whispers softly into my hair.

In my sated state, I nod. He grins, wraps his arms around me and falls asleep.

I sleep hard and wake to find Kurt gone. There are flowers and a note on the dresser.

Babe,

I'm turning over a new leaf. I love you. I'm implementing a new schedule today; we're going to work 10-8 and I'll be home for dinner with you every night. We will be a like a 'normal couple'. Always, K.C.

He gets home at 10, hugs me and drops onto the leather couch. "I'm not cut out for this daytime schedule. I don't get my drive going until midnight. But sweetheart, I'm going to try." He turns an earnest little boy face to me.

I drop down next to him on the sofa. His hands reach underneath my shirt and rest on my stomach and he cuddles me close. "I'm not asking for this, Kurt. You obviously had a good thing going and it's not my intent to change that. It is not the hours that are the problem, it is the lifestyle."

"What do you mean by that?"

"The drugs, the booze, the women."

"There have been no women since you moved in." Abruptly, he changes the subject. "Let's go visit your family. I want to get to know them, and I want them to get to know me. Will they like me, Cassie Burns?"

With his hands playing on my sensitive stomach and inching upwards, I say, "What's not to like?"

"Good answer, baby," and we finish what he started.

Afterwards, he says, "I'm serious, call the troops. Let them know we're coming tomorrow."

"Really? Just like that? What about practice?

"I'm the boss," he answers breezily. "Go to sleep, I'm stuck on the second verse of Heavenly Magic. I'm going to the studio to see if I can pound it out. Now go ahead and call them."

"It's nearly one in the morning, Kurt, they are all sleeping."

"Slackers," he says grinning at me.

"Crazy man," I say throwing a pillow at him as I turn to leave the room.

"Come back here! You can't get away with that," he demands as he fires one, two, three pillows in rapid succession at me.

He catches up with me before I reach the door and wraps me in his arms. "Babe, don't ever leave me. I was so scared when I thought you were gone." He kisses me warmly and I lean into him. Like an ostrich, I stick my head in the sand refusing to review the events of the week.

He slaps my butt and says, "Now go to bed, wench, while I hit the salt mines."

The next morning I call my toughest daughter first and Courtney surprises me by being enthusiastically welcoming, "I'll cook dinner for all of us, Mom, so we get to know your new man."

I feel myself blushing at her description, new man. Really?

Courtney is still talking so I bring myself back, "Is he a vegetarian, Mom? I thought I read that in one of the magazines."

"No, honey, he eats about anything. Just have something decadently chocolate for dessert and he will be happy.

"O.K. I have got to get going. There's lots to do. See you later today. Love you, Mom."

"Love you too, daughter."

When I call Mark next he is more reserved. "What are you thinking, honey?" I ask.

"Is he treating you well, Mom?" I can hear the concern in his voice.

"Yes, why do you ask?"

"I saw him on T.V. trying to get into your hotel room. What were you doing in a hotel?"

I don't watch T.V. so I hadn't seen the news. I shouldn't be surprised, though. The media is always rabid to find out more information on K.C. Troy.

"You can't believe everything you see on the television, Mark. We can talk more when I get home. I'm looking forward to spending time with you."

Lila's is home but distracted when I call. She asks bluntly, "What's going on with you two? I'm not used to turning on the television and seeing my Mother."

"Can we talk when I get there, honey?"

There is a long silence before she says, "Yeah, sure, Mom. See you later." I stare at the phone after she hangs up trying to figure out why I got the attitude.

Lucas answers his cell on the first ring. "Mom, are you O.K.?"

"Yes, of course, Lucas. Why wouldn't I be?"

"Well on the television…"

"It wasn't what it looked like Lucas."

Lucas is silent for several beats before he says, "I worry about you. We all do. And we haven't heard much from you lately and with the T.V. and papers…" again he trails off.

I take a deep breath and say, "Will you be able to come to Courtney's tonight."

"I have a class so I may be late but I'll be there. Love you, Momma bear."

"I love you, baby bear."

Chapter Fifteen

Kurt drives with a boyish recklessness and sings to me. I start throwing out names of songs and most of the time he can sing at least the first verse. I am entranced and the three hour drive passes in what feels like minutes. We find Courtney's condo and she welcomes us effusively. My beautiful daughter! I study her; she looks relaxed and happy. I notice a red streak in her dark hair; that's new. Kurt hugs her and she blushes. He compliments her on the condo and she smiles proudly. I leave them talking to answer the door. It's Mark with Lila and the girls. The girls entwine themselves around me like limpets. Finally, I sit on the floor and they all try to squash into my lap. I breathe in their little girl smell and hug them close. Everybody is talking at once. Lila stands back, frowning, "Girls…" she starts but I put up my hand. "We're fine, Lila. How are you, darling?"

"O.K." But the dark bruises under her eyes tell another story. Mark moves to put his arm protectively around her shoulders. She leans into him and flashes him a look of gratitude.

"Hi, Lila and Mark. I'm Kurt. Your mother has told me so much about both of you. Nothing but good stuff, of course." he adds with a smile, putting his hand out.

Matthew shakes his hand and says quietly, "It is nice to meet you."

When Kurt turns the full force of his personality on Lila, unexpectedly she moves backward and awkwardly sticks out her hand. So instead of a hug Kurt changes mid stride and gently shakes her hand. "You have beautiful girls." He turns and adds, "Let me see if I remember your names." He points to Sandy. "Mickey Mouse, right?"

She gives him a disdainful look. “Sandra Marie.”

“Well, Miss Sandra Marie, would you like to dance?”

“There ain’t no music.”

“You can’t hear it?”

“Nope.”

“Well, let’s find some.” He flips through Courtney’s CDs, finds one of his, *If I Ever*, and flashes me a smile before putting it into the CD player. He fiddles with it a bit and *Sassy Cassie* fills the room.

“Hey, my grandma’s name is Cassie. But she isn’t sassy. Are you, Grandma?”

“I try not to be, sweetie pie.”

“So are we going to dance, Mickey, oh I mean Sandra Marie?”

They waltz around the living room, a giggling Sandy standing on Kurt’s feet. After the first dance she comes back to snuggle on my lap. Kurt sits down pulling me and all of the girls on his lap. Sandy stands up, eyes him seriously and asks, “Do you like my grandma?”

“Very much. Do you like your grandma?” he asks teasingly.

“Very much,” she mimics him, and then sticks her chin out. “My grandma is married to my grandpa so you can’t like her.”

There is a moment of awkward silence until Lila warns, “Sandy…”

“That’s O.K. Lila. Sandy please come here and we will discuss this.” She sits down facing me. “We can like lots of people. You like your mom and Uncle Mark and Aunt Courtney. And I like you and your sisters and your mom and Uncle Mark and Aunt Courtney.

“Well, I think married means loving grandpa.” She turns her stubborn little face away from me.

“Baby…”

“I’m not a baby.”

“I’m sorry, sweetie pie.”

“And I’m not a sweetie pie.” When I take a deep breath, Kurt chimes in, ”And you’re not a chicken and you’re not a mouse; you’re not a piglet and you’re not a house.” Reluctantly Sandy giggles then says, “I’m not a cow and I’m not a dog; I’m not a car and I’m not a…. I’m not a frog!” She flashes a triumphant grin and the tense moment passes. Kurt pulls me back until I rest against his chest.

“Grandma, will you play bowling on the Wii with me? Oh, I rhymed again, Wii and me." She pulls my hand. "And you can play, too," she offers Kurt.

"I'll warn you, I'm pretty good."

"Well, I am gooder." She tells him hands on her hips.

We play Wii in the guest bedroom until Courtney calls us for dinner.

The meal is full of chatter. Mark finds out that he and Kurt have motorcycles in common. Courtney asks Kurt about life on the road and he tells funny stories about fans hiding in his room and about the crazy stuff women throw onto the stage. "One woman tossed her kid to me so I kissed him, sang a verse with him in my arms and passed him to security to get him back to his mother. Another time a woman flashed me and she had my initials tattooed on her well, the pair she flashed at me." Everybody laughs and then Lila asks if that's where he got the inspiration for Forever Tattoo?

"Not really," he tells them. I feel myself blush and I send him a warning glare.

"Actually, it was your mom. Did she tell you how we met?

There is a chorus of no's.

"Well, your mother was walking in downtown Chicago just a-swinging her purse like she had never heard of purse snatchers. So, I grabbed her arm intending to give her a lesson in the proper way to carry her purse in downtown Chicago and…I couldn't let go. I was hooked. Although it took a while to make her realize that we were good together, eventually my charm or something convinced her. Maybe it is my cooking." He stops and grins here. Kurt never, ever cooks and then continues, "Whatever. It is a miracle to me." Everyone looks at me for the rest of the story and I just shrug. Kurt gently touches my lips with his. "I felt this soul connection with her and I had to write about it." Well, that's the PG rated version of our relationship.

"Ew," Sandy says.

"Ew," my adult children imitate.

Just then Lucas enters and I'm spared the need to continue the story. We fawn over my handsome, youngest son. To my critical eye he looks too thin and very tired. He hugs me fiercely and for a moment I feel his heart beating against my cheek.

Courtney fills up his plate and he begins to eat like he hasn't eaten all day. We watch him for a moment before he looks up and grins. “What were you talking about before I dropped in?”

“Mom and Kurt’s relationship.” Lila’s voice is hard. I glance at her but she refuses to look at me.

“O.K., Mom, spill.” Everyone turns to me expectantly. Courtney’s look is eager and open, Lucas is grinning, Mark looks like he is reserving judgment, only Lila’s eyes are narrowed slits. “Kids, you may play on the Wii for another half hour.” The girls run out squabbling about who would have the number one controller.

“With the girls gone, Mother, now you can tell all,” Lila announces. Mother? Why am I feeling so defensive? Kurt massages the back of my neck and I’m grateful for the support.

“It happened pretty much the way Kurt told it. I got lost in Chicago…” There are groans, “Mom, you get lost on the way to the store,” Mark comments affectionately.

“Do you want to hear the story or not?” I ask. They nod. “I don’t remember swinging my purse, but maybe I was. It was a beautiful night. I had heard about Bully’s Pizza Palace and was planning on walking there when I was accosted.”

“She was lost,” Kurt stage whispers.

“Was not. I had a map.”

“You were going in the wrong direction and if I hadn’t steered you in the right direction you would still be walking.” Kurt throws in.

“Who is telling this story, Kurt Charleston Troy?”

“You’re in trouble now, mister. When mom uses your full name, it’s time to back pedal.” Lucas winks at me.

“Forgive me, Babe.” Kurt takes my hand and kissed my palm.

“Oh, grow up,” Lila snaps, throwing down her napkin and leaving the room.

“Excuse me.” I follow Lila and find her on the porch smoking a cigarette.

“You don’t smoke, honey. What’s up?”

“I damn well can smoke now if I want to.”

As I wait for her to gather her composure, I sit on the top step. I don’t have to wait long.

“Mom, what is happening to you? You are living with a kid. You show up on the television and in all of the rags. And, it not flattering the things they're saying about you. Mrs. Robinson sound familiar? What should I tell the girls? That their grandma is a slut? You're an embarrassment to the family, and to Daddy's name." Her voice breaks and she asks, "Don't you even care?"

I cringe and wait for her to finish but she is so angry she is silent. "Of course I care, Lila. But I'm an adult. Living with another adult I care about. We are happy together, Lila, despite what you think. And you seem to have forgotten that Gordon is gone. I'm sorry if I have hurt you. It was never my intention to hurt any of you."

"But you're a grandma," she says tearfully.

"Not a dead one." I snap, instantly sorry for my outburst.

"The papers say he raped you."

I take a deep breath and blow it out. "He did not rape me. There was a misunderstanding and I left for a day. Misunderstandings happen to the best couples."

"So now you consider yourself a 'best couple'." Her beautiful face is twisted in disgust.

I move to take her in my arms but she turns away from me.

"What is going on, Lila? This isn't like you. Can we talk like adults? It is not about me, is it? Is this about you and Anston?" She shuts her eyes as if hearing his name pains her.

"Where is he tonight?" She just shakes her head, refusing to look at me.

"Lila…" I begin but she goes inside leaving me standing alone.

"Babe," Kurt breaks my reverie, "what's up?" He enfolds me and I lean against him a moment for solace.

"Come on in. Courtney's pulled out her keyboard and we're all singing." In the living room Mark is quietly strumming his guitar, Courtney is playing *Mean Streak* and Kurt picks up the melody. Lucas is lounging on the couch. Unexpectedly, Lila comes in with the harmony. When did my children become musical? I remember high school band concerts and Mark strumming in his room late at night but making music like this? I curl up in the recliner and let the song wash over me. They switch over to a couple of Dean Martin songs, starting with *Let Me Go Lover* and ending with *You Belong to Me*. Kurt comes over and sits on the arm of chair so he can look at me and sing. He knows I'm a sucker for Dean. I hold his hand and his smile makes me feel sixteen.

Lila announces that the girls need to get to bed and soon everyone is leaving. I walk my granddaughters to the car and buckle them in. Lila unexpectedly hugs me hard and whispers, "Oh, Mom."

"I'm here for you, sweetheart," I whisper back.

"Grandma, I can still be your sweetie pie," Sandy pipes up and we all laugh.

Mark's hug is remarkably gentle. "Thank you for taking such good care of the clan," I say. He looks at me solemnly and asks, "Remember the making good choices lecture you gave each of us?" I nod. "Back at you, Mom."

"Smart ass." I thump his shoulder with my fist.

"Grandma swore."

"Sorry, sweetie pie. Here is a quarter for your piggy bank, and one for your sisters. You hold them all so the little ones don't put it in their mouths."

Courtney and Kurt are discussing music, with Kurt showing her some chords when I return to the condo. I sit next to Lucas and ask, "How's school?"

"I love it, Mom."

"And Gia?"

"I love her, too."

I hug him. "You amaze me, youngest son."

"That's what Gia says, too." I swat him; he ducks and pretends he is going to tackle me. I throw up my hands in mock surrender. He gives me a hug, thanks Courtney, shakes Kurt's hand and is gone.

Chapter Sixteen

Kurt and I hug Courtney and say our good-byes. It is after midnight and I'm sleepy but for Kurt this is prime time. In the car heading north he asks casually, "Well, did I pass?"

"Pass what?" I tease.

His hand moves up my arm and starts massaging my neck. The hum is strong tonight. Maybe it is the wine; maybe I was a little worried about what tonight would bring. I turn my head and kiss his hand. "You were brilliant, Kurt. Charmed everyone, well almost everyone; Lila is going through a hard time. Tonight we were collateral damage."

"Hmm," he says as his hand trails down my blouse deftly opening buttons. He strokes me through my bra, his fingers playing with the front closure. Sleepily I ask, "Are you watching the road?"

"Nah, I'm concentrating on the action in the front seat. Ms. Burns. Would you please take off your blouse?" I only hesitate a moment before complying. Then I unsnap my bra and throw it in the back seat. Kurt's smile lights up the car so I unbuckle the seat belt and climb out of my panties. I'm only wearing a silky green peasant skirt. I move my foot to his crotch and massage him with my toes. He sucks in air. His hand moves under my skirt and it is my turn to gasp. Abruptly he turns back to the business of driving and in five minutes we turn into a hotel parking lot. While he runs in to get the key I slip into my jacket and my sandals. Within minutes, we're on the bed. The humming is so loud that I get lost in our orgasms. When I open my eyes Kurt is watching me. I can't read his expression. "Thank you," I murmur.

He nuzzles my neck and I feel hot tears, "I'm sorry, I'm so sorry," he repeats. I'm not sure if apologizing for what has happened or for what is to come. Tonight, perhaps even he doesn't know.

The revelation wakes me up and solemnly we get dressed. Kurt dashes to the car to retrieve the clothes I left in the back seat. He is impatient to leave. When I question him all he says is, "I have a song in my head. I'm thinking of calling it *Back Road Loving*. What do you think?"

"Is everything a song with you?" I ask.

"Yeah, everything has the potential to be a song. When we're together I have these little epiphanies that lend themselves to music. Like tonight, you in the front seat of the car with your blouse unbuttoned, sleepy-eyed and trusting me, I felt this immense responsibility not to hurt you," he hesitates and sends me a sad little smile. "You're so vulnerable and I can be such a shit."

"Yes, shittiness is solely a trait of the male species," I answer smartly.

He looks at me and sees that I'm smiling so he takes my hand and squeezes it. "Sleep," he commands, "You're such a grouch when you don't get enough sleep."

When we get back to the house he heads for the studio without looking back. We're home and life resumes just as we had left it.

The trainer, Ivan, comes and he works us every day, morning, and night for an hour. Sometimes he growls at me when he thinks I'm not giving enough effort; sometimes when I'm sore and exhausted I growl back. Our meals become protein and salads. I would kill for a cookie or a piece of bread, but I don't want to let Kurt down. We get weighed and measured every day and our progress is charted on the wall in the bedroom. Kurt celebrates every pound; every inch.

I get measured for a fitted, sea green gown. My under garments are chosen for me. Twice a week I go to the spa to get pummeled and wrapped and buffed. Weekly, my hair gets its own special treatment.

The local college calls me for an interview. Dr. Karen Johnson interviews me; she is a warm and intelligent woman in her 40s. I'm drawn to her passion for her students and education. She offers me a job teaching Psych 101 and Abnormal Psych; I'm thrilled. I pick up tenderloin and vegetables to grill in celebration on the way home. I stick

Annie's dinner in the back of the refrigerator.

I'm whistling *Amore* when the phone rings. "Hello, Cassie Burns here."

"Hello, Cassie." I'm taken aback; the voice is so much like Winston's.

"Hello, Will."

"How are you doing?"

"Well. And you?"

"I've seen you in the papers and on the television." His voice is carefully neutral.

I hesitate until finally I say lamely, "You can't believe everything you read."

"You didn't return my calls."

"Will, there is not much to say."

"Cassie, I think there is a lot left to say. I need some answers. Why did you run off? We needed you here. The kids still ask about you."

Carefully I answer, "I came to the farm to take care of Winston. He…he no longer needed me. It was time to move on."

"What about us?"

"There was no us, Will. We were just getting to know one another. Besides, it looked like Caroline was filling the empty spaces. Have you forgotten that I was just the housekeeper?" I can hear the bitterness creep into my voice. I switch the conversation to more neutral territory, "How is everybody doing?"

"We're suffering, Cassie. The void Pa left is…is huge. And with you gone on top of everything else, we're floundering."

"I'm sorry to hear that," I answer sincerely.

"Then come back, on your terms." I hear the anguish in his voice and I know that he had to bend his pride to make the request so I think carefully before I respond.

"I'm happy here, Will."

"That's not what it looked like on the television the other day. You looked scared and whipped," he snaps back.

I close my eyes and picture his strong face. My mind flashes to our backpacking trip, our haymow conversations, the trips to Friendlys. I let the feelings of being part of a large family and community wash over me. I remember the contentment and excitement and the work. I haven't done one constructive thing since I moved in with Kurt. I look at my manicured fingers and toes. I walk around a kitchen that doesn't reflect me in any way.

My phone beeps and I check the number. It's Kurt calling from the studio.

"Will, I appreciate your concern. I do miss all of the family…" Kurt pads up from the basement in bare feet with ratty jeans and tee shirt that says K.C. Troy tours 2011. He nuzzles my neck and puts his hands on my breasts. The humming starts and I forget what I'm going to say.

"Cassie!" Will brings me back to the present.

"I've got to go. Tell everyone hello. Good-bye," I whisper.

"Who you talking to Cass?"

"Farm. They're checking to see how I'm doing," I reply

"What did you tell them?"

I lean into him as he pulls off my blouse. "That I'm happy. I tell everybody that I'm happy, Kurt." He pulls me onto his lap. I curl up against him and try to forget about the phone call.

* * * *

"Got to do something with those drooping boobs, botox around the eyes and mouth, hair and lash extensions, probably lipo if she doesn't get those saddlebags off." This is Eduardo talking about me. I'm shivering in my underwear as he and an anorexic looking woman assess my faults.

"Long sleeves to hide those bat wings," the woman, Alexis, declares checking my upper arm. "Ass can use some help, too," she adds. "Teeth," she snaps and I open my mouth. "Passable."

"Done," I say putting on my robe. This has been the most degrading experience in my life. All these people assessing me is ridiculous.

I feel the hurt tears welling up in my eyes, but I refuse to let these vultures see them. I don't want to go to the awards show. Let Kurt take some perfect model.

"Excuse me. I would like to talk with Kurt a minute." Complaining, they file out of the room.

"Kurt, this isn't going to work. Please take someone else. I'll watch from the back somewhere."

I turn to him expecting a protest but he is silent, studying me. I wonder what he sees.

Slowly he responds, “They just want you to look your best.”

“They just don’t want me to embarrass you,” I snap back. “Take Foxy.”

“I am. I mean we’re all going together. She is part of the group.” Belatedly, he adds, “I want you there.”

“Do you? Do you really?” I stand before him and take off my robe and the slip and say, “Because this is what you will get.”

He pulls me to him and whispers, “Do it for me. Please.”

I put my robe back on, open the door and announce, “Please schedule all of the ‘improvements’ you suggested and any others you can think of as soon as possible.”

Kurt puts his arms around me beaming.

“Excuse me; I’m going to the exercise room.” That night is the first time I force myself to vomit after eating dinner, but, it isn’t the last time.

Exercising and not eating become an obsession. I ask Alexis for help and she leaves a bottle of pills on my dressing table. I don’t ask any questions; just take three a day instead of eating. They take away my appetite, but I can’t sleep.

Kurt is so busy perfecting the songs for the awards night I don’t see much of him. I roam the empty rooms unable to sit still or concentrate; it takes two days to complete my lesson plans.

Bailey calls, “How are things going?”

“Fine, just fine,” I babble, “I have a job teaching two sections of psych at the local college.”

“Does that fill up your days, honey?”

“Not really.” I cast around for something to add, “I exercise and go to the spa and the salon…” I trail off.

“I saw you on Entertainment Weekly and you look,” he hesitates then says, “kind of pale. You sure you’re feeling O.K.?”

“Must not have seen me with my spray on tan, Bay,” I joke.

“Cassie, actually you looked like shit. How much weight have you lost? And please tell me that you haven’t been ‘surgically altered’.” I can hear the concern in his voice but glibly I say, “Only trying to roll back the ravages of time, dear one.” I’m scheduled for more injections tomorrow.

"What are you using, Cass? And don't try to fool a bullshitter. I know that you're popping something."

I'm silent, angry at him for calling me out. Who is he, a pathetic alcoholic, trying to tell me what to do? I'm exercising four hours a day now and watching what I eat. *Damn him.*

"Cassie, it is because I love you that I called."

I feel hot tears running down my face. "You don't understand," I sob, "I'm a grandmother in a world of perfect 10s."

"If Kurt loved you he wouldn't ask you to be anything but who you are, darling." His voice is soft and melancholy.

"What are you saying, Bailey? Kurt loves me. You don't know anything about us. You're wrong and I'm doing the right thing. So don't call me again until you can be supportive, like I have always supported you. You alcoholic loser," I scream, hang up and throw the phone across the room.

I start shaking. What is wrong with me? I'm fighting with my best friend. I pull myself together. It's not me. It's about Bailey; he can't stand to see anyone happy so he has to question everything. It's Bailey's problem not mine. I don't need that kind of relationship messing with my head. Screw Bailey. What does he know? What did he mean saying I look like shit? I look good without those extra pounds and the crow's feet. If he loves me like he said, he would support me.

I go to the workout room. One more hour and maybe these damn saddlebags will disappear and the batwings; maybe they should just be sliced off. I count the days; there is still time. I'll call Alexis and she will know how to fix it. Look at how well the botox in my hands eliminated that ropey look.

I pick up my cell from the corner of the room. It's still working so I call Lila. "Hi honey, how are you doing?"

"Better, Anston called and we're going to see a marriage counselor. But Mom, what about you? I saw you on television and you look…" She hesitates before she says, "different."

Not her, too! I try to hold my temper in check. "Just losing some weight that should have been gone twenty years ago. Exercising. Eating right."

"But your face," she blurts out, "it looks frozen. Sandy didn't believe that it was you."

"Don't you start on me, Lila. I'll just hang up if we can't have a civil conversation." I snap.

"Mom, we all care about you. We want to know that you're O.K. and you just don't look O.K. You haven't called for weeks. What are you doing?"

"I told you, exercising, eating right and teaching two classes at the college." Oh my gosh, I should be at class right now; it is 10:15 and the class started at 10. I have to call, what's her name? I must have her number here somewhere. I have never been this scattered.

Lila interrupts my thoughts, "Mom, mom!"

"Lila, I have to go, I'm late. Talk to you soon." My stomach rumbles. Alexis said that it would stop soon. I grab my quart bottle of water and take a swig to diminish the hunger pangs.

Kurt races in. "Do you remember seeing those notes I was scribbling about 'Tomcattin'? You know the new song?"

"Piano? Desk? I'll help you look."

"Got'em. Love ya, nymph." He grabs his scribbling from the piano, drops a quick kiss on my head and is gone. Kurt has taken to calling me nymph, his idea of a joke but it makes me feel cheap.

The phone rings; it is the university.

"Dr. Johnson I'm so sorry. I should have called you but I haven't been feeling well and I just noticed the time. No, it won't happen again. I'm sure I'll be feeling better by Thursday. I'm really, really sorry. Yes, I'll let you know if I can't be there on Thursday. Good-bye."

My head is spinning. I sit down and fall asleep. I awake with a start two hours later not feeling rested. I put in an old western and watch it with zombie-like fascination. This one has John Wayne as the hero. I start crying; there are no heroes anymore. When Kurt comes in he removes the remote from my hand and urges me to bed. I check the clock; it is 3:30. I have watched the same movie three times. Where did the time go?

"You're losing your boobs, babe," he says as he runs his hands down my body.

"I thought that's what you wanted," I reply.

"No." He drops his head and starts kissing me on my now prominent collarbone. For the first time there is no humming. I can't lie still. I'm exhausted. I feel raw, like I have no covering; like my skin is gone. I start to shake.

"Babe, what are you taking?"

"I don't know." I get up to pace.

"Let me get you something to calm down." He rummages in his drawer, brings out a handful of pills and hands me one. I dry swallow. Still I shake as I pace. And, I'm cold. I'm always so damned cold.

"It's not working. Kurt, it is not working."

"Give it a minute, Cassie. Come here. Let me warm you up."

"No, no, no I need something now." I pounce on the drawer, grab a handful of the pills and ask, "Which ones, Kurt? Which ones will make me beautiful enough for you?" Suddenly I know the answer lies in all of the pills, so I stuff them in my mouth—blue ones, white ones, green ones, big and little. I swallow and choke.

"Cassie, NO!"

Reflexively I swallow two more pills as he shakes me. His fingers are in my mouth, then he's slapping me on the back. *I don't understand. I thought this is what he wanted. Now I'm too tired to care.*

Chapter Seventeen

"Mom. Mom. Talk to me, Mom."

Courtney? What is Courtney doing in my dreams? She's crying. My independent, oldest daughter is crying? I try to raise my arms to hold her but they are so heavy. I was having a good dream. Gordon and I were dancing. Only wait, Gordon, doesn't dance. Who is this? I don't recognize his face and then I see it is Winston. I smile. 'Thank you for coming back', I say in my dream.

"Mom, it's Lila. You have to wake up. The girls are asking about you."

"She looks horrible."

"Stop it, Courtney, she can hear you."

"Well, why isn't she responding? Do you think she has brain damage?"

Who are they talking about? Brain damage? I want to ask them what's going on, but somebody has put pennies my eye lids like they did in the old days when people died. Wait, I want to say. I'm not dead. Am I?

The next time I wake up my eyes go to a sliver of light under the door. I can see again; the light is beautiful. I hear voices and I want to respond but my mouth is so dry. I can't think of what I might have eaten to leave such a horrid taste. I need to brush my teeth. And my stomach is sore. All of my muscles ache. I can't see; my hair is in my eyes. I can't lift my hands to my face to brush it away. Why can't I move my arms? Why? Why? Why? I can hear someone screaming, "Please, take care of her, she's in pain. Why isn't anyone helping her?"

Later.

"Mom?"

"Lucas," my brain is finally sending messages to my mouth. I open my eyes and see all of my children sitting in…I look around curiously…a hospital room. Why are we in a hospital? No, I amend that observation, I'm in a hospital bed, and my children are looking at me; watchful. *Why am I here?* I close my eyes in an effort to concentrate but I can't bring answers forward.

"What happened?" Is this croaky voice mine?

"What do you remember, Mom?" Mark sounds apprehensive.

"Nothing. I mean, really, nothing. I…" I go to brush the hair out of my face but I can't, "Why am I restrained?"

I catch the guilty look they pass among themselves and finally Mark answers, "The doctors are afraid that you will hurt yourself, Mom."

"Why would I do that?"

"Why did you take a handful of pills, Mother?" This is Lila and she is angry. Each word is carefully enunciated and she bites them off.

A handful of pills? I have a hard time swallowing my vitamins. Why would I take a handful of pills? Finally my brain kicks in; they think I'm suicidal. My children think I would voluntarily leave them. I choke on a sob. My nose is running and I can't even wipe it. Mark leans over with a tissue and I blow.

"Please remove the restraints. I would no more kill myself than I would—" I cast around for some foolish comparison--"jump out of an airplane."

"You went skydiving, Mom, remember on your 40th birthday?"

"Oh shit, come on, little birds, you know that I would never even contemplate weaseling out on all of you. You're stuck with me until…forever. Now untie these or I will. *With my teeth. With my toes. Something.*

A nurse hurries in—her name tag says Sally. "Why are you so agitated, Mrs. Burns?"

"Please remove the restraints, Sally," I say, perfectly rationally.

"I need to talk with the doctor before I can do that, Mrs. Burns."

"Then please do that as soon as possible."

After she exits the kids all look at me. "How are you feeling, Mom?" Lucas's sad, scared voice makes me want to cry.

"I'm starving," I say and for some reason they laugh.

"Why is that funny?" I demand.

"Because you had your stomach pumped so you should be hungry."

That explains a lot. "So I took a handful of pills?"

Lila spits out, "Yes."

"Why would I do that?"

"Why did you do all of the crap that you have done the last few months? Like diet yourself into anorexia? Or have vanity surgeries? Or botox? Or cut yourself off from all of us?" Leave it to Lila to give it to me straight.

The nurse, Sally, comes back into my room and unties me but I lay still taking in the accusations. I sit up and swing my legs over the edge of the bed. I'm so tired and so weak. How long have I been lying here? That doesn't matter right now. I need to get up. Lucas puts his arm around me and gratefully I lean on him as I walk to the mirror. I study the image. I push up my bangs and see tiny scars; I touch my lips, they look inflated. I study the hollows of my cheeks. When I lift my gown there are more scars and a stomach so concave I have to touch it to see if it's really me or if this is one of those fun house mirrors; it is really me.

"I'm sorry," is all I can think of to say as I smear away the tears with the heels of my hands. Lucas wraps his arms around me and I can feel his hot tears falling in my hair. I don't have enough strength to put my arms around him as he guides me to a chair. Four expectant faces turn toward me. I want to go to bed and cover my head instead I ask humbly, "Please tell me what happened."

Courtney, who has been surprisingly quiet, begins the recitation. I listen, flinching at the descriptions of the aborted telephone conversations, the revealing television appearances, the withdrawal, the betrayal. She talks about Kurt's frantic call. Her sweeping arm, taking in the entire hospital room, indicates the ending.

A new nurse, her name tag says Dawna, hustles everyone out of the room leaving me alone with my twisted thoughts until the phone rings.

"Cassie?"

"Hello Eduardo," a wave of pain so visceral I stop breathing halts the conversation. I remember the surgeries, I remember the obsessive exercising, and I remember sticking a handful of pills in mouth. I gag. I will myself to breathe. Someone is sobbing and I feel tears flood my face.

His voice softens, "Are you going to be alright?" he asks, but I don't have an answer. "Kurt's worried about you."

"Then why didn't Kurt call?" I ask as the sobbing wanes.

When he doesn't answer immediately I recognize the problem. "Publicity," I say.

"Cassie, he is…" he starts but I interrupt, "A multi-million dollar corporation. I remember having this conversation, Eduardo, a lifetime ago."

He changes tactics, "The award show was spectacular. I'm sending a disc."

What a lesson—all the pain and all the heartache and I missed it. I look down at my botoxed hands and rub my index finger over the scars. I willingly chose to become a scarecrow so I could wear a sea green dress and spend a couple of minutes on the red carpet. How did I get here?

"Cassie, Kurt is paying for the hospital costs."

"Please tell him thank you," I say cordially, although I want to tell him to go to hell.

"I'm really tired, Eduardo. Good-bye." I hang up and tell Dawna that I don't want any more phone calls from anyone other than my children. Then I turn over, cover my head and try to sleep the pain away.

It takes two long months before I'm able to eat almost normally since eating is a psychological and a physical event, and four trips to the dentist to fix the damage done by daily vomiting.

I'm living with Mark now and the other children are ridiculously solicitous. You would think I was an invalid. I have gained four pounds and the tremors and most of the nightmares have subsided. I spend long hours communing with nature while Mark is working. I'm happiest when I'm sitting on the front porch with all of the dogs at my feet. I don't carry a phone anymore and I never answer Mark's. I know friends and neighbors are calling, but I always shake my head when Mark arches an eyebrow at me.

Mark drove off the paparazzi that came around the first few weeks and I don't watch T.V. or read the paper so I don't know what spin was put on this event. When I was still in the hospital the headline in one of the rags read "Troy's Tragic Love Affair Ends in Suicide Attempt."

There are sixteen unopened cards on the kitchen table. Each day I stack them in a neat pile but I don't open them. Every week I get a bouquet of flowers, this week's are Gerbera daisies. I ask Lila to drop them off at the nursing home. Every week she takes them to a different facility.

Eduardo sent a large box with my clothes and things. The sea green dress comes in its own plastic see through box. I put them all in the back closet. There is nothing in them that I need right now. Maybe someday one of the girls will go on a cruise or gala where they can wear the sea green dress.

I don't know if Kurt ever tried to see me. I never asked and Mark never said anything.

When my granddaughters visited last week I overhead Sandy admonishing her younger sisters not to jump or crawl on Grandma because, 'now she is breakable'.

I walk every day, usually down Mark's long drive way and back up again. Today the dogs want to go beyond the gate. I'm glad I am wearing a jacket because I am always cold now. I pull it tight around me and put up the hood.

I can't go far, I don't have any stamina yet but we make it to the now empty hay field about a quarter of a mile west of the house. The dogs look to me for permission to run and I smile and give them the signal. They are off; running and playing and I sink down gratefully onto the old culvert.

The sun is shining and maybe I doze or maybe I go into one of the trances the kids tease me about.

A shadow falls over me and I look up, not frightened; there is something familiar about the build of the man standing between me and the sun.

"Cassie." His voice is low and careful. "It's me, Will. Is there room on the culvert?"

When he gets close enough I hear his intake of breath; I should be used to it. Courtney did the same thing the first time she helped me shower. Lucas cried when I couldn't find anything to wear home from the hospital, and I had to use a scarf tied in my belt loops to keep my jeans from sliding to the floor. Even my shoes didn't fit and I had to kind of drag my feet to keep them on. Even though I no longer look in the mirror I know what people are seeing.

"How have you been, Will?"

"Better than you, I would say."

I give a short bark half way between a laugh and a sob. "Never one to mince words, Mr. Harley. Haven't changed a bit."

"You've walked quite a bit further than most days, Cassie. Are you feeling better?"

I consider his question for quite a while before I answer, "Despite appearances to the contrary, I think so, Will."

"What are your plans?"

"I don't have any." I get off the culvert painfully since my ass no longer has any padding sitting is uncomfortable. I call the dogs and they obediently respond. I walk slowly up the ditch. The dogs race for the gate.

"Can I take you home, Cassie?" Will asks, watching me struggle to get to the road. I'm panting when I reach the gravel. I reflect a moment. Will opens the car door. I crawl into the front seat and close my eyes.

The End

About the Author

Rhonda Strehlow grew up on a small farm in Northeastern Wisconsin in a large and supportive family. This is her first novel. I will let you in on a secret: this novel was conceived after a single chance encounter with a "Kurt Troy" of her own. The rest, of course, is fiction.

https://www.facebook.com/rstrehlow?fref=ts